I0761903

A Hat For Two Heads

By

Dana Thomas Weber

To

Laura and Larry Thomas

Chapter 1

The frolic of the intruder irritated her. She burrowed in a house that was supposed to be a home, heeding threats with jaded awareness. Raucous ticks and tocks of a grandfather clock composed earnest attempts to drown out thumps and thuds upon floorboards above, forcing her ears to strain for clues. The senator's daughter remained stuck in a moment as New Orleans went about its way of interrupting life with curiosities.

A leg of furniture scraping unwitting pine floors? A brass ornament meeting its demise upon a rug? Perhaps the housekeeper was still about. Highly unusual for this late time of day and week. Shedding flip-flops to tiptoe across the oriental rug in silence, the twenty-something reached the mahogany desk. She stood before the closed middle drawer, knowing it harbored a pistol. The slight young woman slid the long drawer open slowly, just enough to glower at the weapon held on one other occasion. Hesitation set in at the sight. The casualty of this presumed home invasion rubbed nervous dampness from hands and, during her pause, stole a squinted look through leaded glass panes which offered a wavy view of a serene antebellum oak garden. Mockingbirds darted to and fro under cover of June foliage at early dusk. She admired these feathered fathers chasing naughty blackbirds from nests while footfall above eventually convinced her to gather the gun and secure it in the back pocket of her jean shorts. She would handle this trouble before this trouble handled her.

More frantic than a house cleaner fulfilling menial tasks, the disruptions continued upstairs. She watched the ceiling for clues until the Ruger contorted fear into courage. Her long, naive legs took charge as each step carried her unsure body into the Victorian foyer adorned with rich crown moldings and an oversized fishbowl of gardenias perched upon a round, oily Baroque center table, heavily gilded to impose the family's status upon all who entered. Apparently, the glint attracted the wrong kind of company at times. Toward the curved staircase she proceeded, just to the right of a vestibule she entered in unassuming fashion twenty minutes ago. Rather than leave the way she had arrived, she stalked the source of unrest. It was unyielding with a blatant disregard of the sanctity of the brick Gothic Revival which had been in the LeBlanc family for over a century. Abandoning sane options, the rightful resident pulled the hem of her white tank top into place and began her ascent. Step by dreadful step, she grimaced as usual suspects creaked in familiar spots. She nervously gathered her long tresses about her neck and gently resituated the silky blonde mane behind shoulders and ears for a better listen. Inhaling composure and exhaling trepidation, she finally concluded the climb.

The second-floor hallway was flanked by five oak doors that teased with glistening varnish. One of those doors shrouded what she searched for. Silence reigned, for the moment, and made for an impossible choice. If selected, the door at the end would provide entrance to the walkup attic. On the other hand, the nearest door to the left housed her childhood bedroom. Being ajar, she peeked inside. The target was revealed.

Her gaze fell upon a trim young man with sandy hair cropped to military precision. He halted before her ornate French bureau where he tugged on the handles of the swollen dresser. The edges of his red polo shirtsleeves softly highlighted strained muscles. A small lamp toppled from his effort and he righted it. As he did so, she recognized the embroidered emblem on his shirt as the same donned by the golf caddies at the country club. Untucked, it hung carelessly about the atypical prowler's tan shorts.

Foolishness cloaked in valor inspired her to toe open the door and point the weapon. Being the daughter of a politician had hewed deep sensitivities to invasions of privacy, among other undiagnosed psychological complications after her mother's sudden disappearance from her childhood.

"Who are you?"

The trespasser's posture snapped straight, and he spun toward the female voice before dashing toward the window.

"Painted shut. Only window in the house that way. To keep me from sneaking out in the past, I figure." He remained motionless while her casual banter bamboozled him. She leaned against the doorway for support. "Well? You owe me an explanation."

The handsome invader raised golf-gloved palms in surrender. Faith took mental notice of his features: tan, lofty, fit, blue eyes settled atop high cheekbones. A wide smile emerged to showcase a flawless Cheshire grin.

"What the hell are you doing here?" she persisted, marveled by her own fierce voice.

He swallowed his smile to assume serious and spoke a low and slow local's accent.

"I don't mean any harm. I'm sorry. You see, I, well, to be honest," he stammered. The guy was finding it hard to muster ego amid pink walls and a lacy canopy bed.

"*'To be honest'*", she deliberated, "means you're about to lie. I was taught that by a particularly harsh boarding-school teacher."

Her green glare passed right through the intruder whose own turquoise gaze sparkled with shock. Focus returned when sets of blue and green latched on to one another. Her gaze softened and she exhaled.

"Whatever. The room you want is next to mine. My stepmother's dressing room. Loads of jewelry given to her by my father. Some of it was worn by my real mother? The idea of that makes me sick, so, yeah, it's all yours."

She backed away from the doorway while motioning the firearm toward the next room, never taking her clover attention from the uninvited guest.

Convinced of a ruse and having never been caught in the act, he placed an unsure heel forward, humbled as he followed her odd, albeit alluring, command. Electrified by his closeness as he passed, she silently scolded herself and took an intelligent step backward to avoid sudden moves against her. The gardenia bouquet's aroma floated through the stairway to steady her from behind while intrigue lured her. He stood a good twelve inches taller than she who wielded the power in the current situation. She had never been in a position of power and could now see why her father craved it.

A grey, circular velvet settee squatted in the center of Mrs. Chelsea LeBlanc's dressing room with walls lined with well-appointed, custom built-in closets. Gossamer, full-length gowns whisped from white garment bags unable to contain them fully where they hung from oversized golden hooks. She and the senator were attending a fundraising gala at the country club and scattered sequined heels with discarded dress choices suggested the dedicated wife's big decisions of the day. Sections of exposed walls coated with luscious paper swimming with bluebirds glowed with sconce light left lit in her haste to leave on time.

"Sit here," the charge ordered with the pointed pistol. Afraid to defy, he brushed aside a silky, canary robe to sit awkwardly upon the dainty sofa. Although amiss amid refinement, he remained unfazed. He was accustomed to not belonging. Settling in with elbows rested on knees, he studied his new partner-in-crime go to work on the vault. Her hands started to tremble and he resisted the urge to offer assistance. He could have cracked the safe by now but kept that thought to himself. She repeated glances his way until finally finishing the task at hand then reached for a discarded cream shopping bag with pale blue-ribbon handles that would serve as the dysfunctional party favor. She filled the paper bag and rushed to stand.

"Take this. Leave through that window," she instructed while kick-sliding the flat-bottomed boutique bag now weighted with diamonds, rubies, sapphires and gold. "It has a rolled-up fire escape."

He considered the treasures presented to him by this slender bare foot. His mouth instigated potential sentiments before pursed lips sealed the words. Defeat replaced triumph for this thief who was, in the end, given what he came for and as his gloved hands gathered the bag, she detected insecurities that resembled her own. They stood simultaneously and within arm's reach. Then, it was she who first fled that room filled with inappropriate enticement.

How she prevented a tumble down the stairs was a mystery but her uneasy feet did not fail her in the end. She hurried back to her father's office to return his weapon and take cover behind the locked door. Kneeling in darkness before the tall window, she spied him sprint through the yard and expertly hop the wrought iron fence.

Evening intensified while her adrenaline subsided as she remained kneeling. The deep windowsill served as a chin rest and her weary head took advantage of it. Frantic chirps of a baby bird stirred her mind back into focus and she squinted an intense search until she caught sight of the helpless creature flailing about in towering blades of grass. It was slightly bigger than an oversized walnut and the notion of it being out of its nest for the night was rattling. She fought the urge to rescue it. She recalled the time her father had told her a mother bird would abandon her chick if handled by a human. Today, she had no idea if that instruction held truth. At the time, however, her six-year-old mind only pondered what might have touched her to make her own mother leave. The sharp notion prodded the emptiness inside her.

Shaking jarring thoughts from a muddled head, she crawled to take a seat in the maroon, tufted, leather office chair. The back rest rose above her head and made her appear like a child pretending to be a grown-up. Spontaneity kicked in. Unexpectedly finding herself back in her city before her senior year of college, the summer lay wide open with her birthday-weekend on deck. The sleepy old Garden District had welcomed her back to the neighborhood with uncommon stimulation that she had met with courage. Why should she not celebrate her newly minted strength? She knew Louis LeBlanc would have far more pressing issues to contend with over marking his daughter's twenty-first year. She could hear the trumpets calling her to play in the livelier French Quarter. She pulled a slip of monogrammed linen stationary from the desk and with a Mont Blanc fountain pen in hand, scribbled a note designed to buy a little time.

Twenty-eight minutes passed before the bandit with the enchanting, but seldom seen, smile was trying to blend in on his way back to the French Quarter on the evening Saint Charles Avenue streetcar. The happy clatter of the mossy green trolley eroded the stun of events as the car rollicked along. The city thrummed with the promise of a weekend for the nine-to-fivers and the streetcar was full of residents leaving work and revelers making their way off into the night, all unaware of the rogue passenger clutching stolen valuables. He stretched his tense neck and a little straight thinking returned as he admired the passing cityscape. His furrowed brow leveled, and his broad shoulders slumped in response to the iron-landing scenes illuminated by yellow streetlamps tucked within oak hammocks. The retro vessel creaked along with him slumped against a jittery window. He knew one thing. A shift in operation location was necessary and that meant a move from his beloved New Orleans. The city had hardly returned his love anyway.

The streetcar made its first regular stop and he hunched closer to the window to avoid contact with the unknown who slid in next to him on the vintage wooden seat. He could see a few empty seats in the front of the trolley and questioned why this person insisted on sharing his seat. Then, a trace of floral perfume gave her away before he could confirm his fears. His heartrate quickened.

"You know, I never got your name. I'm Faith." Her green eyes fizzed with eagerness and her mellow voice lacked the bitterness it had employed earlier. She clasped her hands upon her lap and crossed her ankles. Despite her polite arrival this time around, she was decidedly more frightening to the troubled young man. He frowned at the sight of her with his back against the wall.

"What the …," he hissed. Running a capable, ungloved, hand over his confused head, he surveyed his environs in defense before casting his full attention back upon the only familiar face in the tight space. "Do you want this stuff back? You can have it. What do you want from me?" he whispered.

His despondent seat companion returned a whispered response.

"I want you to take me with you.

Chapter 2

Two hours prior, car troubles had left Faith stranded on the side of an Alabama highway. She and her broken down vehicle were deposited back in New Orleans, courtesy of a tow diver reeking of grease and beer, the one-way trip neatly arranged by the senator after doling out instructions along with his credit card number. Now, she strode along the uneven stone path known as Pirate Alley, a pedestrian street adjacent to the massive Saint Louis Cathedral in the heart of the French Quarter. The enormous white structure commanded attention for miles as it cast its slate spires toward its heaven and created a shadowy chill upon those walking below, who were like ants in comparison. Faith rubbed her bare shoulders for warmth. He had begrudgingly scrawled the meeting place on a receipt found lying in the middle of the street car's aisle and with a pen borrowed from a kind elder sitting in front of him. Her seatmate had jotted the address with little more than a grunt that announced his name.

He had called himself Patrick and the desired location, she deduced, had to be one of the unmarked stucco and brick buildings stretching along before her. Faith stopped to count doorways and look for address numbers. Without breaks in the line of buildings, their beginnings and ends were indicated only by the haphazard doorways, shuttered windows, and a few painted facades. Faith narrowed her choices on a block that made a mockery of global positioning systems then slid her useless smartphone in the back pocket of her cut-off jean shorts. As a sixth-generation New Orleanian, she should know better than to trust modern technology to find her way. The Big Easy was ancient in nature and shrouded in oddities that paid no mind to what conventional wisdom had to say.

An amorous couple passing by caused Faith to move from their path as she considered the charcoal, oversized double doors before her. The large hinges kept the doors attached to crumbling brick and black shutters covered the second-floor windows to make the address look vacant like the others. The handwritten note indicated an unmarked address; however, it did mention the black shutters. She stared at his writing, questioning everything, as the cathedral bonged seven. A broken, unlit gas lantern jutted out and Faith imagined it had offered a welcoming glow back when the black paint on the doors was fresh. She considered heading home while looking for a reason to stay.

The couple who had passed by a moment earlier returned. Faith watched the brunette hold her escort's arm that worked to pry open one half of the double doors. Seizing opportunity, she came in from behind and the man held the door for Faith, too.

Four patrons and one imposing bartender stopped to watch the newcomers arriving on nightfall's breeze. As the last to enter, the man re-encapsulated the speakeasy by fitting the doors back together behind Faith while his date sought refuge at far velvet booth. Only when the room darkened did the customers return to their private affairs amid red, velvet semi-circular booths. Faith scurried to the nearest barstool and feigned composure as she absorbed an atmosphere soaked in subdued light. Golden wall sconces proved inadequate, so votive candles were tossed about the room. Her eyes began to adjust as her mind did, too.

What if he didn't show?

She suddenly appreciated the dim interior for masking unnerved eyes that flitted across the aloofness. The heavy, tattooed bartender tenderly shined a cocktail glass while walking casually toward this new customer. Faith's nervous fingers twirled strands of long hair. Before restored judgment could set her free into the night, the barkeep's assertive voice tethered her.

"What'll you have?"

Faith stole a comforting glance at Patrick's note then tucked it safely into the empty pocket of her cut-off jeans. The feel of the rarely-used credit card in the opposite pocket provided a bit of security. The name on the card may have been a pseudonym, but she doubted this establishment would care. Then again, she presumed it to be a cash-only type of place. She brushed that thought aside. One predicament at a time.

Faith attempted to match the man's tone. In the end, she choked out words uttered by a dry mouth.

"A rum and Coke. Please."

Seemingly approved of now, he granted her request with a heavy pour. Before he could walk away again, Faith pushed the limits of his hospitality.

"And a cigarette if you have one? I could buy it off you." Faith pulled a couple of rumpled dollars from the pocket with the note. As she set the papers atop the wooden bar, she noticed the barkeep's eyes landing on Patrick's handwriting.

A box of Marlboro Lights were tossed before her.

"Help yourself. I keep a pack of 'em behind the bar for my favorite customers." His wink eased her and she pulled a cigarette from the box while the bartender flicked the silver Zippo's lid to allow a blue flame to dance around the rebellious stick between her lips and fingertips. She took a long drag with closed eyes and filled her lungs with abuse that felt good.

He let her be, walking to the opposite end of the bar to discuss quiet matters with a middle-aged man he appeared well-acquainted with. The bartender's satisfied patrons discussed taboo words left unheard by anyone outside of earshot. Faith took in surroundings reeking of a past era and saturated with dark mystique. Secrets suspended in the stale tobacco air. A darkly varnished bar ran the length of the narrow confines where the burly bartender held court with societal fugitives hidden among those velvet booths. Although the attractive couple from the alley sat close in a booth farthest from her, she could plainly see his left hand flashing a ring of gold while his guest's ring finger remained bare. It was a setting complimented by liquor and tobacco and boasted liberation. Patrick may have been a fleeting mirage, but she was not letting go of this weightless sensation. With a floating head, she welcomed the dizziness.

Her focus sharpened in the bartender's returning presence, his attention fixed beyond her and on the primal doors which surrendered to a new guest. Like bats in a cave, the denizens squinted at natural light seeping in.

"Hey, Mac. Need anything?" the bartender called out.

"Just a Coke. Thanks," a recognizable voice answered. Faith turned to see Patrick enter. He held himself to a new standard with a fresh polo shirt tucked in a professional manner and her fickle heart palpitated. He guarded his mannerisms as he stepped up to the bar beside her and his aftershave tangled with the stream of smoke which swirled from the glass ashtray. The bartender handed him the drink and directed brief scrutiny toward Faith before retreating. Patrick cupped the thick glass in one hand and leaned in next to her without a word.

"I thought you might be a no-show," Faith greeted.

He took her half-empty rocks glass and placed it on the small round table at the closest booth. He motioned for her to have a seat across from him.

"Yeah. Well, I have to stop back at work in thirty minutes," he forewarned once they were both seated.

“You work at Metairie?” she asked with her eyes on the shirt’s logo positioned upon his chest.

“I do.” Patrick nodded intently.

She blushed now in his presence. Out of her league and thrilled by the conquest. “My dad’s a member there.”

“I know.”

Faith had put herself in quite a dilemma, although she quickly realized that he had as well. Patrick leaned back in the seat and appeared to consider his next move. She downed the remainder of her cocktail and resisted the urge to rest the glass of ice against her warm cheeks.

“Look,” he began in a soft, authoritative voice. “I’m not sure what’s going on here. Although, I realize I owe you. Can we at least forget about how we met?” He closed in with a soft regard.

“What do you do at the club? My dad’s hosting a benefit there tonight,” she rambled.

He exhaled nervously and looked back pleadingly at the bartender who was deep in conversation with the man at the end of the bar. Patrick would not be rescued any time soon. A strain of honesty was his only option.

“Yes, I know he is. I’m a caddy there and I help out wherever else I’m needed. I’m heading back over to finish some loose ends, so I can’t stay long. I know who you are, I know who your dad is. I also know he’s taking big time donations from the same contracting firm he’s persuading the state to hire.” Patrick came up for air. To anyone watching, he was pleading a case as he leaned in across the table. Faith leaned in, too, if only to humor him, as he continued. “It’s a conflict of interest and if you agree to forget about meeting me, I’ll forget about making an anonymous tip to the news outlets.”

It was Faith’s turn to sit back and contemplate. A chuckle defied her smugness and she crossed her slender arms. Patrick’s eyes narrowed, trying to make sense of her reaction. If they were cat and mouse, she was the feline.

“Go right ahead,” she shrugged. “It would serve him right to get caught in his own web.”

Baffled, Patrick held up a quick finger meant to stall their twisted arbitrations. He scuttled back to the bartender who was engrossed with his own deliberations with the gentleman still seated at the end barstool. Faith watched with prying eyes and crossed arms, questioning the goings-on in this vague environment. Patrick whispered to the heavyset, graying man seated at the bar who, in turn, craned what he had of a neck to look at Faith. Their conversation became more animated. Patrick shrugged and the gentleman shook his head. The barkeep fetched another cocktail and a cigarette for Patrick's guest of honor. He returned to the booth with calmness restored, a half-grin and bribes in hand meant to placate the kitten before she grew into a tiger.

"So, like I said, I gotta get back to the club," he started as he slid closer. "Where are you going after I leave? You shouldn't stay here alone. Your bill's been was taken care of."

"Thank you." Faith imbibed with a slight cough. "Is there any Coke in this?" Patrick wiped away his amusement.

"That's Hawk for you. It means he likes you. Here, I'll have him doctor it up." He reached for the glass as she pulled it closer.

With a shake of her head, she continued by taking another deep drink. Unwilling to let him off the hook, Faith shifted her body to address him squarely.

"So, now that we're here, together, I do have a small request." Faith was careful to tread lightly, not wanting to spook him.

Patrick sighed, giving in to her charms as he supported his tired face upon his palm. His eyes grew bluer, even with lids growing heavy in the shadowy bar. Faith's voice had become a purr that soothed and, noticing this effect, she took a chance.

"You said you owed me something. Do you think, maybe you'd be willing to meet up with me tomorrow? Just hang out a little?" Her liquor-soaked mouth became slippery enough for unplanned words to spill from her fuzzy brain. She left the question to suspend between them as she retrieved a pen lying on the bar. He watched her take her seat, silky hair tumbling atop hands writing a phone number on a cocktail napkin.

Patrick registered compassion while Faith concentrated. When she looked up, her hollow eyes struck a chord he had not known to exist. She passed her note across the table and he wavered. Her father was as crooked as they come, and the apple never falls far from the tree. Then again, Patrick knew himself to be no angel. Exhaling defeat, he sided with empathetic caution.

"I'll call you in the morning. I'm off tomorrow."

"You're off?" she asked snidely from her side of happenstance. "No break-ins scheduled?"

He clenched his jaw and examined the writing held between fingers and thumbs.

"Forget about that, alright? Anyway, how do I know you're not setting me up? Like I said, you can have the jewelry back." Patrick's direct stare turned cold. She held hands up in defense.

"I don't care about the jewels. I'm looking for …" she paused and her head dipped low as she rubbed her temples. She looked sad and he tried not to care. "Something else. Something, for some reason, I think you can help me with. Okay? Start over tomorrow?"

He agreed with a slow nod, burdened with suspicion.

Chapter 3

Faith was drunk on resentment and rum. Anger, rooted years ago, finally cultivated while the streetcar rambled on. She ambled to the exit prior to a complete stop and hopped outside to trudge the last two blocks in the dark. Twisted branches engaged in shadowy gossip, their sinewy tendrils reaching for Faith as she went. These southern oaks were eager accomplices to impending scandals. Beneath lush currents of beckoning Spanish moss, she advanced along Prytania Street until the brick mansion came into view.

Gas lamplight illuminated the iron gate entrance that squealed a tattle on her homecoming. The worn brick path was depressed in the center. Faith followed its trough to the proud wrap-around porch painted a variety of colors since construction in the early eighteen hundred's. The beadboard ceiling, however, possessed no other color than light blue to protect the homeowners from restless spirits, or haints as the Gullah called these fearsome souls. It wasn't enough to keep Faith's restlessness away. Her steps resonated upon hollow stairs then gray porch decking. The house was dark inside.

The gardenia blooms welcomed her back and she made haste through the foyer to her father's study where her note remained ready for discovery. The lie about spending her birthday weekend with a friend would be spun into an exaggerated truth. Bounding upstairs, she returned her stepmother's jewelry box into the safe. Lights left lit proved no trace of Patrick's visit inside. Faith reached outside and rolled the escape ladder before locking the window.

Hallway walls loomed as her father's house strengthened its grip. Faith's skin prickled at the smothering and she leaned against the cold plaster, placing a hand on her heart to ease its race. Shallow breaths signaled defiant nerves joining the suffocation process. Standard operations generated adequate relief to carry on: breathe deep, focus, recall a fond memory. She forfeited the last part, as usual, and went about the business of becoming a short-term runaway by packing a leather duffle from her stale closet. Casual tops, shorts and a red University of South

Alabama hooded sweatshirt would suffice. She adjusted the dresser drawers back into closed position and rushed from the room before it became a trap. The gardenia scent ripened to a repulsive state and she paused at the entry. Treachery took a turn upon returning to the office for the gun.

The bulk of the weapon was strangely comforting, empowering in her slight hands. Opening the chamber for the first time, she was now certain the gun was loaded so, she engaged the safety just like that friendly city guard had taught her back when her father was mayor and dropped the gun into her bag. Lastly, she decided to reposition the note to the foyer's Chippendale accent table where it would not be missed alongside the floral decoys. Out on the porch, the night ushered her with honeysuckle and cricket song. She would avoid her usual stops to prevent notice from nosy neighbors. After all, it was not the first time she escaped incognito.

As she had occasionally done in the past, she would now assume the role of Josephine Beaumont. The name on her fake – or secondary as Faith preferred - ID's and credit card had been pilfered from a French ancestor and had been obtained via a political connection who would keep any secret for a certain price.

A sole tidbit of family history from her mother's side had been discovered through a fifth-grade ancestry research project. Louis had disliked Faith's interest in her mother for the project, claiming the past belongs in the past. She persisted and he gave in by providing details needed for a proper deed search at city hall. Accompanying internet research unveiled the fascinating story of Josephine Beaumont, a respected healer in the village of Orleans, France and whose good deeds were described as witchcraft by the town's leaders. A bias trial had led to a harsh sentence at the stake.

Unimpressed with her push to do the project her way, and the A-plus earned, Louis soon sent his daughter north to attend the Sutton Academy for Girls boarding school. Looking back, the timing was hardly a coincidence. To stray from Louis LeBlanc's wishes meant finding oneself at his mercy in the end.

Ever since, Faith adopted the name when she needed her privacy honored. That seventh great-grandmother from the late 1700's now had an American Express, Louisiana driver's license and United States of America passport. Some political connections are worth having.

The trolley back into the French Quarter was quiet, and the ride gave Faith a chance to check for vacancies in town via her phone screen. The Omni hotel in the French Quarter would provide safe harbor for the night. After a few stops, Faith chose to exit the car and walk the rest of the way. Jazzy trumpets spewed musical confetti from windowless confines and became more prevalent with each step toward Bourbon Street. By the time Faith reached Decatur Street she was treading lightly upon sidewalks bathed in the spirit of Louis Armstrong. Never minding the throngs of tourists, she was alive in her city and its energy lifted her spirits higher. The glowing white spires of Saint Louis Cathedral towered above meager rooflines and she wondered if Patrick was back at the little tavern on Pirate Alley. Discouraging her reckless temptations, a drugstore employee stepped out to reattach a wooden door hook to the exterior wall and the employee's smile summoned Faith to enter the modern pharmacy housed in the historic structure.

Scanning the aisles for guilty pleasures, her guilty conscious, on cue, settled in.

So unappreciative. Selfish like your mother.

Faith shook the voice away and focused on strengthening shades of red lipstick. She tossed a tube of rouge into the plastic shopping basket as her anxious heart began its typical race.

In the next aisle a disheveled mother hushed a baby crying in its stroller. Faith pretended not to see the tub of powdered infant formula poured into a plastic shopping bag near the child's kicking feet and regretted not taking the cash that had lied with the gun so she could help the poor woman.

I pay for your enviable education and this is how you thank me. Her father's voice was always with her.

Rows of confident faces stared back at Faith from the hair color shelves. She placed two fingers against one coy smirk printed on the packaging. The model's eyes were empty without the smile. Faith tossed a box of L'Oréal hair dye into her basket with a particularly smart-looking woman on the cover. Scissors, mascara, a round brush, and sunglasses piled up in the plastic shopping container and Faith headed to the front of the store to wait in line.

Louis LeBlanc's condemnation pierced her mind at regular intervals, tightening the strappings of the emotional straight jacket she had been fitted with early in life. Faith closed her eyes and exhaled, willing the thoughts to cease. It was no use. Decades of being told nothing but shortcomings will take its toll on a person's psyche.

"You ready, miss?" Faith regained focus with the cashier's voice and set her items on the counter.

"Sorry. Daydreaming, I guess," she offered with a sideways glance, recalling that making eye-contact was another one of her faults. Funny how it had not been a problem upon meeting Patrick. Her father might have been proud.

Her heart fluttered the shame aside.

Throwing in a tabloid magazine and paying for the purchases with Josephine's card, she confirmed it still worked and carried her bags outside.

The Omni Royal hotel was a four-block walk. Louis would say it was an appropriate next stop for a wealthy brat to mend her wounds. Straightening her posture and smoothing her long hair, she walked into the grand lobby, channeling her alter ego. Faith slid her credit card over the granite reception counter with insincere confidence.

"You are all set, Ms. Beaumont," the front desk clerk stated. "I was able to upgrade you to a balcony room. Here is your room key. Please enjoy your stay and don't hesitate to let us know if we can be of assistance."

"Thank you," Faith cooed as she picked up her luggage for a trek to the elevator. The enormous chandeliers sparkled amid the regal decor and she pondered what the real Josephine Beaumont would have thought of this stay. She found her room, shut the door behind her, and sunk spread eagle into billows of cotton bedding. Knowing there was little chance anyone would find her here, Faith's anxiety vanished for a minute. One luxurious minute.

Your work ethic is atrocious. When I was your age, I worked twenty hours a week.

The hollow inside her was riled, and she became desperate for a cure. She called room service and in no time, a bottle of Belvedere vodka was delivered for three times the price she could have found it at the liquor store. A silver bucket of ice, a few twists of lemon, and a sparkling rocks glass accompanied the bottle on the service tray.

Typical. You have no clue how the world works. Weak like your mother was.

She had nothing to combat that one with. Unable to deny her actions as unappreciative and selfish. Just like her mother who had left them to fend for themselves. She poured a drink over ice and gave in, allowing the elixir to follow emotional scars that were like streams flowing throughout her, all leading to that emptiness constantly craving fulfillment. If only he knew how she had aimed to improve herself for him over the years. Sitting back, she allowed the alcohol to clip the wings of the abyss before they could envelope her. She had never questioned the existence of the hollow, only worked to banish it.

Her thoughts switched to the mother in the drugstore trying to feed her baby. Gaunt and filthy, the woman certainly had more problems than Faith could conceive. Throughout the city, state, country, world, the sad statistics proved that Faith was not part of the truly suffering set.

What if she could help them? Would those acts fill the damn hole?

I have provided you with everything. He screamed.

Show some appreciation. He demanded.

She winced and eyes clamped shut. Head back on the upholstered headboard, her mind shifted to that first weekend at the all-girls boarding school. Without warning, she had been sent away. Her twelve-year-old self had reasoned she had left too many cereal bowls in the sink and one too many pairs of shorts on her bedroom floor. The C in math could have been the culprit. Any parent would have had enough of her, she had reasoned.

Louis, of course, was far too busy to accompany her to move-in day. Instead, Chelsea, a new girlfriend at that time, had flown along to drop that little southern girl in a very unfamiliar state called New Jersey. After exchanging awkward good-byes, Chelsea left her in the dorm room and Faith then shared an equally awkward hello to her new roommate. The girl's parents stayed for hours and gushed over their daughter, promising to send care packages often until they saw each other for Thanksgiving break. Faith had eventually excused herself to have a good cry in the bathroom down the hall.

Tears flowed again while Faith recalled the harrowing experiences from her plush hotel room. Forced to leave everything she knew and survive among the mean girls had been excruciating and left scars she never recovered from.

Some scars were more visible than others.

The headmistress had worsened matters with a meeting in her paneled office where it was explained that Faith's father had concerns over his daughter's lack of responsibility and confidence. To remedy this,

Faith was handed a list of weekly chores that would be a part of her curriculum.

The girls loved the chance to catcall *Cinderella* while she mopped the cafeteria floors.

A fine education it had been.

Just as she had then, Faith now winced in desperation to disappear. Life can change all it wants but the feelings remain. She drained the glass and sat it on the nightstand. Rolling up in a fetal position, she cried. Not deserving of anyone else's pity, she bestowed the pity onto herself. She cried harder than the time she got word she would spend spring break alone at school because her father was unable to arrange a flight home (and that some time to reflect on all she learned would be good for her). Harder than the times she spent parents' weekends alone in her dorm.

Harder than the first time she felt the edge of the blade draw blood from her arm.

Sitting up, she brushed the tears away and traced the faded scars. Her fingertips soft, they still allowed a release as the memory of the sensation came back. At least in her younger years, Louis LeBlanc was forced to interreact with his little girl once she got home from school. In her teenage years, his disinterest in his daughter grew more apparent year after year and she wilted away in a cold world where she was unable to make friends. His treatment confused her to that day.

She reminded herself that things were different now. At college, she has a roommate who has become a friend. Her grades are good. College will be her ticket out. A ticket purchased by her father.

Another shot of vodka pulverized the walls inside and Faith made a vow to herself. The weekend's conclusion would present a transformed woman. A confident specimen she, with sudden intensity, knew she could become. Despite him. Without bottles or blades.

The tiny balcony adorned with a black iron railing offered fresh oxygen and she swam from her confines to breathe. From the bistro table she listened to laughter bubbling up from the happy people below. She wanted to be one of them now. Couples held hands, families walked in groups. A man kissed a woman amid the soft glow of lamplight. They were all blissfully unaware of the sad stranger watching them. A stranger who had always found herself irked by their kind of happiness. She preferred the solemn and moody side of the city. The parts where the blues evicted marching saints. That authentic grittiness whispered she belonged there.

Exhaling any bad mojo that had gathered inside since the promise she made, Faith took the hair color and scissors to the bathroom. Pressing the light switch, she took a long look in the mirror. She hated what the reflection embodied. A weak and sad person she had grown tired of. She held the box next to her own face and pulled the ends of her tresses up to her chin. She would be the confident woman on the box. The crisp granite countertop and cold tile floor of the hotel bath encouraged a fresh start. Faith combed her elbow-length hair and gathered it into a low ponytail.

In a snip, Faith's life-long look was gone. Would Locks of Love accept her mane? A first gesture of charity and more comforting than eighty proof. Easing the ponytail holder out and wetting her head in the sink, she evened out the jaw-length style that coaxed her jade eyes alive. Next, she fingered the front forward and added a thick bang with the sharp blades.

She greeted her new reflection with admiration for this girl who was light and ready for adventure. Scraps of her old self discarded on the beige floor, surprisingly fickle under the threat of simple household scissors. Faith swept up the mess with wadded up tissue. A new color was next and, in the end, reinventing oneself was a surprisingly easy process. At least, on the outside.

With a towel draped across her shoulders and the ammonia aroma swirling around her head, she retreated to the balcony bistro set wearing a hotel robe. The box promised thirty minutes until a new image set in. Hooves of white horses below clipped and clopped along avenue in celebration. From her perch above the city streets, Faith looked upon the carriage riders with more kindness and humility. She was one of them and knew that now. All part of a bruised and battered human race, knitted together with an intention for comfort. The warm air caressed ankles and toes and she longed to be somewhere quieter. Somewhere where she could reflect and ponder without scrutiny. A mid-west ranch with thousands of stars overhead or a quiet beach in Maine with only the sounds of waves crashing to the rocky shore could do the trick. She would find out. She had a hunch about Patrick. He could teach her a thing or two about living a bigger life.

In half of an hour, Faith was adjusting the faucets to allow the hot water to stream from the shower head. Steam whirled and bloomed as she stepped under a harsh spray that rinsed the dark solution from her head and onto the floor of the bathtub. She breathed the steam into her lungs while she rinsed her short hair clean.

Saint Louis Cathedral proclaimed ten tolls, two hours away from marking twenty-one years of existence. Two hundred fifty-two months. About seventy-five thousand days of opportunity. Faith would not waste one more. The mirror reflected a truth – a new outlook on life. Her green eyes captivated against black hair and reddish lips. Her skin radiated a fresh pink glow from the heat of a cleansing shower. Fresh energy pulsated throughout her body. Dressing in black shorts and white peasant top, she deserved a night out to test her new look.

A block away and on the corner of St. Louis and Chartres Streets was two-hundred-twenty-five-year-old Napoleon's House. The structure built with an intent to bring Napoleon Bonaparte back from Louisiana from exile. He died before a return was possible. Now, this restaurant showed its age with unabashed pride and the patrons were babies in comparison. In passing during off-hours, the structure appeared deserted with its thin stucco and grime. Shame on them for judging this edifice by it veneer of two centuries of patina. The crumbling stucco on the outside matched the unpainted plaster walls housing a thousand spirits who would certainly rebel against their presence being stripped by renovation. Stepping over the mosaic nameplate at the corner entrance was like tripping into a time machine.

The hostess led Faith to an iron café table in the courtyard where an out of place, wide, hardwood staircase led to unknown destinations. Potted palms, a stone floor, and mismatched seating completed the chaotic setting. A waiter clad in a tuxedo shirt and black bowtie approached.

"A drink for you tonight, miss?" he inquired.

"Pimm's Cup, of course," she answered smartly with a request for the house specialty. The waiter soon returned to present her with a pale refreshment served in a tall Collins glass.

"Happy birthday to me," she toasted under her breath with an upward plea. Palm fronds rustled. Gracious stars twinkled above, receptive to guidance.

The eve of Faith's twenty-first was a night of renewed vigor that seemed to have been carried to her by the wind. As she abided the prodding of the universe, a different sort of local spirit sat hidden from view among flickers of light thrown by candles dripping colorful wax. This ageless woman sat silently among the shadows of a parlor's back room. She spun her old-world magic with finely tuned, female sensibilities that went beyond spoken expressions.

She knew that her ancestors had been punished for what this ardent woman practiced. She herself had paid an ultimate price years ago and she would not allow another child lost to ignorance. Those before her dealt within in the strict realms of white magic. The Creoles' teachings included sinister methods that this occultist was no longer afraid to employ. Tonight, however, she sent the good. She knew the workings of life and death beyond the considerations of immature souls surrounding her. Modern conveniences had connected brawnier buildings surrounding her forgotten chamber. Her place was modest, but just as fierce. The deep, tunneled, brick entrance at the sidewalk signaled reasons to continue by. Yet, if one had been looking for true spells, this would be the place for such philosophies. By contrast, voodoo shops served the tourists looking for cheap thrills.

Atop a butcher table, there burned three pillar candles. Black banished negativity. Blue soothed like cool water. Red would elicit the vital power of love. Wax oozed and congealed. The cathedral signaled midnight, she harnessed her force to direct it. A spell to bring a forlorn descendant to her. The wicks crackled and hissed.

So now, a birthday conjuring fermented. The woman closed her green eyes and rested her slight chin on frail fingers. A draft flickered the flames. She smiled at a call sent. The lost soul would arrive on a whim and there was no one better than she to offer guidance.

Chapter 4

Patrick's cellphone buzzed while he locked up the darkened country club pro shop after-hours. His plunder hidden, his tasks done for the day.

"Yeah?" he answered.

"Mac. It's me. How's it going?" the gruff and raspy male voice asked.

"A close call. Got what we needed. It's in your office."

"What do you mean by 'close call'? That makes me real nervous."

"You're nervous? I'm the fox that got caught in the hen house. Have a little sympathy," Patrick answered incredulously.

"You know I'm not a sympathetic person. What happened?"

"Can't talk now. Hawk and Joe know. I think it's all good. Don't worry. I'll make sure it's all good."

"You better. Alright. I'll be at the club all day tomorrow. Stop in?"

"Got plans tomorrow. Better make it tomorrow night," Patrick replied.

A mild headache dialed up its intensity and brought on fatigue. Seated on the motorcycle with helmet in hand, he watched from his empty section of the parking lot. Aging debutants began early exits from the banquet hall. A trusted caddy, even if his judgment off the greens was poor, he recognized many of their escorts. There was no sighting of Louis or Chelsea LeBlanc who were undoubtably still wringing last bits from remaining deep pockets. Faith, he realized, had never been part of the country club scene. No dinners with her father or lounging by the pool. He would have noticed.

Patrick beheld distant fairways displaying greenery matching her eyes. He permitted invading optimism while recalling earlier encounters that left him equally flustered and intrigued. Her strength and courage on full display at her home. Her severe insecurity and vulnerability even more apparent as the night wore on. He considered her potential whereabouts until his cell alerted a call he had been eagerly awaiting.

"Patrick. Glad you picked up. Are you still able to move the Marauder for me? The slip in Tampa is paid for and reserved until September."

"Hi, Steve. Absolutely. When do you need me?"

The last of the sun's pink rays disappeared. He was anxious to witness that feat from the Gulf of Mexico's calm waters.

"Anytime. Hell, you can take off tomorrow if you want. The sooner the better. I'll email you the marina address and leave an envelope of cash to cover your expenses and time. The same as last time?"

"Sure. That works. Man, I wish I could take off tomorrow, but I can't. Sunday?"

"Perfect. I'll have it gassed up and ready to go. Text or call to keep me posted. You know I'll be a nervous wreck till I know my baby is safely tucked in."

"Will do, Steve. Thanks for trusting me."

"I can't think of anyone I trust more to handle my boat. Regardless," he laughed, "I'll still be nervous. Keep in touch."

"Don't worry. I should have her there by next weekend at the latest, depending on the weather."

His energy was renewed by the image of the Cigarette go-fast boat. It was a million-dollar vessel and a dream to navigate on open waters where it topped out at around 120 miles per hour. He smiled. A strong beauty to whisk him from reality. His helmet muffled bullfrog croaks from water hazards filled with gators. Patrick revved the bike more than necessary to leave the parking lot.

Back in the French Quarter, Patrick stowed the bike in a garage owned by Hawk. The one-story brick building was located just off Royal Street and a quick walk back to the tavern. The bells of St. Louis Cathedral signaled ten o'clock as he passed. He assumed he must be invisible to the throngs of people threatening his personal space as he walked. Historic architecture amid a musical landscape couldn't pry attention from phone screens. Patrick feared for the souls of society while sidestepping yapping drunks with grating voices. He prayed the unpublicized tavern was empty. Maintaining unknown status was blissful and, thankfully, New Orleans was proficient at keeping secrets. Locals in the know of the underground watering-hole never dreamed of tattling and most were gone my midnight. Patrick slipped behind the pub's planked doors and closed them as quickly as he could.

"Mac." Hawk was alone at the bar. Relief rushed over Patrick.

"Hey, Hawk. Quiet night?" Patrick slumped next to the burly man. Low light trickled to the tin ceiling.

"Most excitement we had was your earlier arrival." The bartender chucked a kind laugh that mismatched his outward appearance. "Joe was nervous at first, but he calmed down, like he always does."

Patrick leaned elbows on the bar and hid his face in his hands. He muttered something about being glad the day was over.

"Charlie called me. I told him I couldn't talk." Patrick revealed.

"Good idea. That guy's gonna have a heart attack by sixty if he doesn't relax." Hawk finished his pint and waddled for another. His oversized, tattooed arms poured a Coke for Patrick.

"Thanks," he said in exchange. "I think I'm gonna have a heart attack by forty if I don't relax."

Hawk gave his friend a sympathetic look.

"So, take a break," he suggested as he reclaimed his seat.

They looked simultaneously toward curious fingers prying at the rustic door. The panel opened slightly, letting cartoonish wails of merrymakers interrupt their conversation. Patrick ran to pull the barricade bar across the middle before entrance would be gained.

Hawk shook his head. "Animals."

"You're telling me. I was practically run over by the hoards on the walk back." Patrick returned to his barstool and extinguished thirst with soda.

The two savored the isolation, hidden from masses who would enthusiastically reveal their cloak-and-dagger operation. Then, Hawk broke the silence.

"So, think she'll leave us alone?"

Patrick pondered the question with a finger spin of a cocktail napkin upon the bar.

"I'm meeting up with her tomorrow."

Hawk choked on his sip. "Why the hell would you do that?"

A Bourbon Street celebrant fell against the door from the alley. Patrick and Hawk's heads whipped to the left, grateful for the stern lock.

"What the …?" Patrick shook his head before continuing. "Anyway, I know, I know."

"If she's setting you up, the gig is up. We'll be operating from jail cells."

"She knows too much already."

"If you'd buy a shirt from a store instead of stealing from the pro-shop, you'd better your chances of staying undercover."

Patrick shrugged smugly.

"Now, she knows where to find you. If she tells her sad-excuse-for-a-father, you and Charlie will be the first to go. Me and Joe after that," Hawk deliberated, his hulking body rising up from the bar stool to refill their glasses. Across the bar from his young friend, he pointed accusingly. "You need to keep her in the dark and on your good side."

Patrick's blue eyes flashed despite the darkness. His slight grin did not go unnoticed.

"Looks like I have no other choice but to see her tomorrow."

"Hmmm. I see," Hawk said knowingly.

Patrick left with a wink as he retreated to his meager apartment upstairs, his companion left to read between the lines. In the studio abode, he let hot water rinse the day away before finding respite under a cotton cover, eyes heavy with head on pillow. While succumbing to sleep, Faith's words drifted on dreams.

I want you to take me with you.

A hazy morning found Patrick tracing his usual breakfast route leading to Joe's diner. The stench of stale beer loitered empty streets long after last call. Shopkeepers hosed cobblestones, an unrewarding morning chore repeated daily after the return of thankless customers. He nodded gratitude to those maintaining pride in a city favored by enibriates. Eventually, roasted chicory root and coffee beans provided a more pleasant aroma tinged with powdered sugar. The true essence of a city deemed Louisiana's belle of the ball. The door chimed as Patrick walked into his daily destination. An open galley kitchen featured short order cooks working through paper slip demands. The clangs of the grille in full swing as aproned waitresses sashayed. Patrick took one of the last metal stools at the counter and watched bacon sizzle next to eggs turned over easy. Before he could greet anyone by name, a steaming mug of coffee was placed before him.

"Thanks, Rosy," he replied.

"No problem, sugar. Same old, same old?" The woman of Creole-descent eased a paper placemat and napkin-wrapped utensils in front of Patrick with one easy motion.

"That'd be great. How's your morning?"

Rosy adjusted her apron and leaned in against the counter next to him while new patrons shuffled into the narrow restaurant. "Better now that you're here," she teased. "When you're ready for a real woman, you just come on and see me, hear?" Her guffaw drew amused smiles from the cooks.

"Rosy, how come you don't never make those offers to me? You like those skinny white boys?" he goaded a playful welcome to the favorite customer. "How's it goin', Mac?"

"Hey, Curtis," Patrick greeted in return.

"Hmm. And gettin' skinnier by the minute waitin' for your slow self to make him some breakfast," Rosy retorted with a slap of the order slip. Curtis grabbed it before it could drift away and went back to work with an easy laugh.

The banter continued and his coffee refilled until breakfast was before him. Famished, he stopped conversing to eat and while absorbed in his meal, never noticed the owner taking a seat next to him.

"Morning, Mac," Joe hailed. "Talk to Charlie since yesterday? He was trying to reach you," the portly, graying man tutted. Patrick shoved a big bite of egg with toast into his mouth as a response. Joe waited with folded hands for Patrick to stop stalling. In no time, his topic of conversation and musky cologne snuffed Patrick's appetite. He slid the plate forward. Joe cleared the mess and grabbed the coffee pot to deliver a refill.

"Wow. Served by the owner," Patrick mused.

"You know I'm a glorified server here. Let me put this back. Save my seat."

Joe beelined it back to the counter, not letting Patrick off the hook.

"We talked yesterday," Patrick said between sips of black coffee. "And I'll be seeing him later today. I gotta take off for a week, though. I've got a feeling he won't like that."

Joe shrugged and a pout formed on his wrinkled face. "It is what it is. Take a break. You shouldn't push yourself like you do. What happened with the … situation … from yesterday?" To anyone paying attention, the men appeared to be sharing pleasantries.

"I'm dealing with it today," Patrick reacted. Relief set in when Joe abandoned the banter. With a pat to Patrick's shoulder, Joe went about his business and sent his younger friend on his way with a to-go mug of caffeine. Rosy and the others waved him off into a morning where the rising sun had burned off the fog.

Morning time in the French Quarter was his favorite time. Filled with promise and void of crowds, the city basked in her own glory.

Carried by the cathedral's chimes, Patrick found an empty bench in Jackson Square. Squirrels sprung about, playing hide and seek as they searched for hidden acorns on their way to the next oak base. He squinted up at the tall white spires of the church. So-called sinners casually entered the majestic cathedral in search of a dose of religion, or simply admire what religion had built. He considered joining their pilgrimage. Instead, he isolated in plain sight, believing in a creed of seclusion. His coffee cup half empty, he contemplated options waiting at the bottom of his cup. He had carefully folded Faith's note and secured it in the pocket of his tan shorts before leaving his apartment. Now, it burned like an ember.

He did not have to call her, and that option was chocked with temptation. An easy way out of his latest quandary. By tomorrow, Patrick would be navigating a boat toward Florida. Charlie would ceremoniously terminate the caddy's employment while quietly arranging a fresh cover. The new day job would allow a neat fit into society upon his return. Or, he could reinvent himself in Tampa, with Charlie's help, of course. The idea of leaving New Orleans saddened him. The idea of running away was appealing.

Still, he knew better. Difficulties have stamina and his woes would keep the pace.

Ready to make a move, Patrick retrieved the napkin and called her before he could change his mind. Faith answered on the third ring.

"Hope I didn't wake you. I never can sleep in."

"Just wondering if you'd call."

"So, I was thinking of hitting some golf balls today. Care to join me?"

"I've never picked up a golf club."

"No?" He held back his surprise. Louis LeBlanc was a regular fixture on the country club greens. How had he never included his daughter in something he loved? "I can teach you. I know of a par three course out of town a-ways. Always a lot of beginners there. There's a driving range, too."

"Sure, whatever. Where should I meet you?" Faith asked dryly.

A nearby landmark begged noticed.

"In Jackson Square. On one of the benches near the cannon display. Ten o'clock?"

"Ten o'clock. See you there."

From her hotel room, Faith searched through her suitcase for suitable golf attire. A summery red blouse with a collar and linen shorts were adequate. Shoes were a conundrum. Old Navy flip-flops were the closest she had to comfortable. They would have to do. She took extra time to blow dry her new hair and applied a little make-up as an extra precaution. Surely her father would dare not take his sport off coveted fairways?

By the time she was ready, the bedside clock showed an hour until their meeting time. The hotel featured an upscale restaurant for breakfast, however Faith preferred the city's more authentic offerings. She exuded a newfound confidence as she waltzed out of the Omni and bid the bellhop a good day.

A mere two dozen blocks from home, but a world away, Faith traversed in the direction of the Mississippi River which flowed through the urban center like a giant, muddy trough. Not wanting to take St. Louis street most of the way, she turned onto Chartres Street at the crumbling corner walls of Napolean House to cover the sunny two and a half blocks to the restaurant. Residents watered potted plants on balcony gardens overlooking the empty morning streets. Faith bid hello to those she passed. She was happy in her new skin. Before the river could blossom into view, she discovered a corner table at Café Maspero from where she could watch the people go by. The fluffy beignet sticks served by the welcoming waiter were warm and coated with powdered sugar and paired perfectly with cups of strong chicory coffee with cream and sugar. Unexpected events tossed Faith back to her childhood home and the house on Prytania Street spat her back out. The French Quarter would always claim her, chiseling her depression with charisma. At that café table, corners of crimson lips rediscovered their upturned curve.

Caffeine increased jitters as hands of a wall clock raced to reach ten and twelve. She considered passing on his invitation. She considered calling the police – sixteen hours and a couple of cocktails, courtesy of the thief, later? By nine forty-five, she dawdled toward Jackson Square. Horses with carriages aligned the park fence and Faith stepped from the curb onto the grass to begin the concrete ascent. All four benches atop the cannon display area remained empty as touristy photographers milled about capturing timeless photos of the grounds. A full-on vista of the city's crown jewel church lie at the front of Jackson Square and the disarmed artillery atop the viewing deck respectfully pointed away from the divine building. The symbols of war were no match for such a symbol of peace. At ten o'clock on the dot, she watched him approach from the greenery below. He was dressed in another polo shirt from the club, this one red with a white emblem, and she suspected members' dues unwittingly purchased the guy's entire wardrobe. Silently, she observed. He kept his hands in pockets and head low, a sideways glance here and there. Then, disappeared before climbing the stone steps on the other side of the cannon display. A white visor, also from the country club, shaded his face and matched his white Nike tennis shoes. Long strides brought him the bench next her, not recognizing her yet. She took advantage of this and waited for an excuse to leave him there like any reasonable person would choose to do. He leaned elbows on knees, sat back up, stretched his neck, looked to the right, then to the left. Craning his neck, he looked behind and below. Uneasy, but waiting. For her.

Strangers in their midst paid no heed to the loners sitting benches apart. Faith rose to emerge into his view. He remained oblivious when she decided to sit next to him before anyone else.

"Is this seat taken?" she ventured.

"Uh, no," he uttered before a double-take.

"Good. I'm supposed to meet someone here. We're going golfing." A mischievous grin formed on her dark red lips.

"Faith?" he mused.

"Shh. I don't want to be recognized," she whispered southernly. "I assume you're someone who can understand."

"Wow. You look completely different. You look … incredible."

She was struck by his sincerity.

"Thanks. I'm just going for unrecognizable, though. Did I succeed?"

"Yes. Yes, you did," he confirmed, still taking her new look in.

"Good. So, where are we headin'? I don't want to run into my father or any of his golfing buddies."

"No problem. They won't go anywhere near where I'm taking you. It's casual, which, judging from your shoes, is a good thing."

"Then let's go."

Faith stood and marched ahead. Patrick jumped up to follow before rushing to catch up.

"I have a bike parked in a garage off Royal," he started as they walked side by side toward the park entrance. He hesitated when he realized she might not be keen on the idea. "You okay with riding the bike? I have a second helmet."

"A bike? Like a Schwinn or a Harley?" She wavered.

A street band was setting up near the entrance of the park, in front of the cathedral. The hip musicians drew a sizeable audience which Faith exploited to remain hidden.

"Uh, a Honda. Motorcycle."

"Okay. Just don't wreck," she consented, keeping a swift tempo.

"You're safe with me."

These nonchalant words lit fireworks in her heart.

On cue, the band started up with a Saturday morning kind of tune. The rhythms muffled as they slinked deeper down the alley. Patrick stopped before a brick, one story building. As he opened the padlock and the barnlike doors swung open, Faith swore she could still smell the musty aroma of wet hay from use as a stable long ago.

"Just be careful around the exhaust, okay?" Patrick warned as he heaved the cycle from its kickstand and rolled the black bike from the quarters. He handed her a yellow helmet and put his black head protection on. Checking her chin strap, he slid his index finger under her chin. At the sensation, she recoiled. He jerked his hand away from her.

"Sorry, did I pinch you?"

Faith shook her head and finished the job herself. She slid behind an already seated Patrick and held the rigid bar behind the seat with rigid arms.

As the motorcycle rumbled to life, Patrick looked behind for a clearing in traffic and lurched ahead, Faith jolting into his back.

"You'll want to hold on to me for balance," he yelled through a flipped-up helmet face shield. She remained trusting of the metal bar.

Quaint cottages and shotgun shacks drifted by. Regular stops imposed by signs, pedestrians, crossing trolleys, and red lights instilled ease to an apprehensive Faith. Her confidence swelled. Soon, Patrick leaned into a sharp turn and Lake Pontchartrain came into view. He merged onto the causeway that spanned the vast lake and as he increased his speed, Faith took his advice. Her aversion to physical contact cured by an aversion to road rash – or worse. She leaned into him, wrapping her stiff arms around his waist as Patrick lingered in the right lane. Regardless, fifty felt like a hundred as Louisiana shed its urban skin. Thick stands of tall pines blossomed on the other side with glimpses of swampland serving as channel markers off the bridge. Patrick carried them along smooth highways and rural roads and Faith ascertained a level of solace with him. The tires grasped higher ground where a late morning sky caressed wispy meadows. A cautious turn onto gravel and a drift of dust followed them to a section of farmland turned into a mediocre golf course. Cows languished in a far-off pasture. The greens were far less manicured than an expensive course, but just as serene, if not more so. Patrick parked next to a patched-up shack, Faith lifted the helmet. Plummy air bursting with pine and grass rushed in.

"Nice scenery out here, huh? Hope you didn't mind the less than luxurious ride." Still on the bike, Patrick waited for Faith's reaction.

"I think I loved it," she said, dazed with the adrenaline. Surprised, Patrick took the helmet from her and remained on the bike to steady her exit. He offered his hand. She vaulted from the seat instead. Standing next to the bike, she smoothed her hair and regained equilibrium.

"Hardly anyone here today. Perfect." He walked to the office that looked like a chicken coop and requested a few clubs and two buckets of balls for the driving range. The employee stashed the helmets for them and passed out three clubs apiece with the baskets of golf balls.

Faith followed this stranger, again. Venturing deeper and deeper, existing in uncharted realms where she was unsure of finding her way back. The trend was peculiar, and she willed herself not to think too much. As Patrick set them up on the driving range mats, adjusting his crimson country club visor, he appeared more prep school than skids. Ray Ban cool with athletic appeal, unaware of her scrutiny, she felt the pull of his current strengthen. She realized the draw was more big brother than anything else, but felt the danger of shifting emotions plague her.

He set a precarious ball on a tee and waggled into position. A look down, a look left, a look back down and a swing that whooshed and cracked the little white orb to some far-off point on the range. Satisfied, he grinned wide. Faith cast an uncomfortable glance at her bare toes. She had no idea what to do.

Patrick turned towards her. "Love it when it goes my way. Go ahead. Have at it," he encouraged with one gloved hand resting on the driver and the other on his hip.

"Alright," she said meekly and looked back down at the little plastic bucket containing a heap of impossible feats. She placed a ball on the tee like it was a grenade. She looked back at him and smiled nervously. He gave a broad, confident smile back as he leaned against his driver. "Okay. Here we go," she started again.

With a deep inhale, she went for it. Attempting to mimic golfers she had seen in action in the past, she swung hard and failed miserably.

Wondering how the ball still sat in the same place, she quickly repositioned herself and swung the club again. Another miss. She stared at the golf ball, its stamped, brand name, imprint heckling her. Faith continued with five earnest attempts with nothing to show than frustration. Patrick, on the other hand, was impressed by her determination and chose not to interfere. He went on to lob one ball after another high and far out into the field with little effort. She tried to get another swing in before he could watch her dismal routine. Then, she had enough.

"What the hell do any of you see in this miserable game? Here. I'll just watch. You can hit my balls. Thanks, anyway," she huffed as she went back to sit on the bench behind them.

"Wait. You can't give up. I'm sorry. Let me help you. Come back up here," he said softly.

"I'm a lost cause and I'm okay with that, really."

"No, you're not. I shouldn't have let you suffer like that. Okay, let me give you a quick lesson." She begrudgingly obliged and sulked back to her post. Like a pro, Patrick let Faith in on basics when it came to a solid golf swing. He stood beside her and helped her to hold the club the right way and showed her how to swing effectively. After a few weak attempts and his encouragement to relax, she finally made contact and the ball went sailing. Holding the club high in the air, she jumped up and down ecstatically. Patrick beamed in the glow of her ecstasy

"Great shot," he congratulated. "I knew you could do it. Keep doing whatever you just did," he added as he went back to his post and easily made one straight and long drive after another. Faith continued to work at it with hit and miss efforts. Eventually, the hits were more than the misses and the bucket of balls drained.

"So, you up for a round of nine holes?" he asked.

She flinched. "I'm definitely not ready. I'll just be in the way."

"Nah. You're fine. You're not in my way. I'm enjoying the company, for once." Her heart warmed. "There's no one out there anyway. C'mon. Where's your sense of adventure? Try something new." He struck a nerve and she stood a little straighter.

"Okay. Let's go."

Walking the little practice course permitted ample time to converse, however taboo subjects between them shackled the conversation for the first three holes. When muteness became deafening, Patrick opted to tread controversy.

"So, your dad never took you golfing with him?" He clasped the shaft of a nine-iron in his hand and wristed the ball to a few feet from the fifth hole's flag.

"No." She hit her own ball and advanced a measly ten feet, never even getting up in the air. Patrick took it in stride and stayed with her with each of her pathetic attempts. "How'd you learn to play?"

"Ten years or so? I started out in high school and just always tried to keep up with it on my own. Joined a couple leagues here and there. Nothing too formal. I'm really not that great."

"Pretty good in my book. What high school?" Faith stepped for her turn. She could hear his huffy exhale.

"Ah, I went to Grace King, Booker T., John F. Kennedy," he listed. "None still around, at least in their original form, since Katrina. Maybe Grace King faired okay?" he pondered. "I think Booker T. closed. Wait a sec, if you don't mind?" he reached with a gentle hand to keep her from swinging. "Look at your feet."

"What's wrong with my feet? And isn't Grace King High all-girls?" she stated, point blank

"Not since the 1980's and you have perfectly fine feet that are very pretty in non-regulation flip-flops. Good thing I brought you to the right course. Anyway, the ball will follow your lead. Have your toes show the ball where to go." He demonstrated what he meant by lying the shaft of the club at her toes. She repositioned her feet. "That's it." Patrick's steady voice calmed her typically unsteady nerves. "Now try it. Keep your head down, eye on the back of the ball. Relax. Don't think too much. As John Daly would say, grip it and rip it."

Patrick disregarded her confused expression and awaited follow of his instruction. Moving past his words, she breathed deep and shook tension from shoulders. Pulling the club back, her mind went blank and she continued the motions until she heard the crack of the ball and club connecting. Excitedly, she cupped her palm over her eyes as they watched the ball hang in mid-air before dropping.

"How 'bout that. Nice shot, Faith," he congratulated sincerely. "I think you might be a natural."

"Really? I've never been a natural at anything. You know, I think it landed with yours! Wow. That was awesome. I am so hooked. I love this," she rambled with a zest for life that had gone missing long ago. Each passing day made it more difficult to recall a time she was less aware of how life mishandled her. Lately, she looked in from the outside more than ever, unsure as to why people – even her own father – did not care for her. Pushed out of inner circles by stronger individuals for years until there was no longer a place in society for her, permitted only to drift in the draft of those more significant than she.

The euphoria was fleeting, however, as her cloud swiftly returned to smother elation.

"So, what made you target him? You know, when we first met?" she prodded. He walked ahead, pretending not to hear. She grew frustrated of the role of the swatted fly, so she endured while he carelessly made his putt on the last hole of the day. Faith reduced distance to be heard. "That's all I need to know before you go."

Standing three feet apart on an island of turf and mistrust, there was no escape. She read between the lines of his furrowed brow, anticipating his personal techniques for brushing her aside. He walked to the hole, leaned to retrieve his golf ball, and intrigued her with his return. Removing sunglasses, standing close enough to read misgivings, his comeback thwarted her charge.

"Who says I'm going anywhere?"

The game of cat and mouse intensified. Patrick, the cat with the Cheshire grin and Faith, the meek mouse lured by sleek ways. A grounds worker appeared from nowhere, creating a rift in their exchanges. Unable to navigate the chasm, they moved along, deep in thought. Their worlds had shifted.

Back in the gravel lot, awkwardness reigned. More cars filled unmarked spaces. Neither one knowing where to go from there. Patrick handed Faith her helmet. She hesitated, as did he.

"Well, I guess you can just drop me back off at Jackson Square, if you don't mind?" she ventured.

"And where are you going from there?" His blue eyes were streaked with concern.

"Rent a car? Head back to Mobile?" She said the only thought that came to mind. "If you see my dad at the club, don't say anything."

Patrick laughed. "You act as though I'm someone he talks to." She nodded understanding. He continued. "Anyway, I'm not going back there for awhile." He studied her reaction and confirmed her attention.

"No? Where then?"

"Coincidentally, Mobile. If you need to go there, I can take you. Anyway, what do you do in Alabama, Faith LeBlanc?"

She liked the way he said her name. The way he valued her.

"Nothing now. But, I just finished my bachelor's in premed and still have an apartment until fall."

"Is that right? Smart," he offered with an impressed glance.

Faith shrugged. "What I was most interested in out of the choices I was given. We'll see how it turns out. Anyway, I got into a little fender bender on Friday and my dad arranged for me, and my car, to be towed back here. There's no way I can stay, though. I need to leave."

He capitalized on her urgency.

"You should tag along with me, then."

Chapter 5

"Higgins," Louis barked into the cell phone on Monday morning.

"Yes, senator," the devoted guard answered.

"I have a job for you."

"All ears, sir."

Louis rose from his desk at his Baton Rouge office to confirm privacy. Once satisfied, he retreated to the comfort of a plush, dark leather office chair. Grey clouds hung outside the window. The day was as dreary as his disposition.

"It would appear Faith has gone on a walkabout. Again," he stormed. "She left a note. Claims to be staying with a friend from college for the weekend. Too convenient and vague."

"I see," the experienced detective answered. "Have you called her?"

Louis fidgeted with the black fountain pen in front of him and smoothed his thick, dark hair back in agitation. "No. I must say, I'm a little tired of tracking her down and seeing what she's up to. Still, I should make sure she's okay."

"I understand, sir. Hold on to that note if you still have it and text me her current cell number to make sure I'm tracking the right one. I'll be in touch," Robert Higgins obliged.

"Thanks. Keep it quiet, of course."

"Of course."

Louis disconnected the call and the press photos of his family of three came into focus. The portraits arranged on his executive desk to instill admiration and adoration. Intended to soften his image. Two of the faces were polished and pleasant. Faith wore a slight scowl. More apparent to him than anyone else, it still drove Louis insane. She knew how important a good front was in the political world and had watched Louis rise the ranks and amass solid wealth in his business dealings over the years. Her angst always bubbling just below the surface, surely, just to spite him.

A knock on his office door pulled him from his thoughts.

"Come in."

"Mr. LeBlanc, your nine thirty is early," his secretary of ten years announced quietly through the cracked door.

"Well, he'll have to wait. I have a few things to attend to. Offer him some coffee for now. Thanks, Nancy." Louis adjusted the framed pictures on his desk for a better view.

Nancy cleared her throat to continue.

"Yes, um," she began before entering the office and shutting the door behind her. "I tried that. *She* explained, in confidence I might add, that she'd like to discuss private affairs before her colleagues arrived."

"Well, let's see what she's got. Send her in."

The bourgeoning lobbyist arrived in style with a haughty skirt suit and attitude to match. Her stilettos took her height to new levels. Louis assumed a relaxed position and motioned for her to have a seat.

"Welcome. James, Correct?"

"Yes, sir. Thank you for seeing me early."

"I apologize, I assumed you were a man." Louis chuckled and pushed back from his desk to provide ample space to cross his long legs. He unbuttoned the jacket of his pinstriped suit.

"Short for Jamie. At any rate, I have a bit of an inside track on the team that we're working with that I'd like to keep between us, if you don't mind."

Louis waited for her to make the first move. When she did not, he pressed with confusion. "You mean the team you are supporting?"

"That's right. They are currently embroiled in a lawsuit that I feel could affect their ability to see this job through in a timely fashion."

Louis raised an eyebrow and leaned into the desk. She slid forward, her silk blouse lowered to garner more of the powerful senator's attention.

"Why are you telling me this, dear?"

She ignored the unprofessional term, determined to create leverage.

"I work with another contracting firm who has quietly informed me of what they can offer. I think you will be impressed."

"I already am, I must say." The direction of his gaze revealed true intentions.

She felt the heat of his double-edged comment and knowingly pulled her long, auburn tresses over one shoulder.

"I can arrange the second meeting for this afternoon."

Louis moved to the window to clear his head. He scanned the horizon and admired construction cranes put in place by former deals not unlike this one. This lobbyist, however, did put a slightly different spin on the current one. He struggled to focus on the business aspects. More cranes meant more done deals. More done deals meant more money and power. He walked back to where James sat perkily.

"And regarding these change in plans, there is something to your benefit, I assume?" He looked down on her from his perch on the corner of the desk.

"Of which I will split with you."

"I think we'd work quite well together, my dear. Be sure to arrive early this afternoon."

To ensure ten minutes of privacy, Louis locked the office door.

As Louis finished his intimate meeting with the lobbyist, Chelsea was starting her day at the Prytania Street mansion. She had developed a habit of sleeping in over the years and it was something the former businessowner was ashamed of. Throughout her twenties and early thirties, Chelsea Benton had grown accustomed to rising before the sun to allow breads to fully rise first. During those early hours while the rest of the city slept, she would coax beignets, muffins, cupcakes, and party cakes to full potentials for her boutique bakery. As the sun crested the horizon, the neighborhood residents would begin to arrive. One resident had become a more regular customer than the others his orders increased to an impressive scale. Eventually, all of the senator's morning meetings were to be catered by the petite blonde's bakery. He persuaded the law firm he had been a partner of to order from her. Corporations tied to Louis became loyal to Chelsea's beignets over the better-known New Orleans' bakeries. By the time Louis proposed, Chelsea was ready from a break from the mad rush of business. Chelsea Benton LeBlanc rarely stepped into a kitchen these days, let alone wake up early to knead bread.

Still, she brushed misgivings aside. To anyone judging, her personal life had turned out fine. She had found her footing in more than a few charities over the last five years of the marriage and she was an ardent supporter of her husband's political career. Every so often, however, she recognized her unfulfilled moods. She sat on boards, rarely included in day-to-day operations. Often, her role was to attract donors, not decide how the money would be distributed for greater good. This particular day would be filled with meetings and charitable appearances. Increasingly feeling a void since leaving her business behind; her husband's shadow was cavernous.

Chelsea dragged herself from the plush, four-poster bed. Her slippered feet plodded with soft resistance across the hall to her posh dressing room. The space had been a gift from her husband and arranged through a contractor he had become cozy with. While sent away to a spa retreat, a spare room was converted. She knew it was really designed to convert her. A way to encourage this wife to become more of what this husband desired. Upon her return, she admired closets full of designer clothes and pricey handbags. She had swooned over the expensive fabrics and chic touches. Despite it all, what had really converted her was one of Louis' own monogramed shirts in the closet they had shared before her own quarters were established. Cast aside to be taken to the dry cleaner, the basket hadn't left the house before Chelsea spied the bright pink lipstick smudge on the collar. That Sunday evening had brought a shift in their dynamics and Chelsea accepted a new reality. The romance was gone when she recognized her role was in jeopardy. From that point on, she fought to hold her position.

That pink rouge had hardened her like nothing else had. She played her part and play it well, knowing it would be the only way to leave him one day with her pride intact. Now she sat upon the velvet settee and wondered if her husband had ever sat here with another woman. She sensed a stranger had been in the room. Shaking troubling thoughts from her distrustful mind, she sifted through a dense rack of summer suits, skirts and frilly blouses. With tags still hanging from the garments, she draped the pale canary pleated skirt and creamy blouse across the settee. Plucking a pod of coffee for the single brew system, she had a cup of coffee in hand a minute later and savored a few tastes before walking to the shower. An hour later, her just-above-the shoulder, light blonde hair was dried and plumped at the roots and she descended the stairs with the keys to the Audi Louis had surprised her with on her thirty-ninth birthday last summer. She has been a good wife.

"Good Morning, Mrs. LeBlanc," the housekeeper called sweetly from the round foyer table she dusted. The maid had only been with the LeBlancs for a few months and she still insisted on an air of formality.

"Morning, Marjorie. Please, call me Chelsea. How are you today?"

“Fine, Mrs. LeBlanc. Would you like a cup of coffee to go?” Marjorie held the dust rag in front of her with clasped hands and her salt and pepper hair was styled in a conservative bun. Kind and grandmotherly, warmness exuded her even as she remained professional to a fault. Clad in her usual light blue housekeeper’s dress, white apron, and comfortable white shoes, she stood at attention in the gleaming foyer while she waited for Chelsea’s response. Chelsea smiled at the woman’s refusal to ignore the traditional training she must have received so many years ago.

“No thanks. Oh, forgot my purse. Be right back,” she called over her shoulder as she sprinted back up the staircase.

In the dressing room, the creamy, leather handbag waited for her on the floor, slumped against the built-in armoire. Its location persuaded Chelsea to fetch a few golden baubles for her wrists and she knelt to unlock the safe. Simply wanting a little extra sparkle for a Monday, the sight of the empty vault delivered undeserved shock.

Chapter 6

Room three thirty-one had permitted her transformation and the knock of the housekeeper told her it was time to leave.

"I'm on my way out," Faith called out though the slightly open door. The timid maid spoke broken English and nodded her understanding.

Faith shook day-old memories from the clothes she picked up from the floor before tossing them into the unzipped duffle. Patrick's invitation for a boat ride to Mobile appeared sincere. She smiled at the ludicrous notion. Tempting, but no. Still, she ruffled through the pockets of her shorts to look at the name of the marina he had scrawled on a scorecard. She held the note and recalled the moment. Her apartment bedroom in Mobile waited for her and that was the logical place to go.

The thought of having to return to the world she knew filled her with dread. The freedom she had stumbled upon over the past two days elated her. She still had work to do. Faith picked up her cell phone and sat on the edge of the unmade bed. Her roommate answered.

"Hi, Jane. Can you talk?"

"Faith! Are you back in New Orleans? I got your message late. Sorry I couldn't pick you up on Friday. Are you okay? What happened?"

"I'm fine. Just a little accident that smashed up the rear of my car. Anyway, my dad had me and my car towed back to the mechanic he uses here."

"I'm glad your dad was around to help. When will the car be done?"

"No idea. Hey, um. About my dad. If he, or anyone else, calls you, can you say I made it back?"

A moment of silence set in as the roommate considered the request.

"What's up? Are you okay? You don't sound like yourself, Faith."

"I'm not myself right now." Faith smiled at her refection in the nearby mirror. "I needed a break from home. I just need to buy some time and want him to believe, to know, I'm safe."

"Faith? What is going on? *Are* you safe?"

"Yes. Really I am. Please don't worry. No big deal, just, you know how it can be being me. I think I need a little vacation is all. Maybe I'll end up back at the apartment. I'll let you know. For now, I'm weighing my options. I might just hole up in a hotel by the beach for a few days or something." Roommates since their freshman year, Jane knew all too well the line Faith had to walk.

"Sure, of course I'll cover for you. Although, you need to stay in touch with me. Deal?"

"Absolutely. I'll call you by tomorrow. Like I said, I might just come back to the apartment for the summer."

"I wish you would come back. Well, you're secret's safe with me. Just don't forget to call me tomorrow."

There was another knock on the door with the maid's announcement. "Housekeeping," was called as check-out time loomed.

"Okay, well, I have to run. I'll call my dad now and tell him I'm back at the apartment with you."

"Got it. Be careful."

Faith took a deep breath and called her dad while she had the courage. She breathed a sigh of relief when the call went to his voicemail.

"Uh, hi, dad. It's me. I ended up back at school with Jane. I'm gonna hang out here for a bit. Maybe the summer. Just wanted to check-in so you didn't worry." As she made the last comment, she winced at the credit she gave him.

Unbearable stillness encouraged Faith to swiftly gather belongings before deciding where to go. Simply leaving a message for her father ruffled feathers of the void. The vodka bottle hollered from the nightstand and she answered its willingness to numb her emotional discomfort. By the time the bottle was placed in her bag, the level had reached the halfway mark. The liquor had done good on its promise.

The Omni Royal lobby was abuzz with Sunday morning arrivals and check-outs. Everyone had somewhere to be. Faith placed the card key atop the receptionist's desk and revealed the room she was checking out of before further conversation could ensue. Humidity closed in as she stepped out onto the street. Sober and polite due to recent arrivals to the city, the tourists inspired Faith to stay in the French Quarter for brunch. Her city would tell her the right move to make from there.

Turning onto Bourbon Street, she walked to Lafitte's bar. Named for the famed privateer with greater tendencies toward piracy, the building retained originality, like all structures in the historic district. If Lafitte would happen to rise from the dead, he would find his favorite meeting spot without any trouble, although the fifty stars on the American flag, which currently hangs from the pitched roof, would make him scratch his treacherous head. She strolled through the open doorways that were fasted with shutters in place of real doors. From her perch at the rustic bar, Faith indulged in a spicy Bloody Mary with the ghosts who inhabited the space. Hungover, mortal patrons soon rolled in to join her. She watched them nurse their headaches with what caused them in the first place.

Hunger set in and Café Amelie on Royal Street became Faith's next destination. The café was three blocks from the little place on Pirate Alley and would be easy to reach by foot once she was through with a plate of gulf shrimp and grits. Then, she remembered Patrick advised he would be at South Shore Marina by now. Preparing a boat to leave town. It was on the northern end of the city limits on Lake Ponchatrain and, Faith recalled, next to a small airport. Those private planes could land her somewhere tropical.

As a hostess led her to a table in the restaurant's courtyard, she imagined Florida sun stinging her cheeks and sand on her feet. Perhaps she would take an Uber to the marina to at least say goodbye to Patrick. From there, she could watch the planes take off. Perhaps she would board one.

After a delightful brunch that left spirits restored, Faith meandered down Bourbon Street. Parties were starting, bands were setting up. A saxophonist completed a warm-up riff. Then, an unexpected door opened to her. A muted teal gate at the end of a brick tunnel she had never noticed before. As the gate squealed a greeting on one hinge, Faith stepped closer to inspect then walked the ten steps it took to find another curved door that swayed open to her.

A spellbound Faith peeked in. When her eyes adjusted to the darkness, she witnessed shelves of misty glass bottles and dried plants and petals stuffed in dusty baskets. A shop of some kind. Faith gently pulled the shutter door open a bit more to step in. The floors covered with unmatched boards, rows of candles represented a wide assortment of colors and sizes lined rudimentary shelves. Musky scents wafted through light delivered through pricked holes upon the pin cushion roof. Her thoughts slowed, her mind soothed. The only other source of light came from the still-ajar shutter. No windows, no sign of electric. Statues and dolls strewn about the unpainted shelves were recognized as part of the

Voodoo religion. Beaded jewelry hung from random hooks. She gasped at the long needles and balls of string, indicating the dark side of Voodoo. She shuddered not at the collection, but to her intense attraction to the tokens. She reached for a cloth doll with cross-stitched eyes and glanced about the mildly macabre scene for a counter or register. She only saw more dusty shelves brimming with mystical chattels. And a stone archway from where a reedy voice called out to her. She placed the doll back in its place.

"Do you have the time for a visit?"

Faith followed the pleasant call.

"Rest here," an unseen woman continued. "I've been waiting."

Like a moth to flame, Faith glided toward flickering gold candles being lit. Frail hands scratched matches erupting tiny, sulphuric blasts. New light bathed the tiny room with a butcherblock table at its center and taking a seat across from the white witch, Faith was overcome with an undeniable, and unexplainable, sense of peace. Long, colorless hair flowed over the woman's gaunt shoulders as she readied the space. Discarded matches with burnt tips littered the tabletop covered with melted wax. The woman has been busy.

"You need my help, dear. Let me guide you. Give me your hand." Spirited eyes electrified with flashes of green, her cold and bony hands possessed a feather touch. Candlelight revealed the alabaster face framed by pale, frizzy hair that stretched to the top of the wooden table. The elder gently turned her guest's hands, palms up, as Faith laid forearms on each side of the candle heap. Tempted by soothing ways, Faith's hands stilled in a consoling embrace. There was a familiar quality to this grasp that satiated. She recognized the woman from somewhere. The ethereal lady closed her eyes softly as she continued her remarks.

"My dear, you are on a journey," the woman professed.

"Did my travel bag give it away," she retorted cynically. She instinctively pulled her hand away from the woman who answered with silence and a knowing smile. She reached for Faith's hand once more. Faith gave in.

"Sweetness, not all journeys are of a physical nature. Many are simply journeys of the spirit. Your restless spirit has been suppressed. You mustn't deny the spirit. It will manifest itself in some form. Allow yourself to thrive, my dear." While still holding Faith's hand in hers, the woman closed her eyes again, tilted her head to the side and a tired grin emerged. Her pale skin was bathed in candlelight, her silver hair glowed.

Humming a simple melody, she remained in some type of trance for close to a minute. The melody, too, was recognizable, however, Faith couldn't place it. Uneasiness set in and before she could think about the song any more, Faith prepared to run for the exit by pushing herself back from the table. The woman came to again and beheld Faith with more intensity.

"Don't leave yet, child. Don't turn from the flame." Faith unhid her face from the shadows and remained seated. "I see you are transforming yourself, my dear. Transformation is good. People are rarely what they project. Embody your magic." With those words, the woman grasped Faith's hand with a stronger grip. "A soul companion awaits."

Faith yanked her hands away with a final effort.

"I should leave," she blurted as she leaned to grab her bag.

"Wait, please." The woman whispered in despair.

Faith bestowed pity on the woman who she reasoned my need money. The interaction was rattling her sensibilities all the same.

"Awaken your spirit. Yes, you need to go. Leave now. Go where the open waters run blue. My child, no harm will come. Only freedom. We'll meet again under sweet magnolia blossoms."

Wooden chair legs scraped as Faith rose from the session in a confused haze. "Okay. Well, thanks. What do I owe you?"

"Sweet child, you owe me nothing," the woman whispered, "Until we meet again, I have tokens. For protection and inner strength."

The thin woman stood and revealed herself draped in a long, dark out-of-date dress with a matching V-neck shawl. The whispy attire was more 1970's hippie than voodoo priestess. The matriarch floated past with Faith in tow, tote bag in hand. The enchantress reached for two bracelets from a hook. Their green eyes met as the woman coaxed the youthful wrist.

"This for protection and this for strength and clear intuition. Wear these always." Slipping one then another bracelet onto Faith's wrist, the woman brought her pinkish lips to the beaded bracelets and gave each a gentle kiss. Unsure of what to say, Faith muttered her appreciation for the gifts and the woman's time and rushed to leave.

In her evocative way, the protector made Faith's next move clear. Clear as the tropical, crystal clear waters to the south.

Chapter 7

By high noon Patrick had the red speedboat in shipshape and Bristol fashion. Tossing a used rag into a nearby bucket, he sat down on the captain's chair with a thud as the classic rock channel played Led Zeppelin's D'yer Mak'er. Patrick turned up the radio to let Robert Plant's voice resonate.

"You don't have to go-o, oh, oh, oh, oh ,oh-oo …" he warbled along with one leg propped near the steering wheel and a forearm covering his eyes. An arrival in Panama City by nightfall meant shoving off soon. Still, he allowed himself a little time to loaf. Morning preparations left him depleted of energy. The long, fast Cigarette boat could easily do the first leg in an afternoon as long as good weather prevailed.

"Pat … you there?" the two-way radio crackled. Patrick pulled the hand-held radio closer and pressed the side button to answer.

"Yeah. What's up?"

"Weather's looking good for the next forty-eight hours. I'm thinkin' of pushin' this trip through today for some down time in Panama City," the hoarse male voice announced.

"My thoughts exactly, my friend. Meet in Mobile for fuel stop? Just like last year?"

"Hell, yeah. Panama City's calling me. That place we found last year was a good time. Headin' out in an hour if you wanna leave at the same time? Lemme know, buddy."

"Will do." Keith's upbeat exchange revived him. With top speeds of over a hundred miles per hour and cruising speeds of around eighty, the fifty-foot Cigarette Marauder was a joy to navigate the Gulf of Mexico's open waters, to say the least.

Lean muscles stretched as he reached with a yawn, inhaling a deep dose of salty air before making his way to the swim platform at the rear of the boat. There, he would find a retractable transom shower to rinse off. The cool freshwater cascaded over his head and back. Refreshed, he slid across the expansive sun pad and dropped into the cockpit. Sliding a fiberglass door aside, the elongated, air-conditioned cuddy caddy cabin provided private quarters to sleep, dress, and escape the harsh sun from time to time. White vinyl bench seats stretched along the sides until ending at the v-berth bed made up with dark blue bedding. Patrick quickly changed into swim trunks and pulled on his worn-in red visor. Zipping up the black gym bag serving as luggage, he placed it neatly in a drawer beneath the bed. Satisfied all loose items were stowed properly and the cabin was tidy, he emerged into the sunlit cockpit and situated himself back at the helm. The substitute captain flipped the switch to engage exhaust fans that would blow traces of combustible fumes away from powerful engines. Five minutes later, his heart palpitated when he started the engines. The go-fast boat roared to life. It was a beast of a machine hidden under a flashy, sleek exterior. Freedom guaranteed by horsepower bucking to leave the confines of the slip. At the thought, he felt a chill rise through him. Patrick hopped onto the dock and started to undo the lines. Sensing footsteps behind him, he looked over his shoulder.

"Hi. I tried calling out to you. Guess you couldn't hear me over the noise," Faith greeted.

"Well, well, well. Aren't you a sight for sore eyes." Patrick stood as he admired his muse with arms crossed. "By the way, this vessel does not emit *noise*." Pulling his visor forward, he hid wandering eyes. With tanned skin, a pastel tank top, cut-off jeans, and pink flip-flops, she was a breath of summer. Light and breezy. He suppressed a chuckle at the sight of the Jackie O glasses, blunt haircut, and New Orleans Saints' cap all exploited for masquerade.

"Yeah, well, I wanted to stop by and thank you for a great time yesterday." She rocked on her heels and looked around with hands in back pockets.

"The pleasure was all mine. Sure you don't wanna come along? As long as the weather cooperates, we'll be in Panama City tonight. Like I promised, I'll stop for fuel in Mobile."

Her cell phone rang. Patrick watched a cloud descend from an otherwise sunny day.

"Hi, dad." Shoulders slumped as she spoke.

Her greeting sent him into action. He jumped aboard the vessel and cut the engines. Faith tilted her head back and side to side to allow the tension from her neck to escape as it formed. She took the berating in silence. Patrick pretended to busy himself with something at the helm while he strained to eavesdrop.

“I know. I’m sorry you were late for the fundraiser. I appreciate you driving the whole way to get me.”

She attempted to block his fury with understanding.

“I know you think I was careless, but I really couldn’t avoid it. That car came out of nowhere. It was scary.”

Faith eased down on the dock, legs weakened from tolerating another tirade.

“I’ll be more careful from now on,” she conceded to appease. “Can you give me a ride to pick it up when it’s done? I guess next week sometime?”

The assumption of his availability fueled his rant. She curled further into herself.

“I’m sorry. I didn’t know you were heading out of town. Sure. I’ll figure something out.”

And with those words, she unfurled from her crouched position to behold the fortuitous invitation laid before her. The impressive boat gleamed with temptation, its caretaker ready at the steering wheel. Disconnecting the call, she double-checked to make sure the line was dead before placing the phone in her duffle bag. Patrick stopped feigning disinterest to join her on the dock. Lightheaded, she accepted the outreached hand, attempting to stand steady on the rolling dock. While she remained silent, he implored gently.

“I think it’s safe to say you’ll never get the opportunity to ride in a boat like this again.” Visor now backwards, hands on bare hips, he looked over his shoulder. “That blue water’s callin’.”

Faith tried for a sensible option from her downtrodden mind brimming with insecurities.

“Joining you for one leg of the trip can’t be that bad. I’ll call my roommate and tell her I’ll be in Mobile this afternoon.”

“Welcome aboard,” he hailed with a motion toward the bucket seats. “Make yourself comfortable. Feel free to stow your stuff below. I’ll undo the lines.”

Faith carried her luggage onboard and slid the cabin door open for entry to the sleeping quarters. The interior of the boat stunned with futuristic design. White, uninterrupted seats extended along the sides and ended at a booth-like berth framed within a squared entry. The exterior screamed speed while the cushioned interior beckoned rest. Mesmerized by the boat’s sweet siren’s call, Faith dropped her bag to crawl into the cocoon-like den. She slid onto the upholstered bed and lied still. Water lapped at the hull which gently rocked as she felt Patrick step back onboard.

"Help yourself to a shot of tequila or whatever. We're casting off," Patrick called.

"Don't mind if I do," Faith muttered and pulled herself from the threat of a nap to pull a bottle from a deep holder nearby. With lips upon the cold glass, she soon felt the burn of tequila's comforting distraction.

Back on deck, Patrick stood at the helm and looked behind him as he reversed the elongated boat from the slip. The boat eased out of the marina and into Lake Pontchatrain from where they would lock through the Inner Harbor Navigational Canal. As they motored along, Faith stood beside him and held tightly to a nearby rail. There was no turning back. She slumped down into the bucket seat next to him.

Patrick had promised blue water, but the canal was anything but. A brown waterway dotted with industry. She became immersed in first-mate duties, however, and was unaffected by the scenery.

"Toss those bumpers out along the side?" Patrick asked of her. After a moment, she figured out what he was asking of her and swung the soft, inflated tubes outside the boat. Tied off with their own lines at proper lengths and pre-hung on cleats, they dropped into position and protected the fiberglass sides from the lock's concrete walls. Patrick navigated the boat into position as a worker approached from the lock's upper deck with a long line. Patrick thanked him and grabbed the end of the rope to tie it off onto the boat while the other end was wrapped around a concrete nub to allow the boat to be eased down with the lowered water level in the lock. Fascinated, Faith felt proud to be a part of such an intricate process. The water level dipped and soon the whistle blasted a free to go call. Passing an incoming barge, Patrick steered the boat slowly into the Mississippi River. The New Orleans' skyline blossomed into view. They motored on, flowing with the current toward the Gulf of Mexico.

"We'll take it slow for now, but once we get out of the no-wake zone, you'll wanna hold on. Wait till you feel this baby go."

"Let me call my roommate first, okay?" Faith thought fast to forewarn her companion that someone was aware of her location and would be waiting for her.

"No problem. I'll stow the bumpers. Take the wheel?"

Without waiting, he left the helm unattended. The boat cooperated by keeping a straight course. She leapt into his place and steadied the wheel with a commanding presence.

Jane answered on the second ring and Faith used a shrill voice to address her while keeping one eye on Patrick. In the end, Jane agreed to wait for Faith's call and pick her up if she needed a ride. Although Faith failed to mention an arrival by boat, Jane expressed curiosity at the background sounds of motors and wind.

"I'll explain when I see you later." She placed the smartphone in the nearest cupholder to her left and settled back into her bucket seat while Patrick took over at the wheel. The rush of navigating the lock out of Lake Pontchatrain for the first time, along with the shot of tequila, wore off. Second-thoughts crept in.

"Beautiful day, huh? You just have to soak it all in," Patrick started as he noticed her sullen expression. He couldn't afford her wrath should she turn on him. She remained glued to her seat with arms crossed.

"So, whose boat is this again? How do you know the owner?" she probed.

"Just a guy I know from the marina. I have a little speedboat docked there."

"Hmmm. I see." She digested his words. "How do you know how to handle this one, then?" Her words took on an accusing tone that put him on guard. She analyzed his hesitation behind the safety of her dark sunglasses. Then, with a mischievous grin, he stood to slide the cabin door open and tossed his visor down into the salon. Bare feet and Ray Bans on, he resembled more rebel without a cause versus dangerous liaison and Faith's icy demeanor thawed. The river widened and nature's attitude changed with wind that picked up to create a significant chop on the water.

"I'll show you how I handle her. You might want to take your hat off." His hand outstretched, she handed over her ball cap while smoothing her hair. "Don't bother. You look fine, anyway." He tossed the hat to land next to the visor below and slid the cabin door shut with one hand still on the wheel. Taking a firm stance before the captain's seat, he surveyed his surroundings and pulled back on the throttle. The engines thundered in response and the bow of the boat bucked. Faith grabbed the railing.

"Ready?" he called. Ready or not, the go-fast accelerated to cruising speed in two seconds. Faith's head flew back upon the headrest, unable to suppress elation as butterflies released inside. The shoreline faded as they shot out into the Gulf of Mexico like a cannon.

Chapter 8

At the tavern along Pirates Alley, a determined regular wrestled the hefty door open. He took his usual seat on the stool farthest from the door, the scratch of the legs on the pine floor echoed through the empty room.

"Charlie. Wasn't expecting you here tonight. You get off work early?" Hawk muttered as he sauntered toward the customer and slid a pint of ale his way. Charlie loosened the tie around his thick neck.

"Hi, Hawk. Yeah, well, our boy Mac stood me up. He also left a voicemail saying he wouldn't be at work for the next few weeks. Off to Club Med or something like that," the rotund man grumbled, still catching his breath from the walk after having to park his dated Lincoln Town Car five blocks away. He dabbed at the beads of sweat forming around his thinning hairline with a white handkerchief kept in the inner sport coat pocket. Standing again, he impatiently removed the jacket and placed it on the barstool beside him. Sweat pockmarked his gray polyester button down shirt. The burly bartender arched his back and tilted his head sharply until his neck bones emitted a pop.

"Humph. What's he up to? I didn't know he was leaving town," Hawk lied.

"Good question. Got a voicemail from him saying he was leaving early to run that damn boat down to Tampa again for that guy Steve. Remember him? Member at the club? Seems like a decent guy. Makes me nervous, all the same," Charlie rambled before downing half his beer. Hawk topped it off for him out of habit.

"A boat boy now, huh?" Hawk let out a hearty laugh setting the draft glass on a coaster in front of his old friend. "C'mon, Charlie. We can trust Mac. Where the hell would he really go, anyway?" Hawk laughed some more until a smoker's cough took over and he turned to stifle it with his generous forearm.

Charlie gulped more of the pilsner as a response. "I'm telling you, he's gettin' careless. He told me he had a close call the other night when he was supposed to hit up the senator," Charlie whispered as he looked around. "Then he seems to be getting close to this guy with the Cigarette boat. I think he's hiding something. Forgetting the mission. Our mission. He's flaking out on us and that spells disaster."

Hawk leaned into the bar to rest palms along the edge. "Mac's as good as they come and his heart's in the mission, as you call it. More than any of us. Shit, he's the goddamn poster boy of the mission. Maybe he just needed to get out of town and lay low. Probably a good thing. He knows what he's doing."

The twosome muzzled their words when a young couple tumbled through the door and fell into a booth with a giggle. Hawk made eye contact with Charlie before taking the glass to satiate his high-octane friend. Returning with frothy ale spilling over the top, he walked around the bar to take the newcomers' drink order. Charlie huddled over his beer during the interval. Hawk barked out a customary 'What'll you have' to the already intoxicated couple and retreated to the bar to prepare two gin and tonics. After delivering the cocktails to happy couple nestled in the far booth, Hawk reappeared with plans to change the subject.

"How's everything at the club?" Normal conversation always fell flat among them.

"Fine. Busy with weddings, benefits, baby showers and all the other shit."

"Should allow you to get a few good leads?"

"Suppose so." Charlie's face brightened as a thought came to mind. "Yeah. Know what? I just so happen to know of something in Tampa. A good - house."

"I see," Hawk read between the lines of the thinly veiled statement. He shined a wine glass and returned it to a shelf.

"Maybe Mac can check the place out for us. Now that I think of it, Steve lives part time in Tampa and is close with some slum lord who lives anywhere but the slums, if you know what I'm sayin'. Steve brought him to the club to golf last summer and the guy was a prick. A rich prick, though. I'll find a way to talk to Steve then have Mac pay Steve's friend a visit." Charlie entertained himself with the idea before discretely glancing in the barback mirror to ensure the booth patrons weren't listening. He noticed the man place an arm around his date as she slid in closer and knew listening to his devious plan was the last thing on their minds.

"Now you're thinking," Hawk answered casually while moving on to clean the bar sink. Charlie excused himself and walked back to the men's room. He flipped the light switch and locked the door behind him.

A mellow glow pervaded the dank, one-person restroom with walls displaying a scant amount of black wallpaper decorated with Prohibition-era gold starburst designs. Rust stained the cast iron sink from which he splashed cool water on his blotched face and shook the water from his palms. After drying the rest of the droplets on his trousers, he pulled a burn phone from his pockets and dialed Mac's number. When there was no answer, he snarled his message.

"Mac. Me. Got your message. Don't worry about the club. I'll get someone to cover for you. I need a favor from you in return. Call me at the office tomorrow."

Looking in the mirror, Charlie noticed how the last decade had taken its toll. What he would do to return to days spent with his wife of thirty years. Before time had run out on her wait for an organ transplant. Thick grey hair slicked back to appear distinguished to the members of the country club seemed sleazy in this looking glass. Tomorrow he would resume his farce as a respected banquet manager among distinguished members.

"If they only knew," he deliberated to the tired reflection. "Katherine, you know I do all this in your memory," he added with a somber look toward the heavens.

Chapter 9

The crimson boat sped just past the breakers and Patrick and Faith were on smooth waters now. Tucked into the bucket seat next to Patrick, her short hair whipped at her cheeks amid rushes of cool air. Patrick stood at the helm with bare feet apart as he balanced at the wheel with eyes on the aqua highway. The shoreline a mere sketch in the distance and fellow boaters became a rare sighting as the Marauder's rumbling engines propelled them atop the water that sparked with mid-day sun. Soon, the two-way radio cracked and sounded a loud beep accompanied by a flashing red light. Tuned in to the almost inaudible alert, Patrick adjusted one hand on the steering wheel in order to use a free hand to pull the square receiver close to his mouth. Faith lunged forward as Patrick slowed the boat.

"Hold on, Keith," he shouted. As the boat slowed to a near stop, the wake bobbed them up before plopping them down again and Patrick took a seat. "Everything alright?" He turned the engines off to hear more clearly. Faith looked at Patrick with alert eyes. Again, she questioned her decision to leave the dock with him. Unaware, Patrick went on. Faith glanced at the shoreline that now appeared foreign. "How the hell did you make that kind of time? I can't believe you're there already."

Faith could hear the man on the other end with his raspy reply and it made her nervous. She pictured a ruffian waiting for her on a decrepit dock. She planned how she would bypass this stranger upon arrival in the event her concerns held merit.

"Alright, buddy. We'll meet up with you at the marina's bar tonight. I'll keep in touch."

Keith chirped back a questioned, "We?"

Patrick grinned at Faith. "Uh, yeah. I have someone with me. A hitch-hiker needing a lift to Mobile," he said with a wink. Her smile betrayed her and she was relieved to know this stranger wasn't expecting her. Patrick placed the receiver back into the clip, sat down, unwrapped his vibrating fingers off the steering wheel, and shook his wrists for some relief. Faith stretched her back showing some signs of discomfort as well.

"Mind if I go below for a water?" she said.

"Not at all. I could use a break. Take your time. You know, I think there's a sand bar up ahead. Wouldn't hurt to beach the boat for thirty minutes. We're stocked with snacks and drinks in cubby to the left below. Why don't you grab some food and I'll take us over there to stretch our legs."

"Fine by me," she answered coolly despite feeling anything but. The handgun flashed in her mind and she looked down at the tiger eye bead on the bracelet.

Go where the open waters run blue. The mysterious woman's voice hummed in her mind.

Faith slid the door closed behind her and took a few steps. The boat lurched forward and Faith stumbled onto the berth. Clutching her nearby luggage bag, she sat down on the edge of the bed and rummaged through her belongings. Locating the gun and the bullets, she loaded the weapon in haste. Convinced it would provide protection, she returned it for safekeeping and felt a surge of independence before guilt rushed in with thoughts of home. Maybe her father didn't mean harm by his comments. Insecurity eroded confidence.

The boat made a sharp right turn and knocked heavy considerations loose. She lost her balance. Back into a seated position on the berth, she held her heavy head in her hands. Discouraging sentiments blanketed adventurous notions. Her hand tugged at her cut hair in judgement and the sight of scars on the inside of her wrist recited her weakness. Heavy shoulders sagged in surrender and a tear escaped. She quickly banished it with the top of her wrist. In the process, the longest scar on her forearm caught her watery vision. Each scar took her back to an exact moment when she was unloved and the three-inch mark of shame was raised more than the others. It represented the deepest wound.

She had completed her first year and was home for the summer. Desperate to avoid a return to rampant hazing at the boarding school, Faith resorted to tearful begging. Standing in her father's home office, she tried to explain the bullying that went on. There was the day she was not permitted to speak. When an upper-class student heard her thank a teacher, she was tripped in the cafeteria as punishment. A few sophomores mocked her efforts to clean her spilled tray by barking like dogs as she crawled on hands and knees, baked beans caked to her uniform the rest of the day. On a separate occasion, she had her towels and clothes taken away while in the shower. While running down the hall to her dorm room, naked, a slew of juniors were on hand to document the event with their cell phones. A payment of personal servitude, decided by each photographer, was demanded in order to keep the pictures off social media.

Louis LeBlanc had calmly rationalized that the prestigious school would correct the weakness she demonstrated. After all, knowing how to handle bullies would allow her find success in a harsh world. Then, he promptly left for a dinner meeting. When she heard the front door close, she opened his desk drawer on a whim and found the pistol and weighed her options. The blade of a kitchen knife won and by the time the senator would have had a first sip of a pre-dinner martini, she had successfully stopped the bleeding caused by a slice to a rather large artery. The truth was, she had not cared if the bleeding stopped that evening. In a way, it never had.

She no longer reached for razor sharp edges to release the sadness and anger cradled inside, but it didn't mean the feelings were not there. Now, Faith retrained her focus on the twine bracelets. A polished ball of tiger's eye adorned one of the braided rings around her right wrist. She turned the marble-sized gemstone between her finger and thumb, around and around its intense brown and creamy caramel hues entranced her. The boat slowed and came to a stop. She could hear the pointed hull below gently scrape into the soft sand. The engines went silent. Her ears were ringing. A robust knock on the cabin door brought her back to the present moment.

"Okay if I join you?" Patrick shouted.

"Oh, yeah. Sorry. I was just taking a break from the sun." She tried to conceal her melancholy by pulling the oatmeal tote bag from her leather duffle. Starting to fill it, she placed the gun wrapped in a blue sweatshirt in first then added her hat to the beach bag.

As Patrick pulled a crinkly bag of something from the far corner, she continued to bury her head in her meager belongings.

"So, I've actually stopped here before. It's a decent sized sandbar and usually doesn't disappear with the tide. Patrick said with renewed vigor. Pulling out tortilla chips, salsa, apples, and a few Cokes, he began to drop them into a soft cooler retrieved from somewhere. Zipping the top closed, he turned to see Faith sitting quietly and occupying herself with a lot of nothings. Sensing apprehension, he continued, "It's not as remote as I make it sound. Looks empty now, but other people with probably beach while we're there."

Faith was half listening and emotionally drained. She looked up when he stopped talking and noticed he was now studying her. The red in the whites of her eyes only made the green pupils glow more.

"A break right about now would be perfect," she rasped while rubbing her face.

"Okay," he answered with some hesitation. "Do you mind handing me that blanket there beside you?" Patrick pointed. She twisted around to pull a folded, wool, Mexican blanket from the corner of the bench seat. Handing it to him, Patrick took note of her dejected state. He debated asking her if she was okay. Deciding he already knew the answer, he instead offered a hand. "C'mon. I'll help you up." His hand held hers firmly and as she stood up he caught sight of the faded scars on her fair skin that suggested a painful past. Faith noticed his observation and her face reddened. Feigning ignorance, she turned her head and pulled her hand away from his. Paying no mind to personal space, he remained stubbornly in place with his body only inches from hers. She sensed his strength and had nowhere to go. She looked back down at the bag that held her gun. With a bent index finger, he gently guided her chin back up and their eyes met before she stumbled a little with the rocking boat.

In response to her losing her balance, Patrick reached out gently and steadied her. She held his gaze.

"You good? I got you." He released his hold from her shoulders and, steadying her by hand, he turned to lead her from the cabin with the cooler slung over his shoulder. Faith grabbed her loaded beach bag as she followed. Pulling the cockpit door open, the ocean breeze fanned any negativities away. She followed Patrick up the molded steps that led to long bow of the speedboat. Faith's eyes took in a serene and breathtaking backdrop from where the point of the boat was firmly beached. A scene blanketed by blue waters.

"Here, let me carry your bag for you," Patrick insisted as he reached down for the sagging tote from his position up on the bow.

"No, thanks. I got it," she retorted while instinctively pulling the bag closer to her body.

"Fine by me," he shrugged. "At least give me your hand."

She obliged and reached up as he helped her up the few steps to the top of the boat where they stood together for a moment.

"Peaceful," Faith whispered.

Pale water lapped at a sugary shore. This world was not harsh, at least not in that moment. Only the gentle wind and water made a sound.

Patrick held on to her hand and they balanced each other, and they quickly tiptoed across the hot, fiberglass surface. Like a red carpet leading to a new existence, they hurried along the top of the boat, wanting to feel the cool water on their toes. The sandy shore welcomed her like nothing had before.

Patrick spread the blanket on slightly higher ground, securing the corners with a touch of sand, and sat down with the cooler. Faith lingered at the water's edge, collecting seashells along with her thoughts. Patrick observed his companion go through the motions. He knew that process well.

By the time she had decided to join him, he had the modest snacks spread out on the blanket.

"Help yourself," he offered as he snapped a bite off a crisp apple. He continued to look out upon the water while she took a seat with a sigh. "Did you find any answers?" His words confounded her and she looked to him for more understanding. "A boat, open seas. Hell, a deserted island. If you can't find a clear head out here, you're a lost cause," he stated with a kind smile.

"You know something about that?" she queried with inquisitive eyes.

He nodded. "Yes, I do," then added, "You gotta be kidding me." Faith startled and followed his gaze. The red and white, official-looking boat slowed as it approached the opposite end of the island. Small waves preceded the visiting bow wedged into the sandbar. Close enough now, they could see it was a Coast Guard boat.

Patrick leaped to his feet. "Stay here. I'll take care of this." He walked casually to meet the two uniformed men who were by now hopping down onto the sand and close enough for Faith to hear parts of the conversation. She stayed back, afraid of being discovered.

"Everything okay here, sir?" the shorter of the two uniformed men called out.

"Yeah. All good. Just taking a break. Enjoying the scenery." They glanced past Patrick to notice Faith sitting on the blanket. She looked away and pulled a Coke from the cooler.

"Patrick? That you?" a third seaman shouted from the military boat. Patrick's head snapped toward the familiar voice.

"Campbell?"

"The one and only. Man, is it good to see you. Everything okay?"

Faith tried he best to avoid eye-contact with the group of men, two of whom knew one another, while still eavesdropping.

"Yeah. I was just telling these guys I'm just taking a break from a little cruise. Everything's good."

"You still in New Orleans?" The captain's question was punctuated by a dispatch call on his radio. Patrick waited for him to finish taking the call.

"I am. I'll stop by the station to see you sometime?"

"Hope you do. The guys are all still there. They'd love to see you. Hey, you haven't noticed a wayward fishing boat out here? We received a distress call for a boat that ran out of gas," the man said as his boatmates climbed back aboard the vessel.

"I haven't, but I'll be on the lookout. Stay safe out there," Patrick called out as they backed away from the island.

"You, too, Patrick. Hope to see you soon." Then, as quickly as they arrived, they were out of sight.

Standing alone watching them disappear, Patrick startled at a light touch upon his arm.

"What was that all about?" Faith confronted.

"Nothing. Just checking to make sure we weren't stranded. They were out on a call."

"I see. I was so nervous, but you all seemed pretty friendly by the end."

Patrick started back to the blanket with Faith walking alongside. After a bit, he spoke up.

"I used to be one of those guys."

"What did you say?"

"I was in the Coast Guard. That's where most of my boating experience comes from. Best years of my life."

They reached the blanket and he slumped down, out of breath from the unexpected interaction.

"Why'd you leave?"

He was quiet again. Faith noticed he looked pale and gave him time to recover. The meeting obviously shook him up.

"I was discharged. I can't talk about it," he added when he noticed her quizzical expression.

"Can't or won't?" she pried.

He inhaled deeply and picked up a cylindrical shell from the water's edge. Upon inspection, he noticed it had an inhabitant promptly tossed back into the water.

"The Coast Guard was the best thing that ever happened to me. The closest friends I ever had, too. Sad to say, but I've lost touch with all of them," he offered as he began to pack up. Faith took the cue and started to help.

"I can only imagine what kind of stuff you had to deal with out here," Faith prompted as she placed an empty can back in the cooler.

A gentle laugh escaped from him and Faith was relieved.

"Faith, you have no idea," he said with a shake of his head, She shook the sand from the blanket and they started back toward the boat. "Man, people are nuts, I'm tellin' you. But just when you got tired of the hard times with the criminal-types, you would end up saving a kid's life or bringing a dad safely back to shore from a fishing trip gone awry. That's when you remembered why you risked your own life every day. I'd join back up in a heartbeat. Anyway, we better shove off," he advised with a shade of resentment.

Faith thought about his reference to criminal-types and the way he omitted himself from part of that crew.

"I bet you saved a lot of lives," she suggested as they walked toward the boat.

"It's all I wanted to do. All I want to do." His words carried a double meaning. Before Faith could try to decipher it, Patrick changed the subject. "So, that's that. All in the past and no sense dwelling on it. Let me help you." He arranged the cooler and blanket onto the point of the boat and hoisted himself up first. She followed his technique to join him. Back in the cockpit, he again offered to take her bag from her in order to stow everything below.

"I got it. Here, let me take the cooler and blanket down for you while you do what you need to do up here," she offered. He started the boat's exhaust fans and the engines were rumbling before she was back in her seat.

"Mobile here we come," Patrick announced.

From her first mate's seat, Faith chuckled. As her hand reached for missing long locks of hair to pull over her shoulder, her chuckle turned into an infectious giggle. A laughter that once started couldn't be stopped. She instead tucked her dark bobbed hair behind one ear and tried to catch her breath.

Patrick stared at her. The entire situation was beyond strange and as each ridiculous detail came to her fickle mind, she laughed harder and harder. Through fits of laughter, she tried to talk.

"Sorry," she began as the laughter bubbled over again. "This is all just too much. I think I've gone off the deep end."

Patrick steered the boat calmly back out into the open water. "Good to know. I was worried you hopped into a different stranger's boat every weekend. That would make me feel less special." he deadpanned.

"Yeah, something like that. This is all so crazy." She wiped tears from her eyes as the laughter finally subsided.

"I can't argue with you on that. If you only knew," he muttered just loud enough to be head over the revved engines. The boat sped up and planed off.

"Knew what?" she hollered back.

A wide grin plastered across his charming face. It was reminiscent of the first time they met and it was leading her farther and farther down the rabbit hole.

His self-assured reply came as he sped the boat away from their rendezvous.

"Stay with me 'till Tampa and I just might let you know."

Chapter 10

"Senator, we're all done here. We'll get the evidence to the lab and be in touch with the results."

The investigator turned his back on the LeBlancs who remained stunned in the doorway of the dressing room. Chelsea leaned against the doorframe, weak from the ordeal and dressed for the day's scheduled appointments. Louis towered above his petite wife. When he attempted to lead her from the crime scene, she jerked her elbow from his grip. Foreign perfume on his suit jacket suggested an early morning tryst and that misdemeanor troubled her most. Tenacious despite violations against her, Chelsea walked downstairs unaided, chin out. A uniformed officer followed them to the foyer.

"We'll be in touch as soon as we know more, senator LeBlanc. I'll make sure a rush is put on these prints. In the meantime, make sure you contact us immediately if you remember any other details," the officer instructed.

"We most certainly will," Louis stated with conviction. "Thank you for your service and dedication, officer. This fine city is grateful for every last one of you."

The gray, spectacled maid held the front door open for the policeman and unwound a bit as the last of the investigators exited the house. The dedicated housekeeper rubbed her sweaty palms on her apron as she closed the door behind the officer and the investigator. She jumped with a start as Louis' booming voice called out.

"I sure am sorry you had to go through all that, Marjorie. You know we never had any suspicion of you being behind this horrible act." He circled the women at the bottom of the stairway then resituated a disobedient day lily in the fishbowl vase. Otherwise perfectly arranged, the perky blossoms had recently replaced crestfallen gardenias. Their crisp fragrance drifted though nervous air and masked the unfaithful musk worn by Mr. LeBlanc.

"Oh, of course, sir. I understand. They're simply doing their job." Marjorie wrung her aged hands as apples for cheeks flushed a shade of pink. She adjusted her wire glasses and shifted her weight.

"Well, that's kind of you. You just go along now and try to enjoy the rest of your day. Would you like to take tomorrow off? I know you must be exhausted after all this," the senator offered with pity as he looked down upon the tiny lady.

Chelsea stepped from the bottom step. She leaned her right hand upon the carved newel post and crossed one well-heeled foot over the other and breathed in the refreshing scent of the lilies.

"Absolutely, Marjorie. We insist on a paid vacation." Then, without thinking, she added, "Oh, we have the Burtons arriving tonight. Louis, please cancel that visit. I'm not up to socializing after this morning." Her thoughts turned to the newly minted, younger version of the original Mrs. Burton. Since returning from a honeymoon in Singapore, the mister had been parading his plastic bride through the most notable parlors in the city.

"Oh, surely we could manage? They're only coming for drinks. We might enjoy the distraction."

Chelsea perked up. "I'll bake some savory hors d'oeuvres. Something that goes well with Champagne. Let me think. You loved those mini bacon croissants I kept on hand at the bakery." For a moment, her gaze softened as she recalled the earlier days of their own relationship. Back when she was a new bride on tour with a man about town.

"No, no, no," Louis disapproved. "Don't even think about going to that kind of trouble. Let's just get through the appointments set up for the day and look forward to a night in with good company. How about you put an order in at Marnier's? I'll pick up whatever you decide on my way home around five."

Marjorie watched the husband and wife with patient eyes. "I'm happy to stay and help." Her words were lost amid the domestic discussion.

"But, it wouldn't be any trouble. In fact, it would make me feel …" Louis cut off his wife again with a wave of his hand.

"I won't hear of it. You just be a dear and place the order and I'll pick it up for you."

His long legs strode toward his wife, the heels of his leather oxfords enunciating the effort, and Louis leaned in for a quick kiss atop her blonde head. She managed a smile and looked down as he announced his intentions.

"I have to run now. Tell William at Marnier's I'll pick up the order around five thirty. Don't worry, dear. We'll find out who is responsible for this and he will pay."

With that, Louis rushed out the front door. Marjorie stood awkwardly and turned to Chelsea.

"Well, what a morning. How about I fix you a little bite to eat? What are you in the mood for? Oh, and don't worry about tonight. I'll stay on to help." Chelsea's eyes began to water and before she could get her emotions under control, a flood of tears escaped. Marjorie brought her hands to her face with a gasp. "Oh, Mrs. LeBlanc. Please don't cry. They'll find your jewelry."

Chelsea shook her head vehemently. "I'm so sorry. What a spectacle." She brushed away the unexpected flood of tears. "It's not the jewelry. And, Marjorie?"

"Yes, Mrs. LeBlanc?"

"Please. Please call me Chelsea," she begged in a meek voice.

By the end of the week, Louis and Chelsea were still waiting for a solid lead on the robbery case. Louis was working from home when he heard the phone ring.

"Sir, there's a call for you. It's Chief Mallory," Marjory advised from outside his door.

"Richard?" he answered from his desk phone.

"Hello, Louis." Louis was anxious to hear what the New Orleans chief of police, who he also counted as a close friend, had to say. "Glad to hear from you."

"Well, to get prints back this quickly is not the norm. I was able to pull a few strings for you."

"And for that I owe you. What did you find out?"

"Are you alone?"

"Why? Yes. What's going on?"

"Lou, I had only the best of the best assigned to work this case. I highly doubt there was any stone unturned."

"I don't doubt that, Rick. What'd they find out?"

The chief exhaled sharply. "The only prints on and around that safe, other than Chelsea's, belonged to Faith."

"Well, of course her prints were on it. I assume Chelsea allowed Faith to grab a piece of jewelry now and then. What are you suggesting, Richard?" Despite expressed confidence, Louis began to speak in hushed tones.

"I'm not suggesting anything. Only providing you with the facts. Throughout the crime scene, the only prints, other than your wife's, belonged to Faith." Richard became defiant.

"Please keep your voice down, Richard." Louis sat back and fidgeted with a pen in nervousness. "There had to have been other prints or evidence of someone else somewhere. What about the alarm not going off? Faith would've set the alarm before she left for the weekend."

"She left? Where'd she go?"

Louis winced and cursed himself silently.

"To spend the weekend with a friend. She left a note then I talked to her briefly yesterday." He closed his eyes at his next mistake.

"A note?" Richard interrogated. "I'll need a copy of that, Louis. And, where is she now? What did she say?"

"Why do you need the note? It has nothing to do with any of this. Her car is being serviced. She's getting a ride back to Mobile. You need to focus on finding an intruder, Richard. Not my daughter. I'll handle her." All signs indicated an inside job and a scandal he refused to endure. "You just keep looking into the robbery and in the meantime, I trust you will keep the details of this investigation under wraps."

"I need to see Faith's note, Lou. I'll send an officer by immediately to pick it up. We need to make sure Faith hasn't gotten herself in danger."

Jaw clenched, Louis half-listened as he opened the desk drawer to check for the note. Instead, his heart stopped upon realizing the gun was missing.

"Fine. I won't be here. I'll leave it with the housekeeper."

Without further delay, Louis tried Faith's cell phone. When there was no answer, he scrolled though his contacts until Faith's roommate appeared. He dialed her next and, this time, left a message.

"Jane, this is Faith's father. I'm trying to reach her. Can you have her call me right away? Alright, thanks."

Fishing though drawers was enough to convince Louis that his handgun was missing along with the jewels and his daughter. He contemplated details as he picked up a sloppy clay bowl molded by inexperienced hands. Faith had crafted the ornament as a Father's Day present in second grade. He cradled the art project painted in primary colors, transferring it gently to one hand to examine the lovingly inscribed *To Daddy* complete with an irregular heart. Paperclips scattered across the floor as he smashed the handmade gift against the wall.

Chapter 11

Mobile was attained before dusk. The eye-catching boat pulled alongside the wharf's fuel pump with Patrick behind the wheel and from the weathered restaurant and bar balcony, heads turned in admiration. Unaware of the stir he was creating, he expertly readied the bumpers and lines and sprung onto the dock to secure the boat. Faith scampered into the boat's cuddy to ready her bag for departure when a teenaged gas attendant approached to assist with the fill-up and offer subsequent guidance to the assigned slip for an overnight moor.

Seeing Faith emerge onto the swaying dock, Patrick made an attempt at persuasion.

"Let me buy you dinner before you go?" From his kneeled position near a dock cleat, he squinted to interpret her mannerisms. The light of the late afternoon light was rosy, unlike her demeanor. Arms crossed, sunglasses on, her armor was donned. She watched for signs of the man Patrick was to meet but noted nothing suspicious. Satisfied his nautical knot would hold, he stood aside to allow the attendant to fill the gas tank

"Um, not sure I'll have time. Let me call my ride." Faith intended to leave Patrick alone with his invitation as she bulldozed by in search of a private spot to make her call, but the wake from a passing fishing boat caused the floating dock to bob and weave and tossed Faith against Patrick's bare torso. He steadied her with a grip that lingered while she willed newly acquired sea legs to fortify. Her watery legs found their footing as she muttered appreciation and he slid his hand from the small of her back, watching her amble away along the firm wooden plank. She carried the heat of his touch with her.

"You do what you need to do." He called out after her with his hands now resting on his hips. "I'll move the boat to the overnight slip then meet us at the bar? At least a drink before you go?"

Out of earshot, Patrick cursed under his breath, crouching re-twist the rope around the other cleat with unnecessary force.

Faith wandered the labyrinth of moorings to procure a far-flung seat with a view of the setting sun. Her feet dangled from the dock's edge.

The Gulf reflected orange and pink while water lapped at the rock-lined shore. Absorbed in the splendor, Faith was caught off-guard when Jane answered the auto-dialed call.

"What's up? When are you getting here?" Jane chirped enthusiastically.

"Hi. Uh, I'm at some marina that's not too far from campus. Um … The Mariner?" she revealed, catching sight of a sign. "Think you could come get me?"

Faith supposed the call was lost then Jane finally spoke up. "The Mariner? Never heard of it. Hold on. Let me pull it up on my phone."

Faith could hear enough laughing and chatter in the background to confirm barhopping had commenced.

"Okay. Found it," she replied proudly.

"Well, do you think you can pick me up?" Faith curved into the phone, hugging her shoulder with one arm.

"Faith, you are, like, forty minutes away." Sweet Home Alabama blared from the digital jukebox and Faith knew from experience it wouldn't be the last time a patron would play it that night. What should feel welcoming and familiar was now a scene she felt oddly disengaged from. Laughter mocked her predicament from both the phone and the Mariner's bar and the runaway pictured herself melting through the slats in order to float away from the mess she had created for herself.

"I shouldn't drive. I've had a few drinks. Are you safe? How did you end up there?" Statement and inquiries rattled off and filled her with a deep desire to disappear. She had unwisely presumed Jane would wait for her call. Now she was stuck. Anxiety chewed through sensitivities and left her short of breath with a panic attack waiting in the wings.

"I ran into a friend and got … sidetracked. Sorry I didn't call earlier." It was a sincere attempt at redemption from irresponsible actions.

"I just thought I'd hear from you already and figured you weren't coming. I decided to head out without you. Oh, your dad called. Don't worry, it was just a voicemail asking you to call him. I didn't talk to him." Faith bristled at her roommate's slurred words. She closed her eyes as she remained lost in the dark without a flashlight. "Why don't you call him for a ride or get an Uber and get up here. We're all waiting!"

Faith opened her eyes when cheers from diners on the deck applauded the sun. She caught a fleeting view of the vanishing orange orb. At the end of the day, she could only rely on herself.

"It's ok. I guess it is too far of a drive. Not sure what I was thinking." Awkward silence halted the conversation as a male announced another round of shots. Jane shushed a reply.

"Just call an Uber," Jane happily suggested again, pleased to have worked the situation out in tidy fashion.

"Sure. I'll do that. Don't worry about it. I might just go home. Don't wait for me."

"Okay. As long as you're sure you're safe? Call me later to let me know you're okay?"

"I'll be okay," Faith assured herself as she laid a hand on the pistol hidden among her possessions. She pulled the bag closer and righted her shoulders. Satisfied with the answer, Jane gave an upbeat good-bye and disconnected the call, but not before Faith could hear the chatter asking Jane what was taking so long. Before the call died, Jane offered her report of a ride being needed from someplace and not knowing what the hell she was supposed to do about it.

She recalled the woman's voice from the hidden retreat on Bourbon Street and could see her image afloat on the sea. Peace washed over her with an index finger caress of the tiger's eye bead. Her enchanting words echoed on the sea breeze.

Embody the magic of you.

A soul companion awaits.

Go where the open waters run blue.

The vision evaporated with a polite request shouted from afar.

"Mind grabbing a line for me?" A woman steered a pleasure craft toward the dock.

Faith scanned the harbor for a more experienced seafarer. Coming up empty, she waited on the brink for the tossed rope. She missed and the woman pulled the other end from the water and back into the boat.

"Sorry!" she yelled. "Bad throw. Let me try again."

Faith was eager and the boat headed out into the channel before reattempting approach. This time, as she neared, she tossed the line perfectly and Faith clutched the end with her right palm. She gave the thick, nylon twine a determined tug to gain a better grasp and in doing so was pulled from the edge and into the gray water. The light of day waned and the female captain lurched her vessel away from a potential collision.

"Are you okay? I'm so sorry. I'm not good at docking myself!" she yelled as Faith splashed and splattered about.

Never learning to swim, she panicked and flailed about, gasping for air. After the fourth or fifth attempt to suck oxygen, she fell back under. Useless, reed-like arms sank knuckles grazed the mucky bottom. Her orientation restored, Faith pushed herself up to grab for the safety of the dock.

"Here, grab my hand," Patrick ordered as he came out of nowhere. Her fingers finally grabbed hold of the splintered edge and she hoisted herself up without his help. Embarrassed and unable to make eye contact, she slithered to the middle of the swaying path and caught her breath while Patrick and his friend went about helping the boater finally tie off.

She looked at the beads once more to focus her equilibrium.

The magic of you. Some magical soul I am, she scoffed silently.

"I am so sorry!" the bikini and shorts-clad female gasped as she marched down the dock toward Faith. Her tanned skin accentuated her bleached pixie cut. "You try to help me and look where it gets you. I am so bad at parallel docking."

"It's not your fault. I lost my balance," she stammered through her chattering teeth.

Faith crossed her arms and legs to huddle against the intense chill coming over her while trying to hide curves of her body showing through wet clothes.

"You're so cold. Do you have a change of clothes? Here, take my key for the marina showers to warm up. I insist." Faith took the key ring with the floating marina charm. "Thanks, fellows," she added to the guys as the approached. "First round's on me. See y'all up there."

Mud streaked Faith's arms and legs and she couldn't be sure if her numbness stemmed from her emotional state or the splash of cold water that delivered a shock. Patrick knelt to drape a towel around her.

"C'mon. You need to get out of those wet clothes." She nodded and followed Patrick as he carried her bag for her. "Oh, this is Keith," he added. There stood Patrick's friend, a greasy-haired man sporting a beer belly and a five o'clock shadow that was approaching midnight. She barely acknowledged his sheepish wave as she continued her pathetic march, distress bearing down upon her shivering limbs.

As they stopped before the Marauder's slip for the night, Keith announced he would meet them at the restaurant. Patrick returned from the cuddy with a fresh grey towel and bottles of liquid soap and shampoo.

"Sorry, they're guy brands."

"I don't care," she growled and cradled the toiletries with an arm that held the towel secure around her body while picking up her bag of personal belongings with her free hand. He allowed her time to sulk away before finding his way upstairs to join Keith at the bar.

The shower facilities were located far enough away from the dining area for Faith to slip inside unnoticed. She was relieved to find she had the space to herself and chose a shower stall at the far end of the tiled room. Watercolor prints of sunsets and boats dotted the creamy walls. The white tiled floor was clean and Faith was encouraged by the lather brought on by steamy water. Ten minutes later found her in a better state. Jeans, a clean t-shirt, and dried, styled hair complimented her improved, although still bruised, attitude. She braved the crowded restaurant by first returning the key to the woman now seated next to Keith. An empty stool remained between him and Patrick.

"Hey. There you are. You hungry?" Patrick pulled the seat out for her. She managed a smile and had to admit he was a welcomed sight in his pastel green polo shirt - one that, for once, did not appear to be stolen goods. Keith moved over to give her space without a break in his non-stop with the woman with the boat. She smiled warmly at Faith.

"Hi. Actually, I am," she answered as the smell of fried seafood elicited hunger pains.

Her attention turned to the one person who seemed to care about her in this moment. Patrick slid a full bottle of Miller Lite to her while he took a sip of lemon water.

"So, is your roommate whisking you away any minute?"

"She has to borrow a car. We'll see how long it takes her to get here," Faith lied.

"Sounds like we'll have time to eat, then. Treating my first mate to a meal is the least I can do." He nudged her playfully then leaned closer. She remained motionless before instinctively crossing her arms. His friendly demeanor diminished, and Faith felt a pang of guilt. Displays of affection had never come easy to her, but she decided Patrick hardly deserved her angst.

"You doing okay? You didn't get hurt when you fell in?"

"I'm fine." The walls went up around the folded arms.

"Just making sure. Probably just tired?" he reasoned aloud. He waved off the bartender's non-verbal inquiry of another. "I know I am. It was a long day, but that break at the sandbar was nice." Faith's muscles eased. She took a sip of beer and considered ordering something stronger.

"That sun can do a number on you, but look where you are," he continued, sweeping an outstretched arm. The casual restaurant bordered run-down, but Faith suddenly saw her surroundings in technicolor. Salty sea breezes stirred laughter and steel drum songs together to simmer on a summer night. Faith's combativeness slipped away as she experienced something related to belonging. She decided to live in the moment and go with the flow with a hunch the universe wanted better things for her.

When the woman with the boat excused herself to use the restroom, Keith turned to get better acquainted with Faith.

"A rose between two thorns. How are ya? Feeling better?" he greeted a second time. "I didn't catch your name in the commotion."

"Hi. I'm … how are you?" Faith answered.

He picked up on the verbal stutter and quickly dismissed it. He was carrying about fifty extra pounds on his six-foot frame and wore a silver necklace showcasing a raw gold nugget. His wiry hair was gray and disheveled and a t-shirt with a parrot suggested he had been to Key West at some point in his life.

"Never been better. Glad to be here and glad to have that first part of the trip out of the way. How 'bout it, my man?" he exclaimed as he leaned forward to address Patrick. Patrick held up a shot of tequila in agreement and prepared to toast his friend. At the same time, the bartender placed the same drink in front of Faith.

"Hope you don't mind, I took the liberty," Keith informed as he sloped in close. She shrugged her shoulders and joined in the toast. From there, worries melted away. Keith was the kind of guy who habitually looked for a good time. Deep-fried battered fish, fries, and hush puppies were served with coleslaw and chunky cuts of lemon. One bottle of beer after another was doled out. Faith noticed Patrick passing his full bottles on to them. As a result, Keith's empty brown bottles piled up more than the rest.

"Save my seat, my dear? Don't go giving it way to some other handsome fellow, alright?" Keith said with a wink as he stood. "Be right back, Pat." Patrick acknowledged him with a tall cup of water.

Taking advantage of the alone time, Faith turned to Patrick. "Does he know my name?" she hissed.

"No," he hissed back.

"Good."

"So, when's your friend getting here? It's getting late."

In a moment of tequila-induced weakness, Faith indulged in an honest rant.

"She's not. And you know what else? I'm not so sure I have any friends. You would think I could call my dad to pick me up, but I know he'd point out how busy he is and would certainly not be happy with this ... situation ... anyway. Calling my stepmother is not an option and, well, my real mom's been out of the picture for a while now. So, that's that." She huffed relief and turned to Patrick who took the rant in stride as he casually sipped his ice water without a straw. He slowly took a bite of french-fry dipped in ketchup and stared ahead as he clasped his hands upon the bar.

"So, I'm stuck with you," he said in a slow, monotone voice. A sly smile emerged.

Faith's cheeks reddened with regret for her honesty.

"No. I'll be fine. Don't you worry about me," she said defiantly, sitting up straight as an arrow.

Patrick turned his long frame toward her deliberately. His back to the world, he reached around Faith to reposition her seat. Now facing each other, his intensity caused her to look away.

"No doubt. You're strong. I know you can take care of yourself. I don't doubt that one bit." Faith squirmed, too embarrassed to meet his attentive regard. She had never been showered with such accolades. "However, I, too, have no one I care to count on as a friend. I have no family and, well, I've been charged with taking this beauty of a boat on one hell of a ride. So, I was thinking you might like the idea of joining me for the rest of this trip. Unless you have somewhere else to be?" He propped one elbow on the bar and the other on the back of his seat with his posture open and inviting. A look of intent took on intimate qualities and Patrick clearly couldn't care less about anyone else in the room. His bronzed skin was slightly sunburned and his short, sandy hair highlighted by a day on the water. Faith was under his spell.

"What'd I miss?" Keith bellowed as he clumsily took his seat back. Patrick decided to address his boating companion and Faith gulped relief at the blue-eyed spotlight shining another direction.

"Just trying to convince Fai – uh, my friend here – that there's no reason for her to rush back home. Don't ya think she should join us?" Patrick's ongoing stunt burst at the seams with confidence and flustered Faith. She looked over her shoulder to see if the woman with the boat was paying attention to the net Patrick had casting. The woman was gone.

“Hell, yeah. Why the hell not? By the way, what’s your name, my dear?” Faith gave a tentative glance Patrick’s way before answering.

“Josephine. You can call me Jo.” Patrick winked acknowledgment.

“Miss Josephine. I assure you we are upstanding gentlemen,” he slurred diplomatically. “Will you please do us the honor of accompanying us to Florida?”

Then, to both Faith and Patrick’s horror, Keith stood with one foot on the rung of his barstool and a knee on the seat. He commanded the attention of the patrons with an empty beer bottle as a flag raised high in the air. The steel drum band slowed to a stop.

“May I have your attention?” he shouted to a crowd that hushed with uncertainty. “This lovely lady, Miss Josephine, is trying to decide whether she should join my friend and me on a nautical adventure to beautiful Tampa Bay. Don’t y’all think she should say *yes*?”

Bewildered silence surrounded a swaying Keith. He was undeterred as a few patrons nodded and shrugged in amusement.

“So, dear people,” Keith added dramatically. “Shots all around if I hear a resounding ‘yes’.”

A hundred pairs of eyes fanned the flames of embarrassment which engulfed Faith when the now-boisterous diners shouted ‘YES’.

Chapter 12

Morning fog spread her blanket upon the safe harbor where Faith slept in the Marauder's cabin behind locked doors. Patrick had kept his promise to sleep outside on the cockpit's bench seat below the sun pad and she finally approved the sleeping arrangement when he handed her the key to keep. She had not known about his spare set and he was not about to let her in on that fact after spending the better part of a late night convincing her she need not worry about his motives. By midnight, Patrick was willing to go along with anything if it meant lying down to sleep. Now, his aching, bent legs were not only dew covered, but also covered in sand from the wool coverlet she had tossed out before locking herself away. Throwing the sandy swathe aside, he scrambled out of the boat and onto the dock for a good stretch. Then, like a gruff angel with three mugs of coffee for lopsided wings, Keith appeared from the mist.

"Thanks," Patrick responded and cradled the warm mug in his chilled hands.

"Not a problem. Glad you're up. Here's a cup of joe for Jo." Patrick processed the comment before remembering the fake name Faith had given the night before.

"Oh, yeah. She's still asleep. Here, I'll set it on the dock for her." Yawning a shiver, Patrick set the steaming mug near the boat for Faith to easily discover. He was still dressed in the shorts and shirt from the previous day and wished Faith had tossed out a sweatshirt before secluding herself in the warm nest of the boat. Not wanting to disrupt any trust he had built with her, he opted against using his own key to retrieve warmed clothes and, instead, moseyed with Keith to join him at his boat docked a few slips away. Boarding the smaller Baja speedboat, Keith took his seat in the captain's chair while Patrick eased onto the rear sun pad, trying not to spill his coffee in the process. Unoccupied boats of various sizes were tied to the slips around them and the men took their caffeine in silence, Keith watching mist swirl about and Patrick gazed upon a statue-like heron fishing for breakfast on the shore. The heron speared the water with his needle beak and plucked a slender fish from the salty water.

Unsatisfied with the meal, the tall bird gobbled the treat to resume his patient wait for another victim to swim by.

"What a night. I'm feeling it this morning," Keith groaned.

"You put on quite a show and were free with the shots," Patrick observed.

Keith scratched the stubble sprouting around his cherub-like cheek. "Oh, man. I sure did, huh? Hope I didn't embarrass you guys."

"What? Not me. You were pretty funny. Fai – uh, Jo might kill you, on the other hand." Patrick stretched to rest on his palms behind him. His body started to recover from the less-than ideal sleeping arrangement. The caffeine helped, too.

Keith winced. "I wouldn't blame her. Speak of the devil…" he trailed off.

"I assume this coffee's for me?" Her voice was raspy, but she was otherwise the most chipper of the three sailors. Patrick resented her a little for it as he rubbed his tired, burning eyes. Sleep envy dissolved quickly, however, soon replaced by admiration of long legs rising before him. Unmasked by sunglasses in the early hour, he forced his focus to more appropriate places. Before she could notice the slow path taken by his eyes, he finished the last swig of lukewarm coffee and set the mug on the floor, propping himself on bare elbows on the upholstered sun pad to resume consideration of this woman who would be riding by his side to Tampa. He crossed his right ankle over his left to provide room as she climbed aboard and brushed her hand against his calf in the process. The innocent motion caused a not-so-innocent stir in him. He sat up and swung his legs over the back of the boat while she continued her banter with Keith.

"Peace-offering," Keith quipped.

Faith nodded her consideration and took a seat next to Patrick on the sun pad while facing, instead, into the cockpit. "Have creamer and sugar on this boat?"

"I do," Keith jumped up to retrieve the request and the modest boat wobbled. Pouring powdered creamer and sugar into her mug, he handed her a plastic spoon. Patrick glanced her way to watch her bring the cup to her pink lips.

She relished the morning coffee then answered. "Now you are forgiven."

Keith feigned relief as he comically wiped his sunburnt forehead. Patrick turned back around, now resting his elbows on his knees and sitting a foot or so from his newfound muse. Even at that distance, he could feel her on his skin and her presence alone warmed him. Faith continued to drink in the coffee, unaware of how she was affecting Patrick. He turned his thoughts to food to distract him from other desires.

"What time does the restaurant open for breakfast?" Patrick asked Keith.

"Ten minutes. Nine-o'clock," Keith answered with a look at his silver wristwatch.

"I need food before we go anywhere. Okay with you?"

Keith agreed with a nod. Faith was noticeably silent, so Patrick addressed her to confirm her intentions. "Okay with you, Jo?"

Faith smiled warmly at the moniker, or maybe she was pleasured by her captain's crooked grin. "I have nowhere else to go," she shrugged.

Patrick brushed away his widening smirk.

While the group eased into their day, Patrick's phone recorded another missed call from Charlie. That made five in the past twenty-four hours and Charlie was getting nervous. Charlie was also sitting down to breakfast at Joe's Diner back in New Orleans and still pondering Patrick's loyalty. He chose to leave a second message now that his more recent calls have gone unanswered.

"Mac. It's me again. I know you're in the Gulf and heading south. I talked to Steve. Anyway, I need you to do a job in Tampa. I took care of the other one on my own. I also took care of covering your tee times. You owe me. Call me."

The breakfast rush was still going strong and Joe was rushing here and there while Charlie sat alone with his coffee. He always thought Mac was the most dedicated one of the bunch. Lately, he wasn't so sure. As the ringleader of the errant group, he could not afford treachery. He, along with Hawk and Joe, had worked too long and too hard at their scheme. The fall from grace would be too great now. He would not let it happen.

"You're gonna scare away the customers with that scowl on your ugly mug," Joe said as he slid into the booth across from Charlie. He filled the coffee cup for his friend. To anyone around, they resembled two friends planning to hit the shuffleboard courts later. The reality was far from it.

"Thanks, Joseph," Charlie grumbled as he slurped his black coffee.

"What's on your mind? Tell me before you blow a gasket." Joe's stained white apron fell loosely around him as he slumped back in the seat. His aged left hand held the glass pot naturally.

Charlie looked around. "It's Mac. I think he's flaking out on us and I need to remedy the situation. If I don't hear from him in twenty-four hours, I'll have to do some damage control."

Joe's face twisted. "No way. He's the most dedicated guy we got."

"That's what I thought, too."

Rosy the waitress appeared out of nowhere.

"Joe, the guy at booth five wants a refund. Can you talk to him?"

"A refund? Why?" Joe's temper rose to match his friend's. "Did he eat his meal?"

"All but two bites," Rosy answered.

Joe got up from the wooden seat by leaning hard upon the table. "Refund," he grumbled. "I'll give him a refund. Charlie, give me a minute."

"I'm giving him twenty-four hours, Joe. I'm tellin' you we can't rely on him like we used to." Charlie repeated as Joe waved him off. He stopped to add his final comments on the subject.

"Don't jump to conclusions. You might spook him. Give him some room. He just needs a break," Joe added sympathetically.

"Twenty-four hours," Charlie repeated. Joe waved him off.

Patrick was not the only one sought on the down low. Faith also was becoming one of New Orleans' most quietly wanted.

According to Robert Higgins' cellphone tracking, Louis knew Faith was at a restaurant in Mobile, Alabama the night before. That suggested to him that she could be back campus for the weekend. He had debated driving the entire way to the Mariner Restaurant last night to confront her and bring her home. Instead, he had used the evening to debate his next move. He decided to settle for another phone call for now and possibly a trip to the University of Southern Alabama this week.

"Faith. It's dad. We have a serious situation developing here at home and I need to talk to you," Louis said to the voicemail as he drove to the country club for an early Sunday morning tee time.

The cellphones aboard the empty boat took the messages while the recipients continued to plan their great escape over breakfast.

"So, next stop is Panama City, right? That's about 150 nautical miles. We should easily be able make that on a tank of gas," Keith blurted out while chomping on a bite of steak with eggs.

"Sure we can. Let me just grab my phone to check the weather." Patrick wiped his hands and face on the paper napkin and tossed it on the table. He retreated from the scene in haste. Faith smiled awkwardly at Keith's robust eating habits as she took a demure bite of egg. They ate in silence until Keith spoke up.

"So, Josephine, I mean Jo. How'd you meet Pat?" Faith cleared her throat as she considered what to say. Stalling, she took a long sip of ice water.

"Um, a little gathering at my place. He dropped in unexpectedly," she said dryly.

"Ah, I see. So it was love at first sight?" Keith bellowed with a hearty laugh.

"Was what love at first sight?" Patrick asked as he waltzed back to the table. He allowed his hand to run along her shoulder as he took his seat. For the first time in her life, Faith did not recoil from someone's touch. Facing her full on, he sat with elbows resting on table and backrest. Faith noticed his mannerisms and could see he was a little on edge after his return from the boat.

"When we met," Faith answered directly. She watched Patrick's confidence fade. Still, he remained locked on her. "You know, when you dropped in uninvited." She crossed her arms in anticipation of his response. To her surprise, he quickly regained his cool.

"Yeah. It was," he said pointedly and without backing down from her stare. In contrast, and with reddened cheeks, she awkwardly reached for her cup of coffee. Patrick pushed his chair back from the table and rested an ankle over a knee, an audacious grin plastered on his unshaven face as he decided to keep the dangerous conversation going. "Jo's a killer entertainer. And she really went all out to make me feel welcome despite me dropping by uninvited. Anyway," he started and turned his attention back to Keith, "weather still looks great. Probably some midday showers further down in the Gulf, but that's all. We'll avoid that by hugging the shoreline."

More interested in his meal than anything else, Keith mumbled something that suggested he was glad to hear the report.

"I gotta return a call before we go. Be right back," Patrick announced abruptly as he pulled two twenties from his leather wallet and tossed them on the table.

"Yeah, take your time buddy," Keith said. As Patrick strode off on a mission, he left Faith flustered in his wake. Keith continued to make small talk in his boisterous but friendly way. Faith made an attempt to converse with Patrick's gaze still etched in her mind. As much as she wanted to indulge in that vision, her mind immediately busied itself with the phone call he was compelled to make without finishing breakfast. She also related it to how they first met. If she was to leave this marina with him, she would need to know what he is up to. As Faith half-heartedly listed to Keith and mulled over the thoughts in her head, Patrick returned and briskly sat down. Pushing his plate away from him, he was distant and preoccupied.

"How'd your call go?" Faith tentatively asked. He trained his focus on her as he took a deep breath and offered a weary smile.

"Fine. Just someone from work." Faith speculated on how an golf caddy to amateurs could receive distressing call during personal time. He suddenly looked tired and rubbed his right eye before providing the additional information his tablemates waited for. "Just a mix-up in some scheduling. Some people don't seem know what 'vacation time' means."

Satisfied, Keith moved the conversation on. "So we about ready, kids?"

"Yeah. I'm ready," Patrick said as he slid his seat back. "By the way, I need to get to Tampa by Thursday. I'd like to meet up with someone. Think that'd be an issue?"

Any good sense Faith retained told her she should cut ties with this peculiar crew right then and there. Keith and Patrick were discussing making it to Tampa straight from Panama City. She heard talk of being out at sea too long, pop-up storms, and stocking up on onboard fuel supplies. On the other hand, the thrill of the trip was getting in her blood and being in the company of Patrick was only making everything more intoxicating. Still, something waited for him in Tampa and she was not sure she wanted find out.

"I should check my phone, too," Faith blurted out.

"Good idea," Patrick said. "No signal once we get back out on the water."

She lost herself among a group of fishermen filing in after a sunrise outing. While Patrick pulled in close to the table to continue making plans with Keith, Faith sprinted down the outside steps. Reaching the boat, she clambered aboard and caught her breath by first taking her usual seat. It was comforting and she was confounded by the realization that she wanted to be on the boat when it departed for open seas. A line of pelicans soared overhead, unseen seagulls chattered. Faith knew they were pretty far south of Mobile – closer to the Gulf Shores. That made them an hour from her apartment, over two hours from New Orleans. She needed to make a decision and fast, so she locked herself in the cuddy and flipped on the air conditioning and all available LED lights to start her investigation. She ruffled through drawers and a Coast Guard duffle bag and snickered at the piles of Metetarie Country Club polo shirts. In the end, the shirts were the only suspicious aspect of his belongings. Pulling her smartphone from her own duffle, she noticed one message and it was from her father. She listened to his voice over her own shallow breaths.

His urgent tone held a bit of panic and Faith had never heard her father unnerved. His request for her to call him was laden with frustration and not how a concerned father should sound. She returned his call, desperate for intervention before another reckless move. His generic voicemail answered her plea for interference.

"Dad, I got your message. I'm in Mobile now. Hope everything's okay. Sorry I keep missing you, but I'm beginning to think you're ignoring my calls," she stammered with a nervous laugh. "Just let me know what's up, okay? I'll call you back as soon as I can."

She tossed the phone as it became a hot ember in her hand then leaned back to retrieve it. Adjusting The pillow, she leaned back into the comfort of the full-sized bed and looked up the BMW dealership where her father had sent her car for repair. As she listened to the contemporary jazz hold music, she considered her options. If the car would be done in a week or so, she could get an Uber from the marina and back to the apartment. Then, she would be where her father expected her to be and start making things right. She then considered a ride the whole way back to New Orleans. Facing her father's constant scrutiny and criticisms filled her with dread.

"Brinley BMW," the receptionist answered with a refined eastern European accent.

Faith came to attention.

"Yes, I'm calling to find out the repair status on my vehicle."

"One moment. Let me place you with the body shop."

Resting back against the bed of the boat, Faith closed her eyes and listened to the hold music again. A slow melody was set adrift by a delicate trumpeter. As the boat gently rocked with a passing wake, she was almost asleep when the gruff male answered from the body shop.

"Hello?"

"Ah, yes. Um, I was calling about my car. A BMW 3325i. It was hit near the back wheel and I wanted to see when you expected to be finished with the repair."

"Uh-huh. Last name?"

"LeBlanc. Faith LeBlanc."

"Oh, yeah. Blue one, right?"

"Yes. I know you've probably not even started the work yet, but I wanted to see what you thought."

"That's your car?"

"It is."

"You related to a Louis LeBlanc?"

"I am. He's my father. He bought the car for me. It might still be in his name?"

There was a noticeable pause. Faith sat back up and eased to the edge of the bed.

"Alright, well the insurance adjuster looked at it and we talked to your dad first thing this morning. He told us to put the car on our lot after it was repaired. Looks like that will happen by the end of next week. Maybe your dad's planning to surprise you with a new car? Hope I didn't spoil the surprise. Must be nice," he added with a tinge of disgust.

Faith suspected this was another random punishment dished out by a father who liked only to surprise his daughter with mementos of his control. She knew her father too well.

Hanging up, she laid back down to wait for the shock to wear off. Fitting that the car purchased as a birthday gift should be taken from her upon the end of another birthday weekend. She analyzed the situation in search of justification. He could have at least broken the news over a celebratory dinner or phone call. If he thought this was how to connect with his daughter, he could add it to Louis' list failed parenting attempts. She didn't need the car or his money.

All she had ever wanted from him was his love.

The rap on the cabin door told her Patrick was back. She pretended not to hear his soft knock.

"Faith," the muffled call sounded. "You ready to go? We're leaving for Panama City in ten."

She took her time stowing away her phone and making the bed from sleeping in it the night before. Before the small, round mirror attached to the wall of the boat, she applied a bit of lip gloss and fluffed her easy-to-style haircut and forced a look of confidence like the women on the hair dye boxes from the drugstore. A fresh breeze lifted her spirits when she opened the door to find Patrick sitting back on the sun pad with his bare feet touching the bench seat and his tan forearms resting atop his knees. His head rose slightly to watch her tentatively step from the vault she had been concealing herself in and, as he did so, she could see a hint of pleasure in his otherwise serious face. He was waiting for her. In that moment, there was nothing intimidating about this man who continued to earn her trust. She sat next to him.

"Ready to go?" he asked with hesitation.

"I am."

His demeanor perked.

"We'll be in Panama City by dinner. We could even hit the town a little if you're up for it after the trip."

She appreciated his offer and softened her attitude. Whatever he was up to, he had treated her with nothing but kindness since she forced herself into his life.

"We'll see. I mean, that sounds like fun. But, Patrick?"

His tanned face was rugged by the wind and stubble, but his blue eyes were full of concern. She sustained her interrogation.

"I need to know what's really going on, what I'm getting myself into. It's crazy to think I never had much a problem with what you were doing in the first place. Then again, I'm starting to realize much of my life has been a sham. I don't know who I can trust right now."

The concern spread to all corners of his face and he froze. She suspected he was about to shut down and she held her breath in hopes he would do the opposite.

"You can't have two faces under one hat," he reasoned quietly with an unfocused gaze. Her quizzical expression elicited an explanation. "A Coastie from Jamaica taught me that Jamaican proverb. I think of it every time I look in the mirror."

"I think I can relate to whatever you're trying to say," she offered with an index finger pointing to her cut and dyed hair.

He shook his head in amusement. “You’re as real as they come, Faith. You’ve inspired me.”

His words rendered her speechless.

“You do,” he went on. “I’d venture you’re working through a lot stuff right now. So what? Don’t be so hard on yourself. You inspire me, though, because you’re doing it. Finding out who you really are. Getting out in the world. I wish I could do the same.”

Before they could go on, Keith’s heavy steps sounded on the finger of the dock. They watched him plop down on the boat in an obnoxious interruption.

“What are we waiting for? Let’s hit the water,” he bellowed from the captain’s seat.

“That’s my seat,” Patrick scolded.

“Then use it, my man. I want to get to Panama City before nightfall. Let’s go.”

“Okay, okay. We’re ready?” he looked at Faith for assurance. She crossed her arms and curled into herself. “Give us ten minutes? I’ll radio when we’re about to leave.” Keith picked up on the cue to leave and shrugged his agreement. When he was out of the boat and on his way back to his own, Patrick continued.

“There is no short version of what I want to tell you. If we leave now, we’ll beat the threat of afternoon storms and I’ll fill you in on everything when we get there,” he explained hoarsely. “You can trust me. I won’t let anything happen to you. What I’m mixed up in is my problem, but it’s not all bad.”

She dipped her head, wanting to trust someone. When Patrick’s left hand ventured to her right knee, she drew closer, probing his clenched jaw and tense blue eyes with hers. His fingertips skimmed knee to neck and tension morphed into intention as he slid a grasp to the back of her head, cradling her in place while pressing his lips to hers. Two tender passes preceded a more forceful gesture that ripened to passionate heights. Faith desired to discover the depths from where this fervor flourished.

The crackling two-way radio announced a curt question from Keith and Patrick lost with a frustrated roll of pale eyes. He moved his lips to her ears.

“Stay with me.”

Chapter 13

Emerald flashes elicited powerful influences from her kindhearted face as the woman sailed south along Bourbon Street. Her presence parted the human sea where the French Quarter buzzed with life. When she reached the streetcar line, the trolley's headlight pierced the dusk with prompt arrival. Once inside, an important man in a suit gave her a look of disapproval before rising from his front seat, resulting in a vacancy on the packed, rickety car. The weary spirit took his place. The woman found humor in his ignorance and watched the man head for city hall as she listened to an intuition that suggested the girl was in good hands – for now.

A few additional trolley stops would transport her to the edge of town. After that, she would walk the remainder to reach the sluggish bayou waters she called home. Not minding the trek, she would hitchhike until cars became scarce amid swamp song. The gray afternoon threatened a storm and thunder rumbled. Her thumb never had time to indicate her direction when the old Chevy slowed to a stop at the last busy intersection where a highway led the city's visitors away. The wrinkled man wore a sympathetic expression and a red flannel shirt. She gestured her intent to ride in the bed of the blue truck and he did not protest. When she finally slid from the back, it was under the cloak of darkness.

Stems of dried sage, tied together in a bunch with a long indigo ribbon, was lit and she held the herb torch tightly. The flame died, emitting a protective haze that swirled her embark along hidden trails. A scattered trail of sea salt funneled from the pocket of her coat and untamed brambles snagged at the hem of her shin-length, mustard dress. Rather than slither into tannin waters, the gators simply watched her pass. She forged on until she reached the hidden rowboat within the Bayou Gauche, a long-time fishing community hidden among overgrown brush and battered by hurricanes. Here, the trail ended where the marsh water flowed relentlessly, just like her, and at the water's edge, she knelt. The cairn stood a foot tall, constructed as a piled rock memorial. She set an intention aloud and balanced a smooth stone atop the altar where she also left the stub of burnt sage. The last of the salt was emptied from her pocket. Not wanting to weaken the all the good she had put in place, she pushed away memories of evil acts done from the same spot. She was satisfied with her progress thus far.

In the deep pocket, that one without a hole, of her thin coat, she transported a cherished article to add to her collection. At the thought, glee rose inside of her. That token would have to wait, however. For now, she untied a ribbon necklace. From another band of indigo ribbon, a black velvet mojo bag dangled. The sweet smell of basil and morning glory saturated the tiny pouch of protection and it was sealed with a lock of the girl's own hair. She had not even noticed the tresses plucked while exiting the shop. With this necessary connection to the soul she sought to protect, she was confident in her abilities and ready for him this time. He was no match for the strength she possessed now. She carefully deposited the satchel inside the tiny tower of rocks.

Once the rowboat was set free from lily pads, mud and brush, the swift swamp allowed easy access to her shack across the way. Despite peaceful intuitions, the woman knew a storm was brewing and intervention was essential. The force of nature would be much too considerable for the unassuming girl to handle alone. She rowed on toward the abandoned fish camp. The unpainted, one room shack featured a rusted roof and a dilapidated deck protruding over the swampy shoreline. The teetering dock hung on against the constant current and when the rowboat bumped into the splintered structure with a thud, the woman tied the dinghy to exit. The door of the cabin creaked open without assist.

The bayou fishing cabin was last used for its true intent seven decades ago. From inside its walls, she fished a different sort as she cast spells instead of lines and harnessed needles instead of lures. It was decrepit, forgotten, and forlorn - just like the squatter who used it. In the corner of the dwelling remained a small cupboard. Its missing doors revealed four slanted shelves that housed small figures made of burlap and rope and covered with pins, nails, and strange marks etched with paint. The witchy celebrant pulled a clean canvas doll from her pocket to sit on the shelf with the others and bullfrogs croaked a chorus of approval. When he arrived, she would be waiting.

Chapter 14

Tuxedoed and towering over the elite gathering inside the country club, Louis LeBlanc basked in the mayor's accolades. She had agreed to deliver the campaign dinner introduction speech since they served the same party of constituents, although close confidants knew she did not care for the pompous senator. Now, she listed construction project after construction project that Louis was involved in, including a new entertainment complex that was on the brink of breaking ground, and the attendees applauded politely. The banquet room was filled to capacity with fine apparel accented with lavish jewels and pre-dinner cocktails were served freely by waiters zooming about with silver trays poised at shoulders. The waitstaff could barely keep up with demand. While the mayor showered the senator with praise and thanked him for his tireless efforts, Louis offered a subtle wink to the female lobbyist seated next to his wife. Unaware of the adulterous display of affection, Chelsea exhibited perfect posture in a slimming black, sequined gown while dutifully listening to the mayor's praise of her husband. The lobbyist cast auburn hair behind her shoulder and re-crossed her long legs so that the slit of the dark maroon dress revealed more than appropriate for this kind of event. Louis bit his lower lip, smoothed his thick black hair from his forehead and strategized a reason to move the next business meeting up with the young attorney.

Underdressed and listening from the sidelines was the city's police chief and Louis' long-time friend, Chief Mallory. He was not present as a political supporter. He had business to attend to. Not wanting to appear political nor wanting to cause a commotion, he waited in plainclothes in the adjacent hallway, but within earshot. He had stopped by the LeBlanc's residence unannounced and the housekeeper had informed him where he could find Louis and Chelsea. Richard made his way over to the country club hoping to sneak a brief talk with his friend since junior high before the festivities kicked off. Now, amid the arduous occasion, he considered leaving to try Louis at his office in the morning. Richard chuckled at the difference in the manner they had chosen to serve the public. Alas, the police officer became enthralled by the mayor's over the top adoration of Richard's friend from preteen days and could not prevent himself from listening. Greater applause broke out as the senator took his place behind the podium and Richard used the opportunity to discretely step inside to occupy a lone, extra seat along the darkened back wall. Louis gestured for the attendees to take a seat and they obliged.

"I was born the son of parents whose own parents had emigrated to this great land from their Parisian roots. With little more than pocket change to their names, my grandparents arrived in New Orleans and got to work creating a future. I am inspired by their story every day and it is what motivates me to work tirelessly for you." The gracious crowd applauded again. Louis basked in the applause and waited a minute before continuing. Richard crossed his leg and eased into a comfortable position to hear his friend out. He wondered what Louis' idea of pocket change was nowadays.

Louis began with the story of grandmother and grandfather LeBlanc who, at the turn of the twentieth century, found a way to purchase a stern wheel paddleboat for a ferry and sightseeing business. That boat turned into a small fleet and eventually the LeBlanc Steamboat Line was hosting fancy dinners during cruises along the Mississippi. Louis' parents inherited the money from that business and kept the wealth train rolling with city contract work earned from political connections. It was an impressive story, as Louis related it. Anyone better informed would know a darker side to the tale.

Richard was amused. His friend had them on the edge of their seats with this terrific family history narrative. Richard recalled what he knew of the LeBlanc's business acumen. Yes, they had grown the business into quite an empire. The broken-down ship initially acquired was practically given to them from an owner who was unable to keep up with the repairs. That owner had disclosed the multitude of hazards that needed immediate attention. Never mind that the LeBlancs knew nothing of boats, they were undaunted. Assembling a crew of wharf misfits, they instructed the crew and captain to do whatever necessary to keep the vessel afloat and in working order to complete as many excursions as possible with little to no expense. That paltry business plan allowed them to purchase three more ships, none of which in better condition than the first, having been used and abused as cotton haulers. They completed modest renovations to the ships to add ballrooms and beautiful staterooms but left the mechanics up to a crew with neither experience nor funds.

This plan went well until one disastrous evening in 1919. During a cruising vaudeville show, a boiler exploded on one of the ships. Naturally, none of the LeBlancs were onboard, but hordes of high paying guests and employees were. The exquisite-looking boat was in the swift channel of a particularly wide stretch of the river and many of those who lived through the explosion were unable to swim to shore. Most of the maintenance crew perished and the captain was severely burned and unable to provide useful orders. When the ship caught fire and sunk, the majority of those onboard perished a painful and dramatic death. While all of this is bad enough, the most chilling detail of the story, in Richard's mind, was how the LeBlancs dealt with the aftermath. City residents and tourists were curious and fascinated with the horrific details that emerged from the survivors. So, seeing a way to capitalize on a devastating incident, they paid the survivors to appear on added broken-down cruises that floated past the half-sunken ship and tell first-hand accounts of woe. The LeBlancs made a small fortune until the public lost interest, the country was thrown into the first World War and they, in turn, conveniently donated the fleet to the war effort in exchange for a hefty tax write-off.

Now, one hundred years later, impeccably dressed guests sat ready with deep pockets in this glittering ballroom and listened to the present-day LeBlanc recount the virtues of his lineage. Richard shook his head. The modern-day LeBlanc still profited from smoke and mirror self-promotion along with development schemes he was perpetually apart of.

Louis finished his dissertation and the waitstaff marched from the kitchen with plates of steaks, haddock, pasta, or chicken. The senator made his way through the room, shaking hands, kissing cheeks, and offering spirited slaps to broad shoulders. His handshakes too hearty, his kisses too demonstrative to be sincere. Chelsea LeBlanc hung devotedly by his side. Soon, he caught sight of Richard and inconspicuously made his way back to greet him. As all attendees immersed themselves in food and drink, they never noticed their chief of police standing by.

"Richard, this is a surprise." Louis bristled as he neared. "Chelsea, do you mind grabbing a couple of waters from the bartender for us? I'm parched."

Chelsea paused, sensing there was more to this impromptu meeting, then obliged. "Of course. Richard, would you like anything from the bar?" For the first time, Richard recognized her discomfort in her role. He declined with a shake of his head and she retreated, leaving her expensive perfumed scent behind.

"Richard? We had agreed to talk later this week?" Louis scolded.

"I need to keep the file updated from the burglary to keep it quiet and moving along for you. I also need to talk to Faith as a part of this investigation, for obvious reasons. Is Chelsea aware of the developments? The stolen items *were* hers."

"Oh, yeah, yeah. Sure, she knows," Louis said flippantly. "C'mon. You're throwing a lot at me. This isn't really the time." Richard looked at his friend sternly.

"I'm no dummy, Louis. Talk to her before I have to and I need Faith's cell to get ahold of her for questioning."

"Rick. This is all in the family right now. No need to make a big deal of it. Faith is a little … fragile. I'll handle it."

"What if Faith's in danger, Louis? You don't seem to even know where she's at." Richard tried to quiet his voice to avoid attention.

"She is an adult and capable of taking care of herself. Trust me, I will get in touch with her and have her call you directly. Hear me when I say I don't want her talking to anyone without our lawyer present. Not even with you." Louis' feathers were obviously ruffled and Richard was offended.

"Lou, I'm starting to think I'm the only one with your daughter's best interest in mind. I don't care how this goes down, but if I don't hear from her and Chelsea by tomorrow, I'll move this investigation forward without you."

As Richard left the room, Chelsea returned with two waters. "What was that all about?"

Beet red, he guzzled the water to cool himself. Chelsea took a sip with one eye on her husband. Placing a hand on his forearm, she asked, "Honey, is everything alright? What did Richard have to say?"

The senator regained his composure and reached for Chelsea's hand. "Nothing you need to worry about, dear. Shall we make another round?"

Chapter 15

Tampa was still a long way from the drama about to leave Mobile. While the Alabama shore boasted quaint beach bars and seafood eateries, the Ybor City section of Tampa was rife with crowds that, on certain nights, could rival those in New Orleans. At the turn of the twentieth century, Ybor City was a world-leading manufacturer of cigars. Today, this hip neighborhood featured blocks of brick rowhomes that now housed shops, restaurants, spas, and salons. Singled out as one of the trendiest hair salons was The Cut, owned by a woman named Francine who worked long days and many evenings to satisfy her clients. Little did they know, she worked to mask the pain of losing a child decades ago.

So, while Patrick, Keith, and Faith worked through the rituals of preparing the boats for safe departures, Francine was experiencing a ritual of her own as she began her day. To most, the habitual string of words would be maddening, but as she shampooed a woman's hair, the routine was therapeutic and, for a moment, she was with her child again. The stylist caressed the young woman's scalp methodically, feeling the various contours that were as different as snowflakes from person to person. She felt her client relax and she did, too, as she began to work shampoo into a thick lather. Cue the memories and a warm smile came to Francine's thin lips.

"A, B, C, D ..." Her fingers moved to the rhythm of the age-old preschool song in her head. The tiny voice came alive and stumbled through the verse along with her. The head cradled in this woman's hands was not a toddler, but it made no difference.

"M, UM, NO, NO, P," the frail, cheerful voice sang out proudly. What she would do to return to that time. Knowing what she knows now, she would fight tooth and nail to keep her baby after the brief bout of homelessness she and her baby had endured deemed her an unfit mother. Newly evicted, scared and living in a car in what most would call a rough neighborhood, she had believed there were no other options. She had believed what she was told and allowed the system to provide what they promised would be a better life for her baby. Hindsight is twenty-twenty

and within a year she had gotten back on her feet with a job at a hair salon, however, by the time she had an address again, there was no turning back. The damage was done and her child, they had said, was in the adoption system. Days and months turned into years and she was unable to locate the sweet child that would have found a place in another pair of arms. The shampoo, lather, rinse, condition, and rinse again took her right up to *next time won't you sing with me?* And, just like that, Francine was back to reality.

Chapter 16

Chelsea slowed the Audi to a stop to allow a trolley to cross the intersection. A young professional with a powerful stride crossed the street simultaneously and the to-go coffee cup he held was redolent of the paper cups served at her old bakery. She speculated, again, on whether she made a mistake by selling the business. The doubts were piling up. The regular profits she had garnered were small but would have grown. In the end, an imagined life with the wealthy senator was more enticing than cupcakes. Had she had chosen well? He had said there was no longer a need to toil away in a dark kitchen before dawn. She guessed he was right. Why make life more difficult than it needs to be? Then there were the signs of infidelity that crept up from time to time. She scanned her memories for the details and the sunny morning allowed sunny outlooks. Louis had neither time nor privacy for affairs, she considered. She felt shame in her suspicions and was relieved she had never confronted her husband.

She pulled the car into a parking space near the main entrance to the precinct and grabbed her glossy, tan Chanel clutch from the white passenger seat. Her polished shoes matched the little purse and she smoothed her mint green skirt and hair as she locked and stepped from the sedan. The concrete added heat to the already sultry day, and she commended herself for choosing the lightweight, sleeveless cream blouse. Chelsea's pride in her appearance left her feeling painfully out of place once inside the police station. There was a time when she was comfortable in any surrounding, even this one. Now, she had become accustomed to a certain level of civility and posh environments. Walking toward the reception area with the click of her heels attracting the interest of everyone in the room, she found herself making judgments about the questionable people already seated and waiting. Glimpses of tattooed faces, missing teeth, greasy hair, and tattered clothes were unavoidable. She chastened herself for evaluating surface qualities, although, it was clear they were doing the same. She stepped up to the counter and politely addressed a woman who couldn't care less about serving the needs of anyone in that room. She cleared her throat uncomfortably.

"Excuse me, Chief Mallory requested I stop by to see him. Is he in?" she stated in an authoritative voice. The woman glanced up without raising her head.

"I said I would be right with you. Have a seat." The dissatisfied employee went back to her work. Chelsea chose not to point out the woman had not addressed her before then and turned on her heels to take her rightful place among the misfits. Karma had mediated the situation.

Her stomach knotted as she scanned the room for a seat. A snarled grin from a waif of a man missing most of his teeth announced that she 'smelled real nice'. She changed course when she realized the customers behind him were even less inviting. A set of parents remained in the back row of blue seats. A purple-haired woman with pock-marked skin wore tattered clothes and bounced a fussy baby. Chelsea smiled at the woman and took an adjacent seat. Her smile was met with a blank stare. If Richard didn't see her soon, Chelsea decided, she was leaving.

"Ma'am?" Chelsea snapped to attention three minutes later.

"Yes, you. Come on up." Like some twisted version of The Price is Right game show, she advanced to the front. "Go ahead on through that door there," the woman ordered as she pointed to her left. "I'll buzz you in."

The buzzer sounded and Chelsea pushed the heavy door open. After only a step or two, she was met with Chief Mallory.

"Hi, Chelsea. Thanks for coming by. Here, we can duck right on in here," he hailed warmly. He opened the door to a stark, gray room and allowed Chelsea to enter first. She took a deep breath and continued with the click, click of her heels echoing loudly. Richard pulled out one of the four chairs and motioned for her to have a seat. She conceded, clutching her purse tightly on her lap. He sat across from her at the short, metal table. With the long mirror on one side of the room, it appeared she was in for interrogation. Her wide gaze shifted to the door and he recognized her discomfort. Richard eased into a casual position and crossed ankle over knee to continue his ploy. "So, Louis at the office, huh? Man, that guy works more than me. I tried calling him," he said with a smile. "You want some coffee? I just wanted to go over our findings so far. No need to be nervous."

"No. Nothing for me, thank you. Yes, he certainly works a lot. He cares about his constituents more than anything," she uttered out of habit.

She wished Louis would show and regretted agreeing to the meeting without telling her husband. She could hear him telling her now that she should let him handle things. She repositioned in her seat uncomfortably.

"Boy, do I know it. We're lucky to have him. Anyway, I won't take too much of your time, Chelsea. I know Louis is busy and, well, frankly, the items stolen were yours. I didn't see the sense in waiting for Lou to be available." Richard made a point to show respect for her. He was certain she rarely received reverent interactions.

"Well, now that you mentioned it," she answered. He was pleased as he noticed her straighten her posture. "I have been a tad annoyed that I haven't heard anything yet. Were you able to retrieve anything from the prints yet?"

Right out of the gates, she told Richard what he had called her in for. Louis had not told his wife anything about the matter. He chose to tread carefully.

"We were able to lift some decent prints and I apologize for the delay. The lab is always backed up, but I did put a rush on things for you." He decided to get down to business before Louis called or realized what was going on. "We do, in fact, have a name associated with the prints and it is causing me some concern. Before I get to that, I have to say that I believe there was another person involved. Someone who was careful about not leaving any evidence."

"I see. Well, the prints don't lie, do they? Who stole my jewelry, Richard?"

"Faith's prints were on the safe, Chelsea."

Chelsea's face went noticeably pale. "Faith?"

"Yes. And I'm worried about her, Chelsea. Louis says she's back at school, but I haven't been able to talk to her yet. I don't think Louis has, either, despite what he's told me. I'm of the mind we need to find her and make sure she's okay before making accusations." Chelsea looked away. Was that a tear Richard noticed? He had never seen Chelsea show much emotion before.

"Why would Faith steal from me?" Composed, she turned back to face Richard. Her face had reddened in the meantime and her shoulders sagged under the sleeveless, silk blouse. Her blue eyes were indeed watery. "I mean, I know she doesn't think of me as a mother. I don't expect her to. Really, I don't think she thinks much of me at all. But, I can't imagine her stealing from me, or anyone else, for that matter. Tell me something, Richard. You told this to Louis the other night when you called, didn't you?"

Richard sensed Chelsea was coming undone for reasons he could not place a finger on yet. Not wanting to tarnish his own reputation for the politician's, he nodded slowly. He suspected honesty would get him everywhere with Chelsea.

"I suppose he was caught off guard and didn't know what to do," she said, not wanting to believe her husband was dishonest with her. Still, the truth stung. She sighed.

"As far as I know, you're right. Faith is with her roommate back at college and I haven't heard any news of her calling or touching base with Louis. I guess there's nothing suspicious about that. Faith does her own thing and knows Louis is always so busy with work. I kind of feel bad for her. Their relationship has become more strained over the years," Chelsea admitted with a downcast glance. She continued to ramble and Richard continue to hang on her every word. "Losing her mother all those years ago. Having a father who is wrapped up with work every second of the day. I should be doing more for her. You have me concerned about her now. What are we going to do?" Chelsea remained focused as her eyes pleaded for Richard to confide in her.

Richard had seen that look of despair before in this room. This woman was willing to be his liaison. He didn't skip a beat and leaned in with clasped hands.

"I can't imagine Faith waltzing in and stealing the jewelry on a whim. I also know Louis works hard to be a good father and husband," he added to protect Chelsea's ego and prevent defensiveness toward her husband. "Either someone was at the scene putting pressuring on her or she was in a tough spot and is on the run. We need to track her down and make sure she is safe before we jump to any conclusions. Do you agree?"

"I most certainly do. Have you tried calling her?" Chelsea asked.

"I don't have a number to reach her. I can search the database and get that info, but that information isn't always reliable. It sure would help to get a good number right from the start," he said with his best puppy dog eyes.

Chelsea opened her clutch and pulled out her phone. "I'm embarrassed to admit I don't even know her number without looking it up. Do you have a pen and paper?"

Richard pulled a memo notebook and pen from his front shirt pocket and slid the items toward her. She wrote two phone numbers in ultrafeminine script.

"The first one is her cell. The second one is her roommate's number. Sometimes Jane is easier to reach and Louis has called her in the past to get a message to Faith," Chelsea explained with a sheepish grin.

"Thanks, Chelsea. I'll get on this right away and get back in touch with you and Louis by tomorrow either way."

"That's fine. I am so worried about Faith. The jewels can be replaced, but … well, let's just make sure she's safe first. Oh, and, do you mind leaving out my being here to Louis? I'd rather him believe you were able to get those numbers on your own." Chelsea flashed a charming smile that no doubt helped her get her way in the past.

"Absolutely. It's the least I can do for your help. Don't you worry about him. I can handle the guy," he said with a wink as he led her to the door and out into the hallway. Chelsea shook his hand and thanked him sincerely.

"And please. Let me know that Faith is okay as soon as you know more? I can only imagine what that poor girl has been through since the death of her mother. I'm intent on filling that void for her from now on."

Richard bid his accomplice good-bye, otherwise speechless. Why would Chelsea believe Louis' first wife was dead?

Chapter 17

Panama City blossomed into view. Patrick had kept the boat at full throttle most of the way and Faith had remained motionless in her seat with a permanent scowl. With the impending conversation looming along with the Florida city that would serve as their next stop, Patrick was all nerves. He looked over at Faith now and then and wondered why the daughter of a rich senator was with someone like him - dyed, cut jet-black hair, self-inflicted scars and all. He knew enough to trust the cut of the blade was nothing compared to the emotional pain that caused them. He wanted to know her better, to pick up where they left off in Alabama. He thought about questioning her on her wellbeing but had a distain for asking questions he already knew the answers to.

He turned his red visor backwards and slowed the boat to a crawl as he looked for the channel leading to the popular Florida city. Choppy water hid the deeper qualities he was in search of. The route Patrick committed to was dicey and shallowness was all around. He backed the boat up to avoid running run aground now that the tide had lowered. Faith shook the angry look from her face as she became more alert of the situation at hand.

"That trip went fast," she exclaimed.

"Weather and winds helped. Damn it," he blurted.

"What's wrong?" Faith stood to see what Patrick was craning his neck to see.

"Nothing. I think I passed the entry point to the channel. I need to backtrack a little."

"Oh." Faith sat back down and inspected a hangnail.

"Shit," Patrick muttered.

"Now what?" Faith blurted.

"I think I entered the channel wrong. It looks like there might be a sand bar ahead. Hold on. I'm gonna back out of here and try again."

"Why don't you just turn a little to the left? It looks clear over on my side." Faith lifted her glasses a bit to gain a different view. Patrick set his jaw. He looked behind him and beads of sweat started to form on his forehead.

"Damn it. You gotta be kidding me. What the hell?" Patrick yelled out as the engine sputtered to a halt. He tried to restart it and heard nothing but clicks and whirs.

"What's wrong now?" Faith cried out quietly as she arched her back and craned her neck to look around. "What can I do?" Patrick ignored her and lowered the anchor. Once satisfied they were hooked, he proceeded to look over the aft of the boat.

"Shouldn't you have made sure there's no coral down there before you anchored?" Faith called out matter-of-factly from her passenger bucket seat. Patrick wiped his brow and turned his visor back around to shield his eyes. Faith easily caught a glimpse of the exasperated look he shot her before doing so. Faith followed to see what he was looking at. Peeling off his t-shirt, he tossed it aside and jumped into the water. "Patrick. What is going on?"

Again, she was met with silence as he slid under the water's surface for a few seconds. She leaned over the sun pad as he held on to the rear corner of the boat from the water. Finally, he addressed her.

"Hey, can you go below and grab something for me?" he gasped with water dripping down his face. "There's a pair of goggles hanging in a net of supplies near the cabin door. Oh, and don't turn the ignition key whatever you do. I'd like not to be maimed by these propellers. Again, do not turn the ignition for any reason."

Happy he was speaking to her again, Faith quickly retrieved his request. Lying on her stomach, she handed the goggles to him. He put them on and disappeared under water for ten seconds. Springing back up, he pulled off the goggles.

"That's what I was afraid of," he said, more into the air than to Faith. "Stay there and don't touch the ignition. Whatever you do, do not touch the ignition." He made eye contact that held an intenseness that changed from their last intimate interaction. Faith was disappointed in his harshness.

"I won't, I won't," she said with annoyance and resorted to stretching out onto the sun pad to soak in the hot rays. She lifted her tank top to allow the warmth of the sun to heat her flat stomach and considered needing a bikini if she continued this crazy trip much longer. Patrick continued to pop up now and then for air. Faith's curiosity, and concern, got the best of her and she leaned over the back of the boat to see what was going on.

"Should I call for help or something?" she asked.

"No, you should not call for help," he snapped flippantly.

"What is your problem, anyway? It's not like it was an unusual question. The sun's getting lower and we're out here like sitting ducks."

"Is that right? Well, I'm sorry your three-hour-tour is turning into an inconvenience. I'll have us on our way soon, ma'am."

She swung her legs over the sun pad to address him more clearly. "I don't know what your problem is, but I sure as hell don't deserve the attitude from you," she shrieked. Patrick knew he had touched a nerve and was going to pay for it. His fingertips were turning blue as he tried to hold on in the cold water while keeping his legs away from the engines' propellers. His mask was positioned across his forehead and she berated with bright light ensconcing features he longed to see better from his lowly view. "I never have anything but good intentions and I'm tired of being ignored and talked down to!"

"Simmer down. I'm sorry. I'm just a little frustrated right now. You're right. You don't deserve it."

" 'Simmer down'? 'Simmer down' you say? I just, you know, I don't even know why I'm here and it's obvious you don't really want me here, so, whatever. I'll arrange to go home when you get me back to land. If we ever make it."

"We'll make it," Patrick said with more aggression than intended. "I just need five uninterrupted minutes and I'll have this fixed."

"I think I need go home from Panama City." She tested the waters with the comment. "I shouldn't be here, considering how we met and all. I don't know what you're up to and I don't want to be a part of it anymore." As the words slipped out, she stood up to make sure she could get to her bag in case she needed to fend him off.

"How the hell are you getting there? Daddy Warbucks' copter?" Patrick wiped his face and looked back at a sun that was indeed rushing toward late day. "I'm not holding you here against your will. To tell you the truth, I'm not sure why you're here, either." Embarrassment and sadness written on her face, she recoiled to the cuddy of the boat, sentencing herself with solitary confinement. Hearing the door slide shut filled him with remorse – and worry. He went under water once more to finish the repair on the propeller, all the while hoping she would refrain from drastic actions. He considered removing the keys from the ignition to be safe.

Finished with the task, he pulled himself back up onto the swim platform and wrung out his shorts. Slicking as much water from himself as possible, he went back to the helm and, with a silent prayer and closed eyes, turned the key. The boat came to life and relief washed over him.

"That's what I'm talkin' 'bout, baby. Nice," he yelled with a slap to the steering wheel. He banged on the cabin door.

"Hey, Faith, you hear that? We're good to go."

Faith slid the door wide open and revealed shock. Patrick cut the engines.

"What's going on? You look terrified. It's all good. Look, I'm sorry. I do want you with me. I really do. I was just frustrated trying to get this fishing line pulled from the prop. That's all it was." He held the matted clump of line in his palm for her inspection.

"A message showed up on my phone. It was from the chief of police back in New Orleans. He thinks I might be in danger." Faith studied Patrick's apprehension for a glimmer of virtue. Barely skipping a beat, he tossed back an answer.

"I think it's time we had that talk."

Patrick slithered the vessel from the channel and motored south along the panhandle of Florida, leaving a muddled Faith to process the voicemail without him. Currently, he had three things on his mind: arriving in Tampa, talking to Faith before she called the police, and getting to a hospital. That last need was a personal problem he preferred to keep to himself. He throttled the engines enough to instigate low roars and iced further discussion, but Faith still scorched him with her frosty stare. She stood ready and willing to illuminate his dark path, wanting to know where it led. He was running out of time and her silence was a powerful tool in getting him to talk as she held her cell phone in her dangling left hand and remained standing at the cabin's open door. He navigated the boat further away from shore and, in the process, all cellular towers. The sun mocked him from its three-quarter position in the cloudless sky, coercing him to make a move. If he could convince Faith to give him a little more time, and the weather remained calm, he was confident they could make it to Tampa before nightfall. Shore birds were no more and when he was content with a random off-shore location with calm waters, at least in a literal sense, he quieted the engines to attempt peacekeeping. Anchor stowed; the boat drifted. Faith fell into her seat, defeated and despondent. Patrick strained for common ground.

"I never knew my mother's love, either."

Faith wore inquisitiveness as she considered his words. With all that had been left unsaid up until that point, she was intrigued by the conversation starter.

"Unloved, abandoned, well, they leave holes that are hard to fill."

The boat turned its bow west. The horizon spilled endlessly, making it difficult to decipher between sky and water.

"Mine left me before I was five. I don't know why." Her voice assumed a childish quality. Patrick noticed the scars on her arms were browned by the sun as Faith fidgeted with the tiger eye beads.

"I guess you could say I took to rebelling against unfair systems – how unfair life is."

"Petty crimes and robbery," she ventured, mesmerized by light bouncing off water and not bothering to pull down her sunglasses.

"If you want to call it that."

His inability to conceal offence broke the water's hypnotherapy. She regarded his denial with disbelief, and he clammed up.

"How do you fill the void? What do you call it then?" Faith challenged, squinting accusation.

His seat constricted, so he ejected himself with lean muscles pulling taut under tan skin. He secured his hands behind his head. Faith sucked air, intimidated by sudden moves. He moved to the backseat and hung his head low before rearing back with long legs extended. Unable to keep an eye on him, Faith moved in turn, leaning against the port side of the boat and in time to catch a boyish grin that melted her defenses.

"Charity," he countered with an air of arrogance that bordered cockiness.

She raised an eyebrow.

"What would you say to skipping Panama City and heading straight to Tampa? I need to fuel up, but I know we could make it before nightfall."

He gauged Faith for some type of reaction. Her poker face remained, he forged on.

"I'll get a hotel room for you, you make whatever calls or do whatever you need to do. I'll arrange a ticket back to New Orleans. I'll help you in any way, or I'll leave you alone forever." He winced at the promise.

Faith remained blank while pulling down sunglasses. Patrick babbled additional pleas. "Can I ask one favor? Please don't call the police until you give me a chance to explain more? I'm not a bad guy. There's more to this story." She could see his desperation and lifted her cosmetic shield by placing sunglasses atop her head. Keeping her distance, she articulated unhinged thoughts.

"You sure do ramble when you're nervous. Look, I'll pay for my own room in Tampa. I also need to a visit to a hair salon pretty bad. As far as talking to the police, I'm just as scared about that as you and I'm thinking you'll be better at devising some kind of reasonable explanation." Her sly smile said it all. She and Patrick had officially formed an alliance. "Lastly," she went on, "you might be catching a flight back to New Orleans, but I'm not." She shrugged and put her sunglasses back in place.

"Okay. First, we need to get in touch with Keith. He's a great guy, but I'm not a big fan of traveling with others after a certain point," he stopped upon realizing the impact of his words. "Except you, of course." Faith shrugged, he went on. "Knowing him, he'll never make it to Tampa in good time. He'll hole up in some port with a few good bars and moor there for a month."

His relief was sustained by Keith picking up the two-way call.

"Hey, buddy. You all good?" Keith greeted.

"Yeah, fine. Finding that inlet to Panama City was rough. You navigate that alright?"

There was a noticeable pause.

"Shit, I haven't even gotten there. You ever been to Miramar Beach? There's this place called the Whale's Tail. I just stopped back down to the boat for something and I'm heading back up there in a few. You have good timing."

Patrick gave a *What did I tell you* glance toward Faith who was now back in her seat. Once it was clear that Keith was more than happy to be left alone for a while, Patrick and Faith were free to travel at will.

"Move it along, captain," Faith ordered.

"Hold on tight. Gonna be one hell of a ride."

And with that, he throttled the boat and did a fast one-eighty-degree turn. When the tip of the vessel collided with the wake just created, the front of the boat flew up out of the water and landed with a dull thud. Faith was in hysterics.

"That was incredible!" she yelled over the thundering motors.

"You like that?" he asked.

"Yes!"

"Just wait. There's more where that came from."

Once in high gear, the boat planed off effortlessly. They careened over water at a high rate of speed that bombarded them with a constant rush. The mess of last Friday would not be swept up anytime soon.

A brief stop for fuel was all it took before arriving at the Tampa Bay marina and the slip that had been arranged by the Cigarette boat's owner. The private marina belonged to a residential enclave of snowbirds and retirees. A few couples sipped sundown cocktails from flybridges and aft decks. A twenty-something employee locked the door of a small marina supply store on site. In the waning light of day, Patrick was noticeably wiped out from pushing the last leg of the trip. He looked pale despite being in the sun all day and kept sitting down in contrast to the last of the trip where he stood in nautical glory. Faith gathered her belongings quietly and now stood atop the dock to help tie knots in cleats. She had begun to learn the ropes and now knew from where that phrase was derived. She waited for Patrick to toss a bowline and she fashioned a lazy knot, knowing he would make proper adjustments anyway. Her purse sat with her overnight bag, ready for departure. Faith sat down cross-legged next to her bags. She had reserved a room for Josephine Beaumont at the Tampa Bay Courtyard Marriott and a hair appointment for the next morning at a salon close to the hotel.

"Is there anything I can help with?" she asked as Patrick tugged a rope with heavy breathing. She gasped. "Are you alright? You don't look so good." He wiped his brow and started to stand before opting to kneel.

"I kinda feel like maybe I'm coming down with something," he admitted between labored breaths. "I'll be fine after a good night's sleep," he added with a weak smile.

"Are you sleeping here? That can't be comfortable. Do you want me to reserve a room for you at the same hotel? It's the least I could do after tagging along," she asked sincerely.

"No," he hastily blurted out before softening his tone. "I mean, thanks. Really, I appreciate that, but I'll be fine here. I get my best sleep out on the water. If I decide to I can always get a room somewhere." He attempted to stand before succumbing to gravity. He steadied his wobble and chose to remain seated, looking up at Faith as she gathered her duffel and swung her purse over a shoulder.

"Well, if you're sure. I guess I'll be on my way. How about I bring you some food or ginger ale. What sounds good to you?" she asked softly with compassion in her voice. Patrick was touched, unable to remember the last time he was shown concern. It also made him uncomfortable. He mustered up as much energy as he could to sound more normal.

"No, nothing. Don't worry about me, please. You need some rest, too. You go do what you need to. I'll talk to you tomorrow. Dinner, right?" He reminded her before she could forget about the plan suggested at the stop along the way.

"Okay. If you insist. Well, I'm staying at the Courtyard Marriott under Josephine Beaumont, in case you change your mind or need to find me." Faith picked up her bags and shuffled her feet a little as she prepared to leave. Patrick didn't stand and she waved an awkward farewell before walking away.

The sickness and intense pain that had overcome Patrick was nothing compared to the gut-wrenching stab delivered as he watched Faith retreat from a tepid split. Never before had he felt so weak and it killed him to see what his illness had reduced him to. Crouched in discomfort, he watched Faith disappear from view. Not until then did he attempt to stand. Slowly, he uncurled his body to an almost erect position before blacking out. Just like that, his limp body fell to the wooden dock with a heavy blow.

Chapter 18

Dusk swathed Patrick's limp body as it lie upon the swaying dock. The universe looked the other way. Life went on and the end of the day, thanks to the dockmaster calling 911, the paramedics rolled Patrick's body to the ambulance via stretcher and readied him for a swift trip to the hospital.

Had she known the dire nature of his condition, Faith would have kept him in her thoughts and prayers. Instead, Patrick's only well-wisher checked into a Marriott room with a view of the bay. And, after booking a hair appointment for the following morning, the privileged fugitive indulged in hotel amenities before sinking into sleep.

Louis LeBlanc held the phone hard against his ear as he marched down a hot Baton Rouge sidewalk. The voicemail intensified the scowl he flung to each passersby. The body shop's manager questioned Louis' intent and referenced the call received from Faith so, without hesitation, Louis answered the voicemail by confirming plans to sell. With satisfaction, he dropped the phone into his jacket pocket, knowing Faith had received word of her punishment. The car would be the first of a few ways he would teach his daughter to respect him. His thoughts landed on the seventy-five pairs of eyes on him from the most recent dinner hosted at the club and he imagined the stun of those supporters if they knew the scant appreciation shown for the life he afforded. The stone steps of the tallest capitol building in the United States loomed and Louis was winded upon reaching the doors of the limestone powerhouse built for Louisiana's political elite. The building reached past thirty stories and Louis' ego swelled when he stepped inside the cavernous marble entry, sensing recognition from others. He collected his thoughts once alone in the elevator. Yes, he would make his daughter realize his generosity by ending it. Cutting her off would bring her crawling back. Adding fuel to the fire were the three missed calls from Richard logged by his phone the day before. If Faith expected Louis to stand idly by while she caused potential scandal and chaos, she had underestimated her father's capabilities.

Meanwhile, Chelsea LeBlanc regained her suspicions. Sitting down alone, again, to a dinner at home, she was painfully aware of her husband's preoccupation. She brought a forkful of salad to her mouth despite longing for a juicy bite of steak. She followed the low-calorie choice with water while a desire to share a bottle of red at a table for two raged. Her current table for ten was occupied by one and she looked at the heavy drapery in a room designed by a stranger and felt depressed by it all. More disturbing was her inability to speak up. He had called to say he would be staying in Baton Rouge for the night, she had told him she understood. Somewhere along the slippery slope that was her marriage, she had lost her voice. At the head of the oversized dining room table, she considered how satisfying a slice of rich chocolate cake would taste. She considered how she had lost the urge to bake one.

Chief Mallory paced the halls at the station. A sixth cup of bad coffee guaranteed to keep him restless past midnight. Louis ignored his calls. Faith would not answer a cellphone now registering in Florida. Questions swirled like the cream in the dark swill served in a Styrofoam cup. Thoughts expanded then dissolved and the only solution to decelerating his silent interrogation was a more overt path in ensuring Faith LeBlanc's safety. He would face the senator's wrath later and shamed himself for having been intimidated by Louis in the first place. A breach in trust

While Patrick, Faith, Louis, Chelsea, and Richard took their places, Hawk, Joe, and Charlie deliberated backstage. Whiskey mixed with ale ignited a late-night debate between the men hidden behind the speakeasy's doors, all three crammed into a u-shaped booth. Hawk and Joe contended with Charlie who was convinced Mac would fail them in Tampa. Charlie suggested they close shop in New Orleans and head to a new town, the others supported a wait and see approach.

Wheeling above a tempest created by a cast of ornery characters, sat the eye of a storm. In this calm place, the voodoo woman continued to weave her magic. Still in the Bayou, tending to unhealed wounds from long ago, she no longer looked to inflict revenge. Instead, she strived to shower love on those she longed to protect. The years had taught her that revenge was over-rated. By saving that one most important soul, she knew she could save herself.

Chapter 19

"Welcome, Miss Josephine. I'm Francine. Follow me."

Francine immediately adored this new client. Guarded, yes, but her warm smile indicated another side. Francine knew she would loosen her up in no time. Sitting down in the salon chair, she addressed the young customer once more.

"So, what are we doing for you today?"

Faith assessed herself in the mirror. With her suntanned face and salty hair, her looks were becoming more and more unrecognizable. Adventurous. She liked it.

"Well, I've been traveling with a friend and I'm a mess. Can you shape up this rough cut and freshen the color?"

"Not a problem," Francine's voice was soothing. She inspected the strands of hair. "I see you're experimenting with new color?" Faith tensed with the observation and looked aside.

"I guess you could say that."

"How fun. Are you up for some suggestions?" the stylist asked tentatively.

"Sure. Why not?"

The stylist's thick brunette hair was shoulder-length and the layers in the cut allowed the style to move along with her animated hands. Ruby nails reflected flashes of light and Faith caught sight of a tattoo of two hearts on the inside of her wrist. It stood out as a contrast to her otherwise upscale, conservative style. She continued to run her fingers through Faith's hair as she fluffed and arranged the frizzy tresses.

"So, are you willing to go shorter for a spell? It will help get you back to a healthy state."

Faith wanted to tell this woman this is the healthiest state she'd ever been in. "Yep," she said instead.

"Your natural color's pretty and perfect for Florida beaches. I'll bring you back to that with some highlights to give you a little lift. Sound good?"

"Go for it," Faith confirmed.

"Alright then. Come on over to the shampoo area, Josephine." Francine's rhinestone sandals tapped along. She adjusted the water temperature while wrapping a black, plastic cover robe around Faith before easing her back into the chair.

"Please, call me Jo," Faith cooed as she relaxed under the stylist's expert scalp massage, herb-scented shampoo eroding more insecurities.

The hospital room was dark, except for bedside machines blinking red and white. A florescent glow seeped in from the hallway. The hum of equipment had soldiered on while Patrick had slept. Waking slowly, he examined the uncomfortable IV in his wrist and his foggy brain tried to tell him what had happened. His fate realized upon remembering the worst collapse yet. He was going nowhere anytime soon and that posed a few problems in his groggy mind. Exhausted, he closed his eyes and wondered how long he had been there. He tried to remember other events, however, Faith walking away was the only memory he could recall.

"You're awake," a brunette nurse said nonchalantly, checking the computer before turning toward her patient. "How are you feeling?"

"Tired. How long have I been here?" Patrick tried to raise his hand to rub his eyes. A system of plastic tubes caught on a white sheet and he winced as the IV needle tugged at his vein. His cloudy disposition unable to remedy the mess with weak arms. The kind nurse noticed his dilemma and adjusted the sheet while gently lifting then settling his forearm. Her soft touch pacified him.

"Oh, since about seven?" she pondered with a tilted head. Her hair twisted high upon her head with a clip and a few loose ends fell to the side. "About seven hours now," she added with more certainty as she glanced at the clock on the wall.

"What time is it? Can I just leave now?" he blurted.

The nurse paused and gave him a stern look. "No, you need to stay put. It's a little past two in the morning. Where are you going at this hour, anyway?" She placed her palms on the bedside rail with a motherly look of concern.

"Nowhere, I guess," he said with a sound of defeat and looked toward the glimpse of darkened sky beyond partially open blinds.

"That's right. Can I get you a snack? You must be starving. I could arrange a ham and cheese sandwich and some juice? Not much of a meal,

I know," she offered with a tone of pity in her voice. He didn't want her pity and it irked him to know that's what people felt when they knew his plight. He felt helpless and didn't answer.

"Well, I'll be back with a little midnight snack for you. Sit tight," she ordered with a wink. They both knew a sandwich and a carton of juice would do nothing in the end.

"Thanks," he said, looking away. His coast guard gym bag caught his eye. The nurturing nurse patted him on the arm before stepping away from the hospital bed. "Oh, before you go," he added, "could you grab my bag for me?" He nodded toward the seat below the window and she honored his request. Setting it on the bed, her face leaked sadness.

With the caretaker gone, he quickly rummaged through the bag to find his cell phone. Relief washed over seeing there was power left in the device. He quickly checked his messages and his heart raced as he noticed all three messages were from Charlie. After deleting the third and final one, he quickly typed a text response.

In Tampa now. I got this. Relax.

Chapter 20

"Chief Martin," the Tampa Bay police officer grumbled as he picked up the call from his desk as the station.

"John. This is Richard Mallory. How are you?"

"Richard. Nice to hear from you. What do you need?" His voice softened.

Richard chuckled. "What makes you think I'm calling in a favor?"

"Cop intuition. So?"

"That's why you're one of the best."

"Flattery gets you everywhere. Go on." Chief Martin gave full attention to his respected colleague.

"I have an MIA senator's daughter and her cell phone signal's in your neck of the woods. Mind looking into this for me? I need to quietly keep an eye on her. I stress, quietly."

"Sounds easy enough. What info do you have to start with?" Chief Mallory listed pertinent facts and Chief Martin scrawled on a legal pad.

Richard received a call back before the sun set on the next day. The Tampa Bay PD made quick work of Richard's dilemma and Chief Martin updated the New Orleans chief of police on the progress.

"Her cell is showing up at a Marriott in Tampa. No reservations under the name you gave me, though."

"So, she's using an alibi, hiding away willingly with someone, or being kept against her will. I doubt a rogue captor would take a young adult woman to the Marriott to hide," Richard pondered aloud.

"I have the same hunch," the detective concurred.

"Are you able to continue tracking the phone and keep on the lookout for someone matching her description? Once I have enough to go on, I can get my guys involved with your team? Sounds like we found her, but don't raise any suspicions. Keep it quiet. We don't want to force her to flee now that she's so close."

"Not a problem, Chief. Glad we can assist."

Richard was more anxious than ever. He was getting ready to pounce and bring Faith back, hopefully not as a rescue mission. Without thinking twice, he called Louis LeBlanc as a final shot at cooperation. Louis had the good sense to answer the call this time.

"Hello," he answered.

"Louis, it's Richard. Have you heard from Faith yet?"

"Richard. How are you, my friend? As a matter of fact, I have. Just yesterday she left a message for me. I've been meaning to call you. She said she is fine and doing a little bit of running around with her friend Jane and still in Alabama. No issues. She sounded upbeat and happier than I've heard her be in a while, to tell you the truth." Richard played along, now that he had lost all trust in his friend.

"Good. Glad to hear she's all right. I've been concerned, Louis. Did she mention any specific places they might have gone?"

"Oh, just running around campus now. Their usual haunts, I'm sure. Anyway, I'm on my way to pick up Chelsea at the house. We're heading out of town for a few days. Don't worry about this anymore. We want the robbery case dropped." Richard could hear Louis talking to someone in the background. An order was rung up. A cashier provided a total amount.

"In that case, I'll let you go," Richard said with feigned cooperation. "Where are you and Chelsea heading to?"

"A little R 'n R along the Gulf Coast. You know, spas and shopping for Chels and I suppose I'll find something to do in the meantime," he guffawed.

Something about Louis' tone was grating.

It was at that moment Richard knew he knew he had a bigger case on his hands. He was spinning amid a web of lies and he needed to identify the spider.

His next call was to Chelsea and she, too, greeted him pleasantly. He hoped she would engage in enough small talk to help him cut through binding threads cast upon his meager investigation.

"I hope this isn't a bad time. I just wanted to touch base with you after our meeting. I know you're heading out of town, but do you have a second?"

"Out of town? I'm not going anywhere."

Just as he suspected. "Louis is traveling alone? I probably have my lines crossed."

"Yes, he's leaving for, um, what did he tell me? Oh, yes. A charity golf tournament. That's right. Good riddance," she snickered in confidence. "I told him I'd rather stay home alone."

"In that case, I'll have a squad car patrol your street a little more often this weekend."

"That's kind of you, Richard." He heard a door creak shut. Chelsea adopted a hushed voice. "But tell me, have you heard from Faith? I haven't gotten a chance to talk to Louis much, but I don't think they've talked."

Richard recalled the reason given for the call in the first place.

"Right. Yes, Louis did let me know he talked to her and she is back at her apartment." He waited for Chelsea's reaction.

"Oh. He didn't tell me," she said meekly.

"He also told me to drop the robbery investigation."

"Oh, I see."

"So, of course, I wanted to check with you on that first."

Richard allowed silence to settle between them, wanting Chelsea to find her voice.

"I'm a little offended by him not asking me first."

He cheered her on from the sidelines. "Naturally."

"And we still don't know the depths of or reasons for Faith's involvement?" she ventured.

"Our investigation has not concluded anything."

"Then I say we leave the case open for now. At least, until someone gives me a valid reason to drop it." Each word was weighted with ire.

"I concur." He detected their alliance strengthen. He also detected, for reasons unknown, he was working against a tightening timeframe.

Three for three, Jane picked up Richard's call next. He could hear the buzz of a college bar in the background and she shouted a 'hello'.

"Jane Campfield?"

"Yeah?

"This is Chief Mallory from the New Orleans police department. I'm trying to locate Faith LeBlanc. Her father is concerned about her whereabouts and we're just checking up on her. She doesn't seem to be returning her messages lately." Richard adopted a decidedly more official tone.

Jane shushed whoever was with her and the sound of footsteps and heavy breathing indicated she was nervously finding a quieter space. The thrum of traffic replaced jubilant prattle.

"Um, okay. Sure. I'll help in any way. Is she okay?"

“Thanks. Like I said, that is what we are trying to determine and I’m simply calling you to get a little help with the matter. It sounds like she’s not with you?”

“No. No, sir. She hasn’t been back since classes ended for the summer.” Jane wasn’t sure of what to say. Her last conversation gave strict orders to tell the senator that Faith was there at school. A call from the chief of police was a completely different matter.

“I see. Jane, have you talked to her lately?”

“Let me think. The last time I spoke with her was a few days ago. She wanted a ride from some marina in Mobile. I couldn’t get to her. She brushed it off and said it wasn’t a problem and that she was safe. Then she told me she was with a friend.”

Richard’s concern peaked. “Who was she with?”

“I have no idea. Oh my God. I should’ve went and got her. It’s just that, well, it was late and I had been drinking.”

“You didn’t do anything wrong, Jane. You made the right decision. Listen, I’m going to give you my number. Call me if you hear from her again? Can you try to reach her, too? Let me know as soon as you talk to her. Also, I need you to keep our conversation to yourself for now. Just stay in touch with me and let me know anything you find suspicious. We need to keep this investigation quiet for now and, hopefully, all of this concern is for nothing.”

“Sure. No problem. I know how things go with Faith. I mean, with her dad being in the public eye and all. You can trust me.”

“Thank you, Jane. Make note of the number I’m calling from and you can always reach me at the New Orleans PD station.”

Richard knew there was a detective tracking Faith’s cell phone in Tampa. Now, he needed someone on her father’s trail.

Chapter 21

Nurse Lenora re-arranged the hookups to reach the private bathroom before stepping out to check on another patient. He rolled the IV system with him to find the privacy needed to plan his next move. The reaper may have knocked, but Patrick did not have time to answer. He still had things to do and, having been in this condition before, he knew he was as good as he was going to get. He tugged on the plastic tube leading to his left wrist and winced when the needle resisted leaving the vein. The medical tape peeled from his skin with a punishing smack. Now disconnected, he shoved the bag on rollers aside and dressed quickly before splashing cold water on his face. He strained to hear over the growl of florescent lights, one ear against the door. Quiet enough to risk escape, Patrick slid his ballcap low and sauntered into the hallway as though he had every right to be there. Holding his breath along with his gym bag, he made it down the empty hall to the elevator and banged the G with a force intended to make his descent faster.

The attached parking garage level was full, and he made his way stealthily through the rows of cars, narrowly escaping the view of a security guard in a golf cart, and, finally, out into the dead of night. Trying to stay calm and keep his wits about him, he walked two blocks to a Greyhound bus station where he took a seat against the wall and near an outlet. His breathing was heavy, and he felt clammy. He closed his eyes and willed his breathing to slow to prevent notice from the few early morning travelers. Patrick resumed normal activity and plugged his smartphone in for a charge before pulling up the address and coded information Charlie had given him via text.

1125 Morning Glory Drive. It conjured a serene view of 1950's domestic bliss. While tired trekkers napped upon the benches throughout the station, he reviewed Google Maps to gain his bearings. He barely knew where he was, let alone where he was going. Patrick leaned into the task, absorbing details of a satellite view. It would be an easy walk once he regained his stamina. He walked to a vending machine to load up on Snickers Bars and Coca-Colas while pondering the details of this job, a job that he believed to be his last. Before anyone could take note of his behaviors, Patrick grabbed a city bus map and left the terminal. He made a left turn through the stench of bus exhaust and followed the map etched in his mind. Once the effects set in, he always felt his best right after dialysis and this time was better than normal. Perhaps the hospital version was stronger than the concoction received at charitable centers he normally frequented or maybe it was just the thrill of the task at hand. More likely, knowing he had survived to see Faith at least one more time was supplying a lift.

The house was to be empty for the next three days, that is, if the injury lawyer and his wife had not returned early from a conference in Miami. Charlie's contact at the security company had confirmed the alarm system had been activated the day before and remained engaged. Patrick could remedy that hurdle and would be in and out in no time at all. Still, he knew better than to push it and he settled in for an easy stroll. Early morning hours were his favorite as morning darkness was more optimistic than its late-night counterpart. A quiet time that allowed for reflection and renewed energy. He considered life after this last assignment. A rough start had led to rough paths. Could an easier one wait? He shoved the expectant thoughts aside and chided himself for entertaining such hopeful ideals.

He jumped as a nearby sprinkler system engaged then his thoughts turned to the people from his past as he continued down the neat sidewalk. Foster families. Three of them. All good people who he could have treated better but he had been young and scared and confused.

The Bentons were the first family who took him in. He had lived with them until Mrs. Benton gave birth to their first child a year later. He acted out, they wanted out. He was up for placement.

The second family who stepped up to the plate had been the Manns. They wanted a brother for their adolescent boy who was against Patrick's arrival from the start. The son confirmed his feelings about the situation any time he was left alone with Patrick. Pushed to the brink one Saturday afternoon, Patrick let his own feelings be known and when boy stumbled inside with a broken nose and two black eyes, Patrick knew it would only be a matter of time before he would find himself in a new home. He was right and met the Morris' soon after.

Dot and Bill Morris were a middle-aged couple who never had children of their own. By the time Patrick ended up on their doorstep with the social worker, he had worn out most of his angst. At fourteen, he had somehow mellowed into someone who knew it was easier to play by the rules, plus he never wanted to cause Dot's kind blue eyes to cloud. The three of them lived peacefully in a small ranch house in the suburbs. When he had turned eighteen, he joined the Coast Guard to follow in Bill's footsteps. When his adoptive parents succumbed to different forms of cancer before Patrick turned twenty-four, consumed with grief and alone. His Coast Guard comrades pulled him from his despair and Patrick found his place among heroes.

The Coast Guard years had been the best time of his life until he got his own dose of bad health news. His livelihood came to a crashing halt when he was honorably discharged. It was then he met Hawk, a former Coastie himself. Hawk introduced Patrick to Charlie. Charlie referred to Patrick as Mac from the start and introduced him to Joe and their *business*. Under the guise of a tavern, diner, and country club, Patrick regained purpose and vision for a cause close to his heart. Yes, the undertakings were unlawful, but the foursome justified their actions by targeting unscrupulous individuals. Patrick had never looked back as he did his part. Not until now, that is. This trip to the hospital was a stark reminder. He wanted out. Lately, each job brought visions of Dot and Bill casting looks of disappointment. If his time on earth was coming to an end, as doctors predicted, he wanted to redeem himself and end on a good note.

Back to reality, he glanced up at the corner street sign. He was now deep in a leafy, suburban jungle of oaks trees, palmettos, oleander, and hibiscus flowers. Two more blocks to go. The historic Hyde Park neighborhood featured impressive mansions in the blended styles of Victorian, Colonial, Craftsman, and touches of Mediterranean. Close the bay and lush with hefty landscape budgets to match lofty mortgages, the location was a tropical haven reserved for a few. Charlie always provided a tidbit of incentive for Patrick before a job and from that morsel of motivation Patrick knew the owner of 1125 Morning Glory Drive lived in this bucolic setting while the children of his tenants lived in the squalor that was the hundreds of properties he owned as a slumlord. He hastened his steps as he realized dogs would be walked, morning papers would be delivered, and Saturday early risers would take stock of their neighborhood. He knew the morning rhythm of nice neighborhoods better than he should and for all the wrong reasons.

Morning Glory Drive. Recalling the map in his mind, he strode to the correct address marked on the brick columns at the end of the drive and marched along the winding driveway before ducking around the rear of the house. Golf gloves on, he pulled the palm-sized black box out of his bag and activated the jammer to deactivate the home's security system. The rear French doors had locks that were easy to pick and, with the help of the trusted jammer, the security system emitted no sound as he entered the kitchen. So far, so good. Would the last job be the easiest? He hoped so as he said a silent prayer for the absence of a family dog.

With dawn yet to arrive, a nightlight cast just enough glow for Patrick to find his way. A child's pair of pastel blue Crocs sat by the marble island and he hesitated at the punch of guilt the tiny shoes delivered. Getting over it, he made his way to the wide staircase grandly positioned in front of the main entrance. *In and out. Grab the jewels and leave.* He sped to the second floor.

The master suite loomed at the far end of the long hallway also lit by a single nightlight and he peered into each room as he carefully passed by. One empty room after another featured perfectly made-up beds and neat furnishings. Relief welcomed him to the last room upon finding it, too, was unoccupied. A massive four poster bed was flanked with matching nightstands and bureaus. A door to the right revealed a spa-like bath and a Rolex on the granite caught his eye. The thief checked the timepiece before putting it in his bag. Four Forty Five AM. He continued to slink about the main room to find what he came for.

A floral perfume hung sweetly in the air of a luxury space that served as a woman's walk-in closet. At the far end of the clothing vault were floor-to-ceiling shelves displaying stilettos mixed with Louis Vuitton and Channel accessories. He passed on the leather to find the gold. Holding a penlight between his teeth, Patrick dropped his own ratty bag to claim diamond bracelets, rings, and necklaces plucked from an unlocked drawer fitted with velvet inserts. The next drawer also sparkled when opened under the light he shone. They were the kind of jewels he liked and he grinned at the sight of a two-carat diamond. With each opened drawer, the baubles became more impressive and he continued to dump them into his bag of belongings. The fourth and last compartment did not disappoint and held pieces on another scale. Patrick glowered at the refined mother lode with gems of richer hues. Antiquity fit for royalty. Broaches with lavish peacock feathers swishing with sapphires, emeralds and garnets and blossoms crafted from flashes of citrine and topaz. These pieces belonged in a museum, not to a woman who married a man making money off the injured and poor. Patrick knelt before the display to examine the artwork crafted from polished stones once mined by callused hands. He considered that while holding the glistening peacock on the palm of his hand. The gems most likely mined by forced labor or by those born with little choice in life. Under harsh conditions, regardless, he reasoned. He returned the broach to its spot then carefully eased a tiny, silver ring that lacked the same glint as the others, apart from the diamond. The round cut flashed endless brilliance resembling a room of mirrors. An engagement ring and surely priceless to the young woman it had been given to then inherited by. Patrick placed it, too, back into its velvet cushion before closing the last drawer and leaving the priceless pieces for the rightful owner.

Suddenly, a shadow leapt beyond the partially closed closet door and he gasped as he turned toward a muffled sound. Every inch of his tall frame became paralyzed with shock except for the intense beating of his heart. He allowed his wide eyes to accustom to the dark once his penlight was off and retreated behind a wall of silk and linen. He cringed as hangers scraped. Then, the closet door swung slightly inward. Patrick scanned the opening for an extended arm or leg to suggest he'd been found. From the bottom of the doorway slid a black form whose mew belonged to a harmless black cat with bright green eyes and a swishing tail that ushered him with an evocation that the intruder's time in the home was up. He would have laughed if not still reeling from fear. The cat sat before him, his thick tail fanning the floor with an agitated pace. Patrick revealed himself and gathered his bag, offering a grateful caress atop the eager head of the curious animal and left the way he came. Back on the rear deck in less than a minute, dawn had begun to cast a glow in the eastern sky. His bag was full of gold and gemstones and his heart was full of shame. He reminded himself of the good the money earned from the jewels would do.

Chapter 22

"How do you like it?" Francine held a mirror up and allowed Faith to assess the new style, front and back.

"Perfect! I don't know how you do it!" Faith had never felt so good. Francine was a miracle worker specializing in confidence brought on by beauty. Her sandy blond hair was back, but this time with golden highlights that sparkled a fresh glow. The ends more taped around her chin, Faith was pulled together and ready to take on the world. Or, at least find solid footing with Patrick later that afternoon.

They moved to the reception area and Faith pulled a card from her wallet. Without thinking, she used the debit card linked to her personal checking account. One that her father deposited money into now and then for essential items. Faith continued to admire her new style in the wall mirrors surrounding her. She looked down as Francine swiped the card and started to compliment the woman on her tattoos when she realized her mistake.

"Oh. I meant to give you a different card," she started.

Fortunately, Francine never checked the mismatched name on the piece of plastic. Still, she had already inserted card into machine.

"Shoot. It already transmitted," Francine confirmed as she looked down. "Hmmm. It's not going through. Says 'transaction cannot be completed'. You probably already expected that, though," she went on, in an attempt to lighten the financial hiccup.

Faith tried her best to play it cool despite not knowing why the card would be declined. She hadn't used it since checking the balance a week ago.

"Here. This one is active," she hoped aloud. As Faith passed the American Express in exchange for the bank card, she saw Francine take note of the scars along her arms. She reddened in shame.

A few agonizing seconds later found Josephine's card working just fine and Faith was signing the receipt with a big tip. Bidding farewell, Faith saddened at the thought she would never see this woman again. She squinted to protect her eyes from harsh sunlight before finding her sunglasses. Faith held her head high while taking a walk to clear her mind.

Ybor City's iron railings, trolleys, and energetic sidewalks made Faith think of New Orleans. A pang of homesickness struck. Lunchtime crowds waited for savory Cuban dishes. Open doors allowed glimpses of cocktail hours started early and a scent of lime wafted from drinks delivered by a hipster waitress standing before a sidewalk bistro table. Faith stumbled upon a waiting streetcar and hopped aboard. Centennial Garden beckoned her with a shaded bench so she hopped off at the next stop and once more felt homesick for a home that had never shown her love. Sitting on the bench, she watched people mill about and wondered what she could possibly miss about a man who cared more about his business dealings than his daughter. Then she realized it was the city itself. The music that healed. The Cajun rice that comforted. Buildings boasting weathered facades with pride. The city was proud to show its scars and inadequacies for the details only added to its bold character. She could live without her father, but could she live without New Orleans?

Pulling her phone from her purse, she tapped the bank application and punched in the account log-in information to determine why the card did not work at the salon.

Zero dollars. Shock waves stung her fingertips.

Two hundred twenty-five dollars and twelve cents withdrawn the day before.

He had sold her car and then depleted her bank account. Not talking to her was the norm. Methodically destroying her was a new low. Of course, Faith had sunk to a new low as well when she decided to follow a thief into the night. The cycle would continue until one of them took the upper hand. She decided it would have to be her.

With shaky hands and heart, Faith dialed her father's cell phone. When his voicemail answered, she pleaded her case.

"Dad. It's me again." The tears began to punctuate her words. "I'm sorry. I made a big mistake and I want us to start over. Please call me. Plcasc talk to mc."

She stared at the dead connection, willing the phone to signal a call back. Her shoulders sagged under the weight of her thoughts.

Maybe her final grades were submitted and lackluster? His disappointment in his daughter was obviously stronger than ever. She told herself she deserved what he was dishing out this time around. She pulled up her online university account. If she had misjudged, she could call

Louis to alert him of the good marks and maybe he would admire the work she had put into her studies. She bristled at the grade school sentiments and felt her confidence take another hit.

In minutes, however, she was staring at another punch to the gut.

Faith Saviour LeBlanc: Disenrolled.

Sitting alone on a park bench in the middle of an unfamiliar city, the anvil on her chest threatened to crush her once and for all. The streetcar arrived in front of her like a hearse arriving at a cemetery. This would not be her funeral. Faith boarded the trolley and returned to Francine's shop on a whim.

The Cut salon was open and Francine looked up from her crouched position while shelving a newly opened box of hair products. With a teal shampoo bottle in hand, she stopped mid-task to greet the unexpected visitor.

"Hello, again. Is something wrong with your haircut?" Francine stood slowly and set the bottle on the wrong shelf.

Faith was all business, unable to muster friendly banter.

"My style is terrific. I love your shop and I was wondering if you could use any help? I'm looking for a job."

"Are you in trouble? You look scared. Faith, right?" she observed as she recalled the correct name.

"I'm in a bit of a bind, you could say. I'm reliable."

Francine recognized the look of despair on this young lady's face. "Any help I would need would be rather mundane. Sweeping the floors, stocking the shelves, taking appointments," she added as the phone rang.

Faith walked over the reception desk and in her most professional voice, answered the call by referencing the salon and inquiring as to how she may assist.

Francine was amused and pleased. As Faith placed the caller on hold, she addressed the woman she hoped would become her boss.

"A Sharon Simon is looking to schedule an appointment for next Thursday at three o'clock for highlights and a trim. Are you available?"

Going back to her work at the shelves, she answered.

"The appointment book in right in front of you. Go ahead and pencil the appointment in as long as there's at least a block of an hour available."

Faith confirmed the appointment and found a pencil to write down the details. As she hung up the phone, Francine continued.

"Oh, and Faith?"

Faith looked back with wide eyes.

"Can you finish displaying this product while I prepare for my next appointment? Can you be here tomorrow morning at ten?"

The stylist brushed a trace of dust from her white jeans and gave a friendly wink to her much-needed assistant. As Faith eagerly accepted the chore, a text came through on her phone. Thinking it was her father, she filled with dread then relief at the sight of Patrick's words.

Columbia Restaurant in Ybor City? 7:00?

It took her only a second to reply yes.

Faith was already getting acquainted to her new city. Having no car was no problem in this part of Tampa where the street car would get you where you needed to go. That similarity to New Orleans was comforting. She had left her new job at four with a promise to return the next morning. By seven o'clock sharp, she arrived in style in a satiny, sleeveless, light blue cocktail dress purchased with her one financial lifeline. Fitted at the waist with a matching belt, the pleated skirt reached just above her knees and fitted the mood she was attempting to embody. She assumed if she portrayed confidence and well-being enough, her brain would be tricked into believing it. Knowing the beaded bracelets did not match the retro style of the dress, she still refused to part with them as she recalled the warnings from the woman in the mysterious witchcraft parlor. She reached for the beads for assurance as the maître de showed her to a small, square table for two in a private corner decorated with drooping palms in oversized pots. The tables were covered in crisp, white linens and the lighting was low. The Spanish restaurant could be mistaken for a classic Havana vibe. In actuality, it embodied Mediterranean décor and its satin walls were painted in Dijon hues alongside highly-polished, golden wood accents. Soft chatter was flecked with sounds of clinking glassware and silver. Patrick waited at the table and stood as she approached. Everyone around him disappeared as she focused her eyes on him. She suffered a moment of self-doubt in this moment of truth.

Be kind to yourself. The motherly words seeped into her brain like magic and she felt some relief.

"You look incredible," Patrick complimented while leaning in to kiss her softly on her cheek.

First kiss, she thought. Her confidence soared at the loving gesture.

Patrick took a seat in the chair across from her. A crisp, white button-down shirt complimented his tan and it appeared he had visited a barber. Scented with aftershave that now seemed familiar to Faith, this sharper version reminded her of the Patrick she met at the tavern a week ago. Color had returned to his face and he seemed to be in good spirits again. The table for two was not suited for his frame and his long legs bent out from underneath.

"So, you're feeling better I see?"

"Much. Guess I just needed some sleep to fend off whatever was getting to me. And what about you? I like your hair. And your dress." His eyes wandered.

Faith blushed. "Thanks. I let the stylist have creative liberties and needed something to wear. The dress was at a shop near the salon," she downplayed.

"Well, she certainly knows what she's doing and that dress is ... you look fantastic," he gushed with a trademark grin.

"What'd you do today? Did you get a chance to meet that friend you mentioned," Faith asked to change the subject as the waiter returned to take their drink orders. After ordering a glass of white wine for herself, she noticed he opted for a Coke and she became self-conscious.

"Um, yeah. I stopped by, but they weren't home. Then, I just ran some errands. I paid the marina. Ran to the post office to mail something." Patrick fidgeted with the linen napkin has he placed it upon his lap.

"What did you mail?" She asked before thanking the waiter for the wine.

Patrick took a sip of soda to stall. He had the urge to level with Faith about everything. He knew he couldn't, not yet, so he opted for half-truths.

"Since you asked, a resignation. I think I'm going to stay in Florida for a while. Take some time off. I had to finalize everything with the, uh, club."

"Oh?"

Patrick took one look at Faith's quizzical expression and felt terrible about lying. His near-death experience had certainly done a number on him. He got lost in her bright green eyes that shined with the sun setting beyond the windows of the restaurant. Her new haircut accented her features and an innocence that was not customary for a young woman of her age. The guilt was killing him.

"I just need a change. That's all. I'll make sure you get back. Unless you want to stick around a little longer?"

Faith's initial answer was a playful smirk.

"What? You're up to something," he deduced with crossed arms.

"You're one to talk." Her coy response caught her by surprise and she glanced to check his reaction. He remained fascinated and she reflected his sentiments. "It's a bit of a coincidence."

"What is?" he asked suspiciously, now leaning in closer. She mirrored his advance and didn't bother to blush this time as his gaze took all of her in as she leaned forward.

"That you're staying in Tampa. I decided to do the same today. I got a job at a salon a few blocks from here." Faith buttered a piece of bread and took a bite. "Sorry, I'm famished," she murmured with a full mouth and took a sip of wine before continuing. "I got a job because, as of earlier today, I have no money to my name. I also no longer have a car, courtesy of my father selling it without discussing his plans with me," Faith continued rationally. Patrick stared at her incredulously. "To top it off, he disenrolled me from school. He is systematically dismantling me. I'll have to figure out a way to complete my last few classes for my degree." A smile flourished, in spite of it all.

Patrick spoke in a somber tone. "Faith, I feel real bad you're going through this. This is all my fault. I'll call your dad. I'll come clean. Did you talk to him today? What did he say?"

"No, I did not talk to him. I've tried, but he won't speak to me. Although, that's how it's always been. Not sure why it's taken me this long to get fed up with the treatment," she shrugged while polishing off the rest of the bread slice. "You're not calling him. Don't you dare even think of doing that." She shook her head profusely.

They turned to see the waiter return and explained they hadn't looked at the menu.

"We'll have the empanada appetizer for now. We need a little more time with the menu," Patrick requested.

He leaned in closer to hold her hand. She relaxed in his soft grip.

"Faith, you have to make things right with your dad. I'll make things right."

"What?" she asked with a touch of attitude. "You don't want me here? That's fine. I can handle things on my own. It's a big city. You'll never even see me."

"No. I don't want to leave you. You're misunderstanding." He lowered his voice as he noticed a bar patron look his way.

"Then make me understand," she pleaded.

Faith eased closer until their faces were little more than a foot apart. Her gentle green eyes coaxed him into submission. She let him trace the scars around the inside of her wrists and watched as his fingertips lovingly caressed symbols of darker times.

"Life can be beautiful. Never doubt that," he reassured. She waited for his eyes to meet hers.

"I know that. When I'm with you."

When the waiter arrived back at their table for a third time, Patrick asked to have their meals to go.

A red Mazda mid-size SUV took the couple from Ybor City to the Tampa country club where the Cigarette boat was docked and harboring Patrick for a couple more days. The Uber driver gave up trying to start conversation and turned the top forty station us a little. Patrick reached for Faith's hand in the darkness.

Well-dressed, they now appeared as if they belonged at the members-only facility with a marina that was filled to capacity. Faith and Patrick walked the trail of docks to reach the boat they called theirs for the night. Many of the boats had crews assembled and were engaged in lively cocktail gatherings. With so many guests, no one really took notice of the boater who seemingly rose from the dead from the evening before. In addition, Patrick had made sure the docking fees paid included a bit of hush money and the dockmaster was happy to keep quiet on Patrick's whereabouts in the event anyone came looking for him from his hospital stint. In the end, no one cared. Faith moved in closer as he continued to hold her hand the rest of the way and helped her into the boat.

"AC's on. Let's have dinner down below," he suggested.

They settled into the cabin and Patrick slid the door shut. The bench seating on each side of the interior offered cup holders and room to rest the take-out. Patrick handed Faith a Corona and, this time, helped himself to a bottle as well. She pulled out their containers of empanadas and other tapas from a paper bag and rested the treats between them. He claimed not to be hungry. She offered a handfed olive anyway and he obliged. Watching her demurely lick the juice from her finger caused him to drain his beer. He rose to retrieve another. Faith raised an eyebrow at the unusual act.

"You normally don't drink. Why?"

"It's just something I try to stay away from."

"I should do the same."

Faith popped another olive in her mouth and held one out for Patrick, his tongue tasting her finger on the takeaway. Setting his beer aside, he plucked the juiciest cherry tomato from the assortment and positioned it on matching red lips. Into the slit, Patrick pressed the fruit. Bursting with ripe flavor, she savored the moment as he did the same, waiting for the flash of her green eyes to reveal the same eagerness he now suffered a need to relieve. Her taunts were as innocent as they were persistent, showing no mercy by lifting a skewer filled with shrimp and other delights, enjoying each morsel bite by scrumptious bite. She arrived, finally, to the last salty artichoke and he was ready for dessert. The shoulder strap slipped from her dress and he bit his lip to concentrate on finishing, feeding a spoonful of flan, wanting to fill her with pleasure. She accepted, a drip of caramel serving as evidence of decadence. He kissed her clean. Hungry for more, no longer interested in the role of trusted companion, Patrick knelt before her, sliding strong hands along her thighs and glancing up only to confirm a willing partner. Certainty of her inclination to join in on intentions stirred his frenzy and he forged on, searching every inch of a body he intended to worship. She felt his raw desire, sensing his urges, just as hers, were rooted in something more than lust. Her dress, loosely hanging from her heaving body by way of his sensual explores, fell atop the shirt he had thrown aside and the tipping point of their journey was reached, inevitable, really, from the start. Faith ran her fingertips along his hard torso and brought lips to him as they made quick work of any barriers left between them. Patrick guided her to the bed with tenderness where he practiced restraint, proving to be a gracious lover, never wanting her to question his intentions. With a glorious common ground reached, the release of tension brought a new level to their journey. A kind of peace never experienced settled in and sleep came to their quivering, knotted up, bodies, holding on to the only true love either had ever known.

In the middle of the night, Faith's middle-of-the-night mind bullied sleep out of the way. When she cycled through the same thoughts one too many times, she burst.

"My prints are all over that safe," she blurted out in a voice just audible enough to wake him.

"Your prints are on a lot of things." He tried to kiss her troubles away.

His attempts mildly pacified her. "Patrick, I'm scared."

Hearing her angst tore him up. He felt responsible and would make this right.

"I'll take care of it. I'm making the calls tomorrow to make this all go away for you."

She sat up and pulled the sheet and comforter around her in modesty. He leaned on one elbow.

"Please stop saying that. It will only make things worse. I need you with me."

"I need you, too. I love you, Faith."

His sincerity dissolved her fear.

"I love you, too, Patrick. Please don't leave me alone here. Let me stay with you."

His tone became stern. "I have no intention of leaving you. Ever," he added with a look of despair mixed with willpower. He moved on to her conversation starter. "Has your step-mother ever let you use the safe?"

"Genius! She did! Just a few months ago. In fact, I'll just say I wanted to wear the set of pearls that I she let me store there."

"Um, by the way, that pearl set is definitely no longer there," he pointed out with shame.

"Wow. Very strange conversation. You really need to explain yourself before this goes any further," she scolded with a shake of her head.

"I actually hate that we're having this conversation. You shouldn't be going down this road," Patrick offered. "But, since we're both up, this is a good time for me to come clean." He pulled his shorts from the edge of the bed and began to get dressed. "Meet me out there?"

She waited for him to leave before she took advantage of using the shirt he had worn earlier to cover up with. Faith buttoned it up most of the way and breathed him in. She wanted to tell him to forget about everything and come back to bed. She wanted to tell him that she didn't care. She started to think she was better off not knowing.

There were other things Faith remained blissfully unaware of. For instance, earlier at the restaurant, a busboy had cleared their table and couldn't resist the lure of the expensive smartphone left behind. He had placed Faith's phone on the tray with dirty dishes then stashed it with his personal belongings. Not only did she not realize it was missing yet, she also had no idea multiple people were tracking the device. Furthermore, amid the bustle of the late Friday night restaurant scene, Senator Louis LeBlanc went unnoticed when he entered the exact same restaurant in search of his daughter.

Chapter 22

Cool night breezes drifted along dark waters. It kept nuisance mosquitos away. Faith brought the tan comforter out from the berth and moved between the cockpit seats toward the oversized sun pad where Patrick waited with his back toward her. Using his forearms as a resting point and pensive, he cocked his head toward a nearly full moon casting a glistening glow upon the water. She paused to soak in the moment before they ventured any deeper.

He offered a defeated smile when she did approach and offered some of her blanket, which he declined. Patrick asked if she wanted anything to drink. She snickered at his politeness.

"No, thanks. And, I think you're stalling now," she encouraged.

"I know," he agreed and sat in close. "Not sure where to begin."

"I'll get you started. Did you grow up in New Orleans?" Patrick smiled at the easy questions and, for a moment, considered taking an easier path out of the situation. Knowing, however, he could hold nothing back from her now.

"Yes, but I moved around the city a lot."

"How old are you?"

"Twenty-nine. Do you have experience with facilitating lie detector tests?" he fired back for comic relief.

"No. Moving on, you mentioned you were in the Coast Guard?"

"I enrolled at 18. Medically discharged at 25. Loved it and being discharged was one of the worst moments of my life." Patrick looked out over the water. "Thanks for going easy on me. I'll take it from here. Yeah, so medically discharged from the Coast Guard. I'll save that story for another time, if you don't mind. I was raised in foster homes until eighteen. I have no idea who my real parents are and I don't think I care anymore, although that's all I wanted to know during the beginning years of my life. Once I had to leave the Coast Guard behind, I didn't know what to do with my life. Soon after that, I met Hawk. You remember him from the bar on Pirate Alley?" Leaning elbows on knees, he turned his head to watch her sit up with more interest.

"Sure. The bartender there the night I met you?"

"He was. He owns that building and is always there. I'll tell you this, if you ever need anything and I'm not around, you go to him. He knows everyone and can move mountains. You can trust him."

"You're already planning your escape from me?" Faith asked with a grin.

Patrick's heart ached as she uttered the words. "You won't get rid me as long as I have anything to do with it," he answered before looking up at the stars. Breathing deep, he continued. "Hawk was a godsend. He gave my life new purpose and, until recently, I was fully committed to helping him with a, uh, charity he runs along with two other guys." Faith looked confused.

"What kind of charity?" she ventured.

"Here, let me show you something that will make what I'm about to tell you a little clearer." Patrick pulled out his cell phone and opened the Internet browser. He clicked on a link and gave the phone to Faith. "Go ahead and scroll down. Take a look at the faces and read the captions."

Faith leaned over the phone and looked at the faces of children and young teens. Next to each face, the word "Status" was typed. Various statuses were given. It quickly became obvious these were faces of young patients needing organ transplants. Faith became emotional as she looked into the precious eyes of one toddler, baby and hopeful teen after another. With watery eyes, she handed the phone back to him.

"Sad, I know. But, there is a lot promise and good in those kids you just looked at. Not all have sad endings."

"So, when I caught you in my room? What was that all about? I'm confused. What are you telling me?"

"Here," he pulled up a Facebook page of a little boy with thick brown curls and smiling, baby blue eyes. "Read the note the parents wrote in the last entry."

Faith started to read aloud. "To the angels who helped make Carter's transplant possible, we are forever grateful. Happy eighth birthday to our sweet boy." She looked at Patrick, her own eyes filled with tears.

"Carter needed a kidney transplant. Without it, he wasn't expected to make it past age ten. Now, no hospital is going to deny him one when it comes available. However, the transplant world is a rough one. So many factors come into play and, sadly, money is big factor in keeping that train rolling." Patrick put the phone down and ran his hand over his hair and contemplated his next words. The moon shined like a spotlight.

"You should know that the jewelry I took from your stepmother's safe went to help a child like Carter get his transplant." Faith was speechless. In a matter of minutes, her life took on a whole new perspective. "I'm not justifying my actions, Faith. I know it's not right to steal. But, I also know there's a lot of injustice in the world and the scales are cruelly and unfairly tipped. What can I say? I have more compassion and desire to help save an innocent life that's slipping away."

"Even if it means you have to steal to level the scale," Faith said quietly.

"In certain cases, yes." Patrick waited for her to find fault with his revelations.

"Certain cases?" Faith inquired.

"I don't pick them. The guy who sets me in motion usually tells me a thing or two about where I'm going. A sort of motivation, I suppose," he shook his head at the words. "Let's just say your dad must have really pissed off someone in this little underground charity world I'm a part of. They never send me in unless they know of a wrong that needs to be righted. I could be getting it wrong about your dad, but," he backtracked.

"No need to protect my feelings. He never did. I know my father hasn't climbed the political rungs with all good deeds and he isn't going to help any charity that won't help him win re-election. As far as I'm concerned, that's his burden to bear. Aren't you afraid of getting caught?"

"Up until that night you caught me, no. Since then, yes. Meeting you like that was the first time I ever risked being caught … or worse," he added thinking of her more aggressive nature that evening and the gun she had pointed his way. "I know being caught again wouldn't have the same pleasant outcome," Patrick added with a grin. "Well, now you know. For what it's worth, though, I'm starting to think my luck could be running out and I'd like to find a new way to help."

"Like volunteer with a reputable charity?" Faith laughed.

"Some of those charities have so much overhead and pay their directors so much, it's disgusting. In a lot ways, those directors are stealing from their own cause. No way. My actions may not be noble, but at least I know this organization I'm a part of sends every last penny earned, or stolen," he added matter-of-factly, "to help kids get the transplants they need while keeping their parents out of debt."

Faith scanned the marina in silence. The moon outshined the stars and empty boats barely bobbed on water calmed by halted breezes. Spoken words hung in the still air, anticipating regard.

"Faith?" Patrick said after a minute of silence. "Please say something. You're making me nervous."

Faith adopted a humane expression. "What you do *is* pretty noble, Patrick. I was raised in the world of politics where a lot of decisions are made without any concern for how it might affect innocent people. Everything was about personal gain. What made you get involved in the first place? Did someone you know need a transplant?"

"Yes," Patrick answered slowly. "I guess I was just looking for some purpose in life and an opportunity came along at the right time. By the way," he added craftily, "the so-called resignation I mailed today was not for the country club, although I don't think I'm going back there. I did a job this morning in Tampa that's gonna be my last."

"Hmmm. A job in Tampa," she ventured as the pieces started to come together. "Okay, so I'm guessing that's the friend who wasn't home?"

"Definitely not home and definitely not a friend."

Was it remorse she perceived? His touch punctuated the statement when he slid a tender arm around her waist to bring her closer. As isolated as they were, she desired more, wanting to be on the water without traces of other humans and their achievements – only the moon, the water, the palms, and the nocturnal seabirds would be welcome. She glanced up at this mysterious man who happened to land in her world when she needed him most. She loved him for it. If he knew she watched him, he did not let on, continuing his dark sky watch like a sailor keeping the north star in sight. He had revealed much of what had preceded her that night, although she suddenly felt she knew him even less than before. Fathoming, now, how much more of him there was to know. He stole jewels, she stole glances. The moonlight in his hair, the jaw line that no longer set so tight. Lips that she longed for but was still too shy to claim, although only the moon kept them company. She shivered and he wrapped her closer in the blanket, then his arms. As he cradled her head in the crook of his neck, she dropped her secret glances to breath him in, her heart to settling into a rhythm with his. When his kiss atop her head rippled the still of the night, Faith felt an urge to utter a random thought.

"Do you have any tattoos?"

"No. Need me to prove it to you?" he half-teased as he sat straight.

“Take it easy. I’ll take your word for it,” she laughed. Continuing in a tired, raspy voice, “I noticed the owner of the salon I went to, my boss,” she remembered, “had one showing two hearts entwined. I thought I might be able to get something like it or maybe a vine of flowers to cover these scars. Hers were on the inside of her wrist.” Faith traced the enduring marks on her arms, considering blossoming that pain into beauty.

Her words stunned and, unable to speak, he ran fingers and palms over the skin she scrutinized. Then, lifting the parts she hated to his lips, he brushed the pain away, once and for all, with tenderness. He regained composure. “Tell me more about her … and your new job.”

Faith dared to dream of a new life, together, in Tampa while sharing the more minor details of her day with him. As she talked about Francine and her qualities Faith was drawn to, Patrick sobered with glistening eyes he tried to disguise. The woman’s tattoo and its placement could be a coincidence, but still, he wondered. Was Faith’s recent acquaintance the mother who had abandoned him? A woman possessing that one distinguishing feature his mind’s eye had held on to over all the years.

Chapter 23

Not working in an official capacity, the senator still donned a designer black suit, although, he abandoned his tie in the hotel room. From his table by the window he chose a pricey bourbon from a pushed aside menu and scanned the establishment like a rat sniffing out cheese. He swallowed the bourbon to suppress the mounting rage and the rat became a lion, standing tall to assess his kingdom. Still no sign of his daughter. Louis texted his diligent private investigator in order to get a grasp on the situation.

"Would you like to order now, sir?" the waitress asked politely with hands behind her back. Her white, button down shirt remained crisp despite a long night on her feet delivering meals to demanding patrons. Her long apron showed signs of more wear and Louis' eyes darted from the phone and un-approvingly at the stains.

"I told you I would like to enjoy my cocktail first. I'll take another." He shook the ice at her to prevent additional misunderstandings.

She mumbled her apologies as she took the glass from its dangled position. He stopped her before she could go too far. "Wait, miss?" he called out in a gentler voice.

"Yes?"

"I am supposed to meet someone here. A girl about twenty. Long, blonde hair. About five feet eight inches tall. Have you seen her?"

Now it was the waitress' turn to offer looks of disgust as this older gentleman spelled out a description of a younger female he had no business fraternizing with. "No, I haven't," she answered smartly and walked away to tend to another table.

Louis picked up his phone and sent another text.

Not here. 2117 E. 7th Ave. Right place??

After thirty seconds, the response came through.

Yes. Tracking site showing phone at that locale

His valuable time squandered by her again. Conceding there was nothing he could do but sit and wait, he pushed back from the table to cross ankles and arms. It was about to end. It had to. He thought about all he had done for her as he raised her on his own. The schools, the car, the money he doled out to ensure the right clothes to make the right friends. What more could she possibly want him? He was at a loss. She never had appreciated it and she clearly does not appreciate any of it now. Always an outsider, never making friends. He understood it was not him, it was Faith. The more Louis did, the more Faith distanced herself from him. Well, if that's what the girl wants, that's what she'll get. He tossed a twenty on the table and bumped into the waitress on his way out.

"Sorry. Something came up," he muttered and walked outside. Immediately, he lit a cigarette and inhaled deeply as he made his way to the black Cadillac he had rented at the Tampa airport. He would return to the Marriott to burn more time, now adopting the habits of a snake in the grass, waiting to surprise his daughter.

A small crowd had gathered at the hotel bar and Louis took a seat against the wall to pick up where he left off. More bourbon to fuel more deliberation. He ran through all the ways Faith was turning into her mother more and more. He would put an end to it before she made him look like an even bigger fool. He lit up another cigarette which brought the bartender over immediately.

"Excuse me, sir. Smoking is permitted in the courtyard, but not inside."

"Well, at least I finally have your attention. Can I get a Makers Mark on the rocks?" The bartender watched in disgust as Louis tossed the cigarette into the full glass of ice water. "And another water."

Chapter 24

Dark clouds pelted rain against windowpanes, ushering a wake-up call for Chelsea LeBlanc. She tugged at the ivory comforter in response and nestled her chin in cotton and smirked at the thunder booming in retaliation. She was content with her husband gone for the weekend. No one to judge her for sleeping in. No one to suggest her inclinations were flawed. No one to suggest she was flawed.

Dear, don't you want the red wine tonight? You're having steak instead of salad? Darling, shouldn't you touch base with the Simmons? We haven't seen them in ages. Is that what you're wearing? Oh, you cut your hair. No, sweetie, you needn't cook anything. That's why we have a maid! The echo of his laugh drowned out the thunder. Her peace pummeled by her controlling husband and the charade they called a marriage, even without his presence. A divorce would mean she would have to play the bad guy. Afterall, Louis had an image to protect. That bothered her less and less. There was no other option. Repairing a relationship is impossible when only one side saw the problems.

She gave up by tossing blankets aside, but she would not dress for the day. If Louis could see her now. Shuffling downstairs with matted hair and in bulky pajamas with fuzzy blue slippers, leftover beignets and coffee were on her mind to enhance the rainy morning.

At the base of the stairs, the lilies Louis had requested for the foyer gave her a headache, so she gathered the stems from the fishbowl vase. Whatever type he had selected possessed an overwhelming scent. A trail of water droplets followed her to the kitchen where she stuffed the cut flowers into the trash bin under the marble island and pushed the cabinet door closed. The soft-close hardware prevented the slam she needed so she allowed his favorite coffee mug to drop to the tile floor. The spontaneous act gave the gratification she was looking for. Kicking the larger piece of broken mug out of her way, she set out to prepare her coffee by placing a mug on the Keurig. The start button was pressed, and she leaned against the marble counter to wait. She told herself to leave the mess for later. Isn't that what he said the maid was for? The notion stirred remorse and Chelsea retreated to the broom closet to clean up her own doings. As she swept up the shards, she recalled time spent in the kitchen of her bakery. Her mood shifted; a little calmness restored in the middle of the storm. She hadn't baked a thing in over a year and the realization alarmed her. Who was she if not a baker? A politician's wife. And there she was, living a life she had only intended to avoid. Baby steps into the real world, she had let down her guard and now, despite her resistance, nothing of her true essence remained.

Chelsea emptied the dustpan and left it with the broom on the floor. She readied her coffee with extra sugar and cream and pulled a stale beignet from under a glass dome centered on the island. Powdered sugar sprayed and she wiped her face with the back of her hand while eating without a plate. Rain poured and the morning grew darker. She turned toward a watery window to enjoy the view, the base of her spine coming to rest against the island. Sipping on coffee, she considered what to do with the day. Binge watching her shows, the ones Louis scoffed at, came to mind. Rations would be needed for such a feat.

Not inclined to leave the house, nor dress for such an outlandish idea on such a morning, she searched cupboards with her free hand, wanting to know what baking items were in stock. With enough basics to work with, she collected essential ingredients for her restorative chocolate cake. It had healed many beloved customers in times of need and now it would heal her. Cocoa powder, vanilla, eggs, flour, baking soda, and baking powder lined the counter ready for battle. The remaining ingredients joined in and by ten o'clock, evidence splattered the room. A coroner would rule death by chocolate. Into the Viking stove the cake pan went and a door, again, shut with force. The scorned baker advanced to the icing task, whisking and beating the concoction with a handheld mixer on high. Where had her Kitchen-Aid mixer gone? She looked around the scene of the crime with wild eyes. The turquoise appliance was garish, an obnoxious color, according to Louis.

"You're obnoxious," she declared.

If he had ordered that precious possession, a last stronghold, gone, that would be grounds for divorce. How had she ever let it out of her sight? The slaughter of powdered sugar, vanilla, butter, and milk came to a halt. The cupboards and walk-in pantry were strip searched to no avail. She charged the attic to rescue her weapon of choice, marked with batter and icing from her culinary battle.

The pounding rain was now inches away from the crown of her head and she ducked at the intense claps of thunder. The attic was hot and full of unknowns stuffed beneath steep rooflines. A pull switch bathed the confines with dull light from a bare lightbulb overhead. She searched for a flash of blue along rows of dusty shelves holding treasures long forgotten. Boxes from the day she moved in remained untouched. She recalled that sunny day full of promise and excitement that had withered away.

She finally spotted the mixer and heaved it from its perch. Holding it like a baby, she carried it back to the attic steps. She set the heavy object down to get the light and readjust her grasp when a shoe box caught her eye. It was shoved deliberately between floorboards with only a corner of the box sticking out from its hiding spot. After lifting the loose pine board, she was able to pull the little box from its secret spot. Kneeling, she carefully lifted the lid as a bolt of lightning lit up the room and preceded a deafening thunder boom. Inside was a stack of hand-written letters. Some were in envelopes, some simply folded and lying exposed. Curvy, female, handwriting decorated plain notebook paper. Upon further inspection, she was surprised to find they were all written to Louis and signed by the same woman. Love letters to her husband from his ex-wife? Her heart picked up its pace. Private letters that he would rather her not read. Still, something told her that they represented a time when his heart was softer and in love with his first love. Perhaps she could gain some insight into the man she was once in love with before it was too late. Forgetting the mixer altogether, she gathered the boxed bundle and retreated downstairs into the comfort of conditioned air.

The unmade bed beckoned her to return and she nested amid the fluffy down comforter, luxury sheets and overly soft and abundant pillows. Setting the old box of memories on the nightstand, she carefully pulled the top letter from its cardboard vault.

Louis,
Next month can hardly come fast enough. Six weeks of not seeing you has been miserable. Not much new is happening here and I miss you like crazy. I went out with Debra, Richard, Gabe, and Jean the other night. They insisted I tag along – I still felt like a fifth wheel! We had fun. Lots of laughs, as usual. Still, it's not the same without you. It made me miss you more than ever. Well, good luck with your papers and the bar exam. You'll be incredible. You always are.
Love Always,
Sissy

Sissy? It was a nickname Chelsea didn't expect. Come to think of it, she never knew the name of Louis' first wife. He guarded that part of his past and Chelsea never wanted to stir up bad memories. Louis never wanted to talk about it and had only referred to *Faith's mother* occasionally over the years. When he did, his tone was flat and unemotional, sometimes irritated. Chelsea assumed that was the result of burying those old emotions years ago. Long before Chelsea entered the picture. Refolding the letter, she set it aside and moved on to the next. All were much the same as the first. Sissy missing Louis. Sissy congratulating Louis on university honors and his accomplishments as a young lawyer in Atlanta where he got his foot in the door with a large firm before moving back to New Orleans. Sissy singing Louis' praises. A few lines in the fourth letter, however, caught Chelsea's attention:

... I know this has been a year of ups and downs for us. I know our baby will be a blessing and I know that you will be an excellent father. I only hope your proposal is not solely based on this little surprise. Once you start with the firm back in New Orleans, our new life will begin as a family ...

The letters embodied Sissy, sitting with Chelsea, having girl talk. Two women linked together by the same man. Chelsea could only imagine the struggles they faced as a young couple with an unexpected baby on the way. Chelsea's next thought surprised her. She couldn't help thinking Louis' feathers were ruffled by this unexpected scene-stealer. Was he a doting father? She hadn't seen anything of the sort over the past three years since they married. Maybe he was different back then. She read on. There were fifteen letters in the box and Chelsea poured over them like a treasure map. Hanging on every word and trying to read between the lines. They became fewer and the love letters took on a different tone. The last one held an air of urgency:

Darling,
This baby needs us. We need to leave this craziness behind and start fresh. Let's move far away where it can be just you and me again. I have always loved only you. You need to believe me. I'm not scared anymore and I want you to trust me. I know our love will see us through this mess. By

this time next month, we'll be far away from here - together as a family. I love you. Please take me, take us, away.

Chelsea scrambled to check the box for any remaining letters. That was the last and it was incomplete, unsigned. Had Sissy been unfaithful to Louis as she begged him to trust her? She leaned back against the tufted headboard and held the last letter close with a strange feeling of pity for Sissy. She seemed to be begging for love and showering Louis with attention in every letter. Chelsea wondered about this man she had married and what secrets from his past he held tightly to.

Chapter 26

The full moon coaxed Richard Mallory's active mind into a tailspin. Three thirty in the morning had a way of making mountains from tiny hills of thoughts and, after an hour of climbing, he gave up. It would not be the first time a case allowed sleep to evade him. Bad feelings about Louis LeBlanc led to worry about Faith. He needed a reason to devote on-the-clock time to this case.

The two-story townhouse sat on the edge of town where things got a little quieter. The chief liked it that way. In his out-of-the-way home, his aching knees made a slow descent downstairs. The white linoleum kitchen floor was more forgiving on his middle-aged joints. After a pot of Maxwell House was set to brew in the dark, he sat upon a three-legged stool to wait. He rubbed the tired from his jowls and breathed in the caffeine smell for a start. What did he know? By the time to pot was full of coffee drips, he deduced that his friend was being deceitful about a handful of little things. Experience proved that enough little lies would add up to a big cover-up. A New Orleans' Saints mug in hand, he went to his leather couch that often served as an office. His laptop was ready on the end table and his fingertips were soon firing on all cylinders, fueled by coffee and a mystery. The glow of the screen emphasized the wide-eyed work of a mad scientist in action.

No return call from Faith and, according to the cell tracking service, her phone was in Tampa. Louis claimed Faith was with Jane in Mobile, Jane claimed she hadn't seen Faith for days. Louis broadcasted a weekend away with Chelsea, Chelsea said otherwise. Was Louis a father in the dark? Richard did not buy it. After all, Louis was a career politician.

With those morsels of information, Richard began his cyber snooping. If Faith was with her phone, she was still in Tampa. A Marriot hotel, a salon, a marina, and the Columbia Restaurant. That's where the trail ended for now. The marina peaked his interest. Did Faith travel to Tampa by boat? Why and with whom? Next up was finding Louis. Richard entered the cell number into the system and waited. The findings confirmed reason for suspicion. Louis was also in Tampa. Not only that, but at the same Marriott that Faith apparently stayed at and he had stopped at the same restaurant. Now he was getting somewhere. He entered Chelsea's number and waited. She was home and had been all day.

"So, Chelsea is the only honest one in the bunch," Richard thought. Now what? Perhaps Louis was dealing with his daughter like any caring father would. Checking on her safety and getting to the heart of the matter which, in this case, was stealing her stepmother's jewelry and running off. Of course Louis wouldn't want such details to be leaked when his job depended on his popularity.

Richard started to feel foolish for assuming there was more to all of this. He shut down the laptop and eased back into the leather recliner. Putting the laptop on the small table next to him, he leaned his head back and cradled the warm mug of coffee. As his mind wandered, random thoughts entered. The subconscious mind has a way of telling you what you need to know.

Louis and Sissy. They had been high school sweethearts who had gotten married due to an unexpected pregnancy. That unplanned child would be named Faith. Richard recalled times spent together in high school, weekends and summers home from college, and the early years of the real world. It shocked everyone when they had found out Sissy had supposedly been unfaithful to an always-working Louis. Richard and Debra, Louis and Sissy, and then there was Gabe. The five of them were together more often than not. Always together, that was, until Louis went off to Atlanta to begin his career, leaving Sissy behind waiting for an engagement ring. Louis had repeatedly said he needed to establish himself before they could wed. Sissy said she understood and lived at home with her parents who would never dream of having their daughter live with a man unwedded anyway. When Louis did come back to New Orleans, he was different, not as friendly and always preoccupied with the law firm he was working for. Soon, he started amassing wealth by partnering with contractors on developments and these dealings led to political aspirations. He became infatuated with positions of power and the group of friends saw that one member of the group less and less.

Richard walked over to the kitchen for refill of coffee as he reminisced about the good and not-so-good times. The worst being that fateful night Louis found Richard and Debra at a local bar they all frequented. Louis had rushed in late and unexpectedly. He had looked disheveled and his eyes were manic. Richard and Debra had pulled up a barstool for their friend and, concerned, asked what was wrong.

In the glow of the neon lights, Louis was rubbing his face and was manic. After some coaxing, he explained he had stopped by Gabe's apartment only to find Sissy there with him. Richard recalled the out of control way Louis relayed what had happened. Debra had given Richard looks of confusion and concern and they both tried hard to understand exactly what Louis was telling them. Louis was convinced Sissy and Gabe were having an affair. Gabe insisted Sissy had stopped by as a friend, Louis did not believe that story. Richard shook his head and smiled at the memory. The baby came, Sissy and Louis settled into a domestic rhythm for Faith's sake, however there was little happiness in that home. They all settled into separate paths in life.

The memories faded and Richard relaxed in his seat as he contemplated another cup of coffee or bed. He decided, instead, on a little TV to numb his brain and then maybe see if he could get some sleep despite the caffeine now coursing through his veins. Louis and Sissy's story still pulsated through his brain, though, as an infomercial mindlessly droned on. There was a sticking point in his thoughts that Richard couldn't quite grasp. The scene at the bar turned over and over in his mind. Then there was Sissy who had never been anything but kind and honest and devoted to her high school sweetheart. He recalled her easygoing smile, her blonde hair, those bright green eyes. Richard wondered where Sissy and Gabe were now. Her walking away from Faith never made sense to Richard. Sissy was a doting and loving mother from the start. The night she left had been rainy and unseasonably cold even for winter. By that point, Louis had been voted into the local political world. Richard and Louis were closer back then and Richard was happy for his friend. He knew a career in politics was becoming his focus and no one worked harder at achieving and retaining a political title than Louis LeBlanc.

Then Louis called Richard one night and his voice was flat. Depressed. Richard was worried about him as Louis conveyed the events of the evening. He had never gotten over that night he found Sissy at Gabe's apartment.

"I found a letter from Sissy to Gabe." Richard had tried to comfort his friend and make sense of his friend's words.

"Maybe you're reading too much into it?" he had said.

"I don't think Faith's my child." He was surely jumping to conclusions. Richard asked Louis if he wanted company, He could be at his friend's house in a few minutes.

"They left together. They're dead to me."

"They're dead to me."
Richard's suspicions turned serious.

Chapter 27

"I'm looking for my daughter. She may be in danger," Louis announced to the dock master who was preparing to lower a fishing boat into the water at seven that morning. At the controls of the mechanical lift, Johnny was concentrating at the task on hand. Louis' booming voice jolted his progress to a stop. The morning sizzled with Florida heat. The man decked out in a three piece suit was undeterred by the elements. Johnny eased the boat into the water before addressing the visitor's interruption.

"Hi. Are you a member here? Haven't seen you before." Johnny wiped his brow with a red bandana before using the same swath to rub the sweat from his hands. When he hopped to the pavement and offered a hand in greeting, Louis snubbed the gesture. Johnny did a visual check on the fishing boat instead and missed Louis' face turn a shade of purple.

"No, I am not a member here. I am," he stopped and reconsidered. His actions softened. "Sorry, I am just a little flustered. My daughter seems to be here with a stranger, and I need to reach her. Have you seen a girl about twenty with blond hair? It's very long. And, uh, she is thin, Maybe five, eight? Her name is Faith."

"No, sir. I haven't. Why do you think she's here? Have you filed a report with the police?" Louis turned irate. He would handle this matter himself like he always did.

"Thanks anyway," he snapped as he turned to leave.

Johnny called after him. "Hey, buddy! Wanna leave your info in case I see something?" Louis simply waved him off as he stomped along the dock and back to the car.

The exchange had gone unseen and unheard by Faith and Patrick were slowly waking, still tucked aboard the boat docked at the very same marina. Throughout the night, Patrick's lucid dreams and dim thoughts wove together into a tapestry glowing with impressions of reuniting with his mother. He kept the fanciful notions to himself when he walked Faith down the dock at eight.

"Let's grab a cup of coffee and I'll walk you to the trolley stop," Patrick suggested.

"No need. I'm leaving early enough to grab something before … work. Sounds funny to say," Faith mused.

"New beginnings," Patrick offered. "I could go with you and wait."

She gave a sideways look in return. "I'd like to do this on my own. I need a little time to digest the past few days."

Patrick agreed with a kiss goodbye intended as enticement for a hurried return. He watched her walk along the ramp to the parking lot until the gate closed with a clang. He walked toward the marina office for complimentary coffee and waved to Johnny who had just lifted a boat out of the water for dry storage. Paying Johnny generously the previous day had bought him a new friend. He stopped when he noticed the squirrely dockmaster darting toward him. Johnny was a pro at his job, but still looked out of place – as if he mistakenly jockeyed boats instead of racehorses.

"Morning," Johnny called out in a friendly voice.

"How are ya?" Patrick greeted the young guy.

"Fine. You feelin' alright? I'm worried about you leaving the hospital early and all."

"I'm fine," Patrick lied. "Wasn't going through another round of tests and other stuff that insurance wouldn't cover, you know? Had to protect my wallet and get the hell out of there."

Johnny looked at him intently before turning toward the clear sunrise. "Yeah, I hear ya. Wow. Gonna be a beautiful day. Look at that sun rising higher and higher." He shook his head as he took it in breathing a dose of morning sea air along with the view.

"Beautiful. Shame more people don't stop to appreciate it," Patrick said.

"You're telling me. Like the guy who just burst in here thirty minutes ago. All wrapped up in a suit in this heat. Thought he was real important. Looking for his daughter who probably took the first chance to get away from his overbearing self." Johnny shook his head and laughed. "Nah, I shouldn't joke. But why the hell wouldn't he talk to the police if he really thought she was in danger?"

Patrick tried hiding his personal interest. "Oh, yeah? You think she's here?"

"Nah. Long blond hair, about twenty, he said. I ain't seen anyone matching that description that don't belong here with their own parents."

Patrick looked back out at the sunrise.

"Well, I'll let you know if I see anything suspicious, anyway."

"Thanks, man. That's good of you. The dude in the suit didn't leave his info anyway."

Patrick nodded. "Y'all have coffee on?"

"Sure do. Help yourself. Have good day, man. Let us know if you need to go back to the hospital. You're crazy, you know?" Johnny laughed and shook his tan, shaved head. "I don't wanna find you playing dead on my docks again, you hear?" Patrick offered a nod and a grin as he turned away, however once he got to the modest coffee bar, he broke into a slight sweat and could feel the color run from his face. Louis LeBlanc was here looking for Faith.

Forgetting the coffee, Patrick made a beeline for the parking lot. He reached the gate in seconds and propped it open with a palm branch to keep it from locking him out. It made him wonder how Louis had gotten in. Maybe it had not been him. With no sign of Faith, nor her father, he settled into a state of uneasiness rather than panic. They would need to leave Tampa if they wanted peace, he considered as he took a seat on a nearby coquina rock to catch his breath. In a trance, he used a stick to draw lines in the sandy border of the lot until his heartrate slowed, all the while feeling a strong need to protect Faith. The sun rose higher and he felt the sting of its rays on the back of his neck. Patrick knew Louis had ways of getting things done and had heard from Hawk that his ways were not always on the up and up. He kicked himself for not asking her the name of the salon she was working at. Whether they wanted to or not, Patrick and Faith were in the proverbial soup together and things were heating up on all accounts.

He spent the rest of the morning cleaning the boat to keep his mind off Louis LeBlanc and had lunch at the marina's clubhouse, courtesy of Steve's membership. The tan and mahogany room offered members a place to escape the heat and entertain guests while grabbing light refreshments. The BLT he ordered could not compare to those offered at the greasy diner back in New Orleans and the beer he allowed himself didn't taste as cold. The server seemed annoyed to be there and it made him miss Rosy back at the diner in New Orleans. A few members ambled in with frowns upon well-off, and well-fed, faces and, now that he was able to see things from the other side, he realized he hadn't been missing much when it came to the country club lifestyle. Still, he would love to find a way to hit some balls and calm his nerves on the affiliated golf course. Not wanting to risk overstaying his welcome as a pseudo-member combined with the possibility of Louis slinking around, he figured it was better to stay under the radar and decided against asking about that perk. He tried to text Faith a guarded message of warning. She didn't reply and he was increasingly nervous, so he scrambled back to the Cigarette boat to wait.

By three o'clock, Faith was back with him and fast-talking about her day.

"It just feels so good to make my own money and I love Francine. She is so professional and strong," she rattled as she tossed her purse into the cabin before sitting next to Patrick on the sun pad. Shirtless and shoeless with Ray-Ban's on, he was picture of calm. He hid his emotions well. Faith was dressed in a nice blouse and shorts, but opted for a baseball hat and sunglasses pulled from her purse out of constant habit since leaving the Garden District less than a week ago. "She's patient and I just know I'm going to like working for her. Oh, and she said she knows of an apartment for a reasonable rate and knows the landlord will work with me if she vouches for my character. Isn't that great? You can stay with me, you know," Faith ventured. Patrick knew her green eyes were sparkling behind her drugstore sunglasses. He hated to dull them.

He turned his visor around and leaned in for a kiss, unable to wait. She moved toward him and felt safe in his arms. "You still don't want to go back home?"

"Nope. I never knew I could be so happy." She leaned her head against his chest to listen to his heart.

Patrick felt a pang of sadness. She was hardly living a comfortable life at the moment. He wanted to give her more.

"I don't want you to leave, but, the reason I ask," Patrick started slowly. He now had Faith's rapt attention. "I was talking to Johnny, the dock master here, this morning. From what he said, your dad might have been here earlier looking for you. I could be mistaken, but," Faith cut him off.

"What? No. I'm not going back with him. You have to help me. Forget it. I can't ask that of you. I'll take care of it. Shit. He will turn this city upside down until he finds me. Then, well, I don't know what he'll do."

Patrick was taken aback by the urgency in her tone. "Don't worry, then. We're in this together. Johnny told him nobody here matched the description your dad gave. He must not know you changed your hair. Good move, by the way," Patrick added with a smile to ease her concerns. "Did you tell anyone where you are? Your friend from college, maybe?" They were whispering by now. When a mature couple boarded the yacht in the adjacent slip, Patrick and Faith straightened and waved casually. The unassuming couple went about readying their vessel for a day on the water and the castaways got down to business.

"No, no specifics, anyway. Keith? No. I gave him a fake name. Jane has no idea where I am or who I'm with. I used a fake ID and with a matching credit card for the hotel. What about the owner of this boat? You said he's a member of the club?"

"He's a member of most clubs in the south and he's not political. I can't see how he would have anything to do with your dad. I've left messages and sent texts for him to let him know all is well along the way. He'll be here next week and he's not a concern."

They sat quietly for a few seconds, mulling over the pertinent details.

"Your cellphone," Patrick quickly deduced with widening eyes. "I tried texting you all day, by the way. I was worried."

"That's it! My dad's good friend is the Chief of Police. They must be working together and Richard tipped my dad off. Hold on. Let me find it." Faith ran below and Patrick could hear Faith rummaging through her meager belongings until a mess was dumped on the floor of the cabin. A few minutes later, she returned without the hat or sunglasses and her hair in frenzy to match her demeanor. "I can't find it. Look around that seat. Maybe it fell behind the cushions?" Patrick got up and lifted the removable seat up. Nothing. They spent the next fifteen minutes looking through every possible crevice and found nothing. Faith started to retrace her steps the night before. "Well, if it's not here, I must have left it at the restaurant. Unless I dropped it between there or here? They obviously tracked it here and wherever else I went in Tampa. Let's get out of here. Please, Patrick? Let's just go. Now."

Patrick took one look at here pleading eyes and knew he would do anything for her. "I agree. We'll move on. But, I need to do something first. I hope you understand."

Faith looked confused. "What? Don't you want to leave now, too? Who knows what evidence Chief Mallory has from that night. I bet they're looking for you, too. Let's just go."

By now, Faith was repacking her purse. Patrick stood and leaned into the cuddy opening and inadvertently also looked around for any sign of Louis. The docks were empty other than a few boat owners washing their boats and packing coolers for a day out on the water. He went below to join Faith and sat down while she frantically collected her spilled belongings.

"Faith, I will get you out of here. I promise. Then, we'll go wherever you want. But, stop for a second," he placed his hand on her shoulder and knelt down next to her. She stopped her scrambling.

"I need to talk to you about something. Do you remember how I mentioned I grew up in foster homes?" Faith became irritated at his stalling. "Yes. Whatever it is, it's in the past. Let's move on. Together."

"I know. But, there's a chance my real mother could be here. In Tampa. I promise I'll keep you safe. We'll find a place for you to hide out where you can't be tracked. I know for sure that Hawk can help me with that. I just, I need to make sure it's not her. It's probably not. I'm not getting my hopes up." Patrick sat on the floor, leaning back against berth. He clasped his hands between his knees. Her compassion kicked in and she put her own worries aside.

"What makes you think she's here?"

"The only distinguishing feature I remember was a heart tattoo on the inside of her wrist. One of those strange details you remember from being a kid. I was so small I don't even know for sure, but I do have a really clear vision of it. It's just always been one thing I've known about her."

An image of the woman's faded tattoo flashed in Faith's mind. A few other features instantly came to mind. A stick straight nose. Tall and slender. High cheekbones. A crooked smile. Dark eyes that focused when she talked. Were these features she shared with a long-lost son? Faith had a feeling it wasn't as much of a long shot as Patrick believed. She reached for his hands with hers and pushed the remaining items from her purse aside to sit before him more closely.

"Of course, you have to know. I understand. I think I can help you."

Patrick looked at her with those familiar dark eyes and shook his head. "No, no. I'll take care of this on my own then we'll leave. In fact, you stay here where you're safe and I'll make my way to her salon. I'll try to get a haircut today, make small talk, see what comes out of it."

Undeterred, Faith continued with her plan. "Let's go back to the Marriott. I'll grab my bags, use a side entrance to enter and leave." She shuffled the items in her purse until she lifted the hotel card key in triumph. "In the meantime, we'll have a place to stay close to the salon in case it doesn't go as easily as you think. It's not really the kind of salon that takes walk-ins. Unless you plan on bursting in and asking if she's your mother, your plan's not going anywhere. As far as my dad goes, he might have stopped there, but he's long gone. He doesn't have the time to sit around and wait for me. Besides, he'll never recognize me from afar."

"I don't like it, Faith. He's your dad. He will recognize you. Why risk it? I'll take care of the place to stay. I know Hawk or Charlie can arrange a place you'll never be found."

"That sounds creepy."

"Sorry. Not my intention."

"I need to grab my suitcase anyway. And my gun is there, and my pajamas and I still have the room reserved for two more nights."

Patrick stared at her as though she was from another planet. "Your gun and your pajamas?"

"Among other things."

He inhaled deeply and looked around nervously. "I don't know. He's probably staying there if he's tracking you."

"A gun really belonging to my father that will ultimately leave a trail of my whereabouts. Who knows how that could affect us in the future."

Patrick rubbed his face in defeat, exhausted and too tired to argue. If Faith was returning to the hotel, he would be with her.

Chapter 28

Beaumont had been Sissy's maiden name. Richard could not recall her given first name, so he began the task of tracking down her parents or siblings online. The station was relatively quiet at that eight o'clock hour. He figured the Tuesday night drunks were just getting started and by midnight the dispatch calls would roll in. For now, he took advantage of laying low in his office. By nine o'clock, his data revealed Saviour "Sissy" Beaumont was an only child and her French immigrant parents were now deceased. He also had no solid leads on any extended family. Spinning his wheels, he moved on to see what he could find out about Gabe. Gabe Thiboux was another story. Within minutes, he had one of Gabe's brothers on the phone. The fluorescent lights flickered – a little excitement from an otherwise stale room.

"Is this Brookes Thiboux?"

"It is. Who is this?"

"Chief Richard Mallory with the New Orleans PD. Don't be alarmed and I'm sorry to call so late. I'm just doing a little bit of research on a robbery case. I think we went to high school together?"

"Oh yeah, sir. I do remember you. You were a few years ahead of me. Closer to my brother, Gabe, right?"

"That's correct. That's actually who I'm calling you about."

"I see. Well, what can I do for you?" The man became guarded, not as friendly.

"Thanks. Like I said, I'm investigating an occurrence here in the city. A robbery that is leading me down other avenues. Is your brother, Gabe, still living around here? I think he could really help us with this case and, well, I'm coming up empty in my search for him."

The silence landed with a heavy thud. Richard swallowed hard, preventing himself from rambling as the pause became awkward.

"You know, Chief Mallory. I have some questions for him myself and I wish you luck in finding him. If you do, please let me know."

"When did you last talk to him?"

"When he ran off with Sissy LeBlanc twenty years ago," he stated gruffly. "Although, he was kind enough to drop a letter in the mail to our parents. It crushed them."

"I see. Where were they heading?"

"Didn't mention it. Only said he and Sissy needed to leave town to start a life together. He hoped we would all understand. Well, none of us understood. My sweet ma always assumed there was more to the story. To this day she expects him to show up at her doorstep. Especially on Christmas."

"In that case, I should really talk to your parents." The lights crackled and fluttered again. Richard made a mental note to have maintenance change the bulb.

"Be my guest. I'd like to be there when you do, if you don't mind?"

Brookes gave the chief a number for his elderly parents and asked for the courtesy of letting him talk to them first. Within the hour, Richard was scheduled to meet the Thiboux family at noon the next day. His gut wrenched as he disconnected the return call from Brooks, not entirely sure what he was getting himself into, nor if any of his extracurricular efforts ware necessary. He decided to trust his instincts but call it a day. Tomorrow would tell more.

The Thiboux's home was a welcoming white Colonial impeccably kept in the University District. Pink and white impatiens lined the sidewalk leading to the front door and trimmed, pink azaleas were in full bloom around the perimeter of the house. Southern magnolias graced the sunny property. Richard pulled into the drive, in his personal vehicle to avoid a stir, and walked along the front of the house. The front door opened before he reached the porch.

"Welcome, Chief Mallory," Brookes Thiboux greeted. "Come on in." Tall and slim, he had aged well. A spot of gray hair made him distinguished and his button-down shirt and dress slacks suggested a break from work for the meeting. His round, tortoise-rimmed glasses added to his scholarly appearance.

Richard offered his thanks and followed the man to a sunroom at the rear of the house. The interior was as neat as the exterior with furniture that was older but appeared brand new. The elder Thibouxs sat on a rattan loveseat and were also dressed nicely. Mrs. Thiboux clasped her small hands on the lap of her gray, shin-length dress tied neatly around her tiny waist. Her white hair was curled and framed a round face adorned with wire-rimmed glasses. Her husband had on a white, pressed dress shirt with short sleeves and slacks finished with a shiny, black belt. Richard noticed their shoes were all shined to perfection – ladies black pumps and black oxfords. He felt out of place and frumpy as he took a seat on a wicker love seat. Had Sissy ever sat here with Gabe? He dismissed his wandering mind.

"Can I get you a glass of tea, Chief Mallory?" Mrs. Thiboux asked sweetly. Richard felt pity. As if her hospitality to him would somehow bring her son home.

"No thank you, ma'am. Thank you for inviting me to your lovely home. I'll get right to the point," Richard began under the watchful eye of Mr. Thiboux and Brookes. "I'm working on a case that is entirely unrelated to my visit. During my investigation, however, the whereabouts of Sissy and Gabe came up. You see, there is a good chance one of them might know something about the case I'm working on since the robbery deals with a close relative of Sissy's."

The three Thibouxs looked at one another waiting for someone to respond. Finally, Mr. Thiboux spoke up.

"I wish I could help you, sir. I really do. Gabe left town years ago. He sent us a letter explaining he was leaving with Sissy LeBlanc. We haven't heard from either of them since." He leaned back on the settee he sat upon with his wife and placed his arm around her shoulders.

"That's right, Chief Mallory. I don't think my boy would've left us without a good reason." Richard noticed the mother defending her son from the start and frowned for her feeling the need to do so. "I just know he will come back one day. I always thought," she started in a righteous, but shaky, voice. She looked down to find composure in the folded handkerchief on her lap. "To tell you the truth, I've always thought he and Sissy left because of Louis LeBlanc. If it's true what people say, there is no way the senator wanted a scandal to ruin his political career."

Mr. Thiboux glanced at Brooks who looked at Chief Mallory for a response.

"What exactly do people say?" Richard implored.

"That Gabe and Sissy were close and eventually had an affair. That the senator's daughter is really Gabe's." Mrs. Thiboux shrugged. "They do look alike. If it's true, we'd love to have her in our lives."

Brookes straightened in his seat uncomfortably. Richard got the impression this was not the first time Mrs. Thiboux stepped upon this particular soapbox.

"Do you still have the letter?" Richard asked. "Would you mind if I took it back to my office for a closer look?"

Mrs. Thiboux rose slowly, smoothed the pleats in her skirt, and walked into the living room. A drawer scratched open then closed again with a dull thud. She returned with an envelope in hand and reclaimed her seat next to her husband. "It is the last link we have to our son. Would you mind making sure I get the letter back?" she asked as she handed it to Richard. He rose from his seat to take it from her.

"I'll personally return it to you by the end of the week."

Mr. Thiboux patted his wife's hand and looked back to Chief Mallory. "Thank you, Officer Mallory. Maybe you'll be able to tell us more."

"Please, call me Richard," he said as he rose to leave. "Thank you, again, for meeting with me. I'll be in touch with your letter this week."

The family walked him to the door. As Richard stepped back into his vehicle and drove away, he noticed all three still standing in the doorway; silently watching him leave.

Pulling over once he was out of the neighborhood, he slipped the thin piece of notebook paper from the envelope with faded writing. The postmark was from New Orleans. The letter was hand-written:

Mom and Dad,
It pains me to write this and please know I never wanted to hurt you or anyone else. I need to leave town for a while for reasons I can't disclose. I'm sorry, please trust me. I will make my way back to you, but I need to say good-bye for now. I hope to clear up whatever mess I've caused and when I do, I'll be back. Please know that I love you both forever.
Love,
Gabe

"Where did you go, Gabe?" Richard whispered as he tilted his head back against the headrest, silently ticking off the facts he held in his mind until the cold blasts of air from the vents encouraged him to drive back to work. He pulled the LeBlanc robbery file from his canvas briefcase and placed the letter in the file for safekeeping. Upon doing so, the official police report caught his eye. The facts of the robbery were well detailed by the responding officer. Louis LeBlanc's signature was an even bigger detail. Richard rubbed his wide eyes. Louis LeBlanc's signature perfectly matched many of the letters written on the letter from Gabe. The L in the closing was a perfect match for the L's in Louis' signature on the report.

As if on cue, his cell phone rang. It was Chelsea.

"Hey, Chels. Everything okay?"

"Yes. I just wanted to see if he talked to Faith yet." After a quick pause, she added, "And, Richard, whatever happened to his first wife?"

Richard was caught off guard. Was it possible that Chelsea suspected something as well? The coincidences in this case were becoming too much to ignore any longer.

"Why do you ask?"

"Louis never told me how his wife died. Not wanting to bring up bad memories, I never asked. Seems silly now. Why wouldn't a wife ask a husband something like that? And then, I found letters in the attic written by her, by Sissy."

"Are you serious?" Richard asked in disbelief. "I'll be right over."

Chapter 29

Patrick collapsed on the king-sized bed at the Marriott, spread eagle style.

"How about I call and have a pizza delivered? My treat."

"Anything's fine by me. Just wake me up when it gets here. I'm exhausted." The arm that rested across his face muffled Patrick's voice.

Faith found an extra blanket in the closet and covered Patrick for a nap. The rhythmic sounds of his breath indicated he was already nodding off.

"Alright, then. Can I see your phone to find a place?" Patrick did not answer her quiet question.

She helped herself to his phone that was sitting on the nightstand. Surprised to find there was no password, and that the screen hadn't locked yet, she sat on the other bed and pulled up local pizza shops that would deliver. While she scrolled through her options, a call from Hawk came in. Faith looked over at Patrick who was peacefully lying where she had left him. She declined the call. Pizza ordered; delivery promised in forty minutes.

Minutes dragged on with the phone alerting Faith to a recent call and voicemail. Still cradling his phone in her hand, she resisted the urge to listen to the voicemail by engaging in a standoff with the device. Patrick slept, unaware of the moral debate raging seven feet away. Faith's curiosity got the best of her, and, justifying her actions, she told herself it was only prudent. She needed to ensure her own safety, after all. Accessing the voicemail screen, she touched the play icon and took the phone into the bathroom. The bartender's voice started talking into her ear.

"Hey, buddy. Well, color me touched. You used my number as an emergency contact. You plannin' on goin' back to that Tampa hospital you ran from? I think those doctors know a thing or two. Call me so I stop worrying 'bout you."

Faith stood against the granite sink counter, dumbfounded. The words were not what she expected to hear. She slowly opened the bathroom door, afraid of her deceit being discovered. Seeing Patrick still had not moved from the position she had left him in, her concern grew. Then again, she considered, he may be getting the rest he needed to recuperate from being under the weather. She walked softly, appreciative of the carpeted floor that silenced her steps, and placed the phone back where she had taken it from.

An hour went by. The dinner had arrived, but Faith's hunger had subsided. The pizza went cold in the unopened box on the desk in the corner of the hotel room. She resorted to making noise. Television volume up, a dresser door slammed shut, luggage items moved around clumsily. Patrick did not budge. She called out his name and gave his shoulder a shake. He would not answer, his breathing shallow and irregular.

Permitting instincts to be her guide, Faith returned Hawk's call from the privacy of the bathroom. She bit a thumbnail as she waited for the accomplice to answer.

"Oh, man. You had me worried. You doin' alright?" Hawk's voice was suddenly comforting.

"It's not Patrick. I'm a friend of his. I met you at the bar a week ago. Can you hear me?" Faith strained.

"Of course. Is he okay?"

"I don't know what to think. I don't know what to do. I'm scared. Maybe I'm overreacting."

"Ok. Hold on." Faith heard muffled conversation and footfall. "I'm back. Needed to find a private place to talk. Is he with you?"

"Yes. He's been sleeping for hours and now I think something might be wrong. He never told me he went to the hospital. He was real sick a few nights ago. Then, he didn't mention anything when I saw him the next night. Now, he's sleeping and I think he looks pale. Maybe it's just my imagination. Should I call a doctor? I listened to your message. I know I shouldn't have, but …"

"Slow down, dear. Yes. If he doesn't look well and won't wake up you need to get help. Trust your instincts."

"What do you think is wrong?"

"I'm guessing he didn't tell you. Typical Mac."

"Tell me what?" There was a noticeable pause before Hawk continued.

"Honey, he's terminal. Been on a waiting list for a kidney for some time now."

Chapter 30

Speechless and numb, Faith watched the medics load Patrick onto the stretcher. He was unresponsive by now. The EMT's were eerily quiet as they went about their business. Faith watched from the sidelines. The hotel room shrunk like a balloon losing air. She tried to pull the last of the oxygen into her shaky lungs from her seat at the desk. It was the only surface unused by the workers.

"Are you a relation?" a second police officer asked. She looked up in a daze, wanting to ask where he had come from.

"No. No, just a friend. Is he …" she trailed off with a blank stare. She heard the officer continue in a monotone voice. He asked for her name and how she knew Patrick. She figured it was time to be honest and gave her real name, not concerned about hiding any longer. "Can I go with him?" she asked meekly as he was wheeled out of the room.

As he wrote her name on the report, he stopped midway, then continued without looking up at her. Faith watched the officer motion his intentions to step out into the hallway.

"I'm sorry, but you can't ride in the ambulance. They're taking him to Tampa General," the remaining officer stated. Faith could hear his partner now in the hallway and calling in some kind of official notice.

Faith blinked back tears. The emergency responders were gone as quickly as they came, taking Patrick with them. The lone police officer stood by the door, watching Faith in the now silent room. A stranger walked by in the hallway, craning his neck to catch a glimpse of the happenings.

"He has a bag of belongings here. He thinks his mother is in town. Can I call her?" The officer nodded and Faith moved to where he had been, the bed still warm. She resisted the urge to lie down in his place, to feel his warmth one last time. The front desk clerk answered her call. She requested the number for Francine's shop and jotted down the number on a hotel notepad. The officer stood by as dialed it. The salon voicemail picked up and Faith left a message.

"Francine, it's Faith. Oh, I wish you could pick up. How do I say this? I'm with someone who needed to talk to you. He is twenty-nine years old and lost his mother years ago. Just a shot in the dark, but if you happen to be that woman, your son is waiting at Tampa Bay General Hospital. You'll want to ask for Patrick Morris. You might not have much time." She stared at the receiver, trying to process the events of the past twenty-four hours. The officer broke the silence after a brief consult with his cohort in the doorway.

"Miss LeBlanc? I can give you a ride to the hospital."

"Thank you," she answered gratefully.

The lobby was bustling with curiosity. She could see the stretcher lifted into the back of the ambulance and it took all strength she had left to not rush out to join him. The hotel guests whirred by in muted colors. The ambulance lights and siren engaged. He was gone. She felt weak and lost focus. The kaleidoscope whirred until one man moved from the blur and deliberately toward Faith.

The adventure was over.

"Faith. I knew I would run into you if I was patient," Louis exclaimed as he neared. "I barely recognized you. I'm so relieved to see you," he added as he reached his long arms out and pulled her into him with a strong embrace that smelled of aftershave and bourbon. Standing stone still, she passively resisted the strong embrace.

"Is there a problem?" He asked the police officers who was now standing a few feet away, closing in on the senator.

"We should get going." The officer stated. She looked down at her shuffling feet.

"Ready for what? Where are you taking my daughter?" Faith felt her father grip her elbow.

The officer relaxed and looked back at his partner. "Daughter?"

"Yes, my daughter. I came all the way from New Orleans to find her." He wrapped his arm around Faith's shoulders, claiming her as his own. The second officer returned while Faith lost her voice all over again.

"Sir, may we have your name for our report. Before we let you leave with your daughter, that is."

The lobby crowd grew and guests milled about, finding seats for the show.

"Senator Louis LeBlanc. Should I spell it for you?"

"No need," the officer said dryly. This time Faith could hear him speak clearly into his radio.

"We have Miss LeBlanc's father present. A Louis LeBlanc. Is it okay to leave her in his care?"

Louis stiffened and pulled Faith closer to him as he waited for the response.

"Alright then. You two are free to go," the officer confirmed moments later.

Faith was emotionally drained and terrified for Patrick. She suffered under the weight of defeat and nodded as her father placed a heavy hand on her shoulder. With Patrick on her mind, she spoke.

"Dad, I need to get to Tampa General Hospital first. Please."

"Come on, Faith. You're safe now."

"I've been safe all along," she stated blandly as she walked with him towards the valet. "You'll take me to the hospital, right?" she asked wearily.

"Of course, dear. Just get in the car." Louis smiled at the valet and handed him a tip. The valet held the door of the black Cadillac open for Faith and she slipped back into the passenger seat of her reality. The valet shut the door on Faith's newfound spirit. Louis pulled out into the light stream of traffic and cleared his throat.

"So, I've been worried about you. Why did you lie to me?" Faith could only stare out the window at the buildings and people flashing by, unable to answer at first.

Eventually, she spoke up. "I don't know. I just needed to get away, I guess."

"I barely recognized you. New haircut. Running around with a stranger. Faith, what's going on? Are you in trouble? Who is this guy?"

Faith started to come to life again with her dad's questioning. "I just needed a break, dad. He's just a friend. He works at the country club. I helped him move a boat for a member."

"I see. He didn't look well at all, Faith," Louis started to explain as he glanced at his daughter cautiously. "I don't think it's a good idea for you to see him right now, sweetheart."

Faith shot him a look. "No, you need to! Take me to that hospital right now. You promised!" Her words sounded childish and she took a breath to calm down.

"Alright, alright, Faith. Calm down. We'll go. It's just, I want … I want you to be prepared. From what I saw and overheard, well, I just think you need to be prepared for … for the worst." Louis chose his words carefully. Faith began to shake uncontrollably.

"Are you cold? Need the air turned down?" He reached for the temperature control.

"Then, just let me say good-bye. Please, dad. Please take me to him to say good-bye. He doesn't have anyone else. Please?" she begged with sad, watery eyes.

Louis' was unsure of what to do. He placed his hand on Faith shoulder and gently caressed it to comfort her. "Okay. We'll go. I just need to put a little bit of gas in the car. I'm on E," he explained and pointed to the gauge as if he needed to prove it to her. She nodded and wiped the tears from her cheeks before looking back out the window. A station with a convenience store loomed ahead and Louis pulled the car into the lot.

"Wait here, I'll be fast. Can I get you Coke? I'm gonna grab one for myself. Looks like we might have a long night ahead of us."

"I don't care, dad. Please, just hurry?"

"I will, dear." The door slammed behind him and he engaged and propped the nozzle before briskly walking into the convenience store. He quickly emerged with two fountain drinks in hand and walked to the passenger window. Faith put the window down and turned her blotchy, tear-stained face toward her father. "Here, hon. Take a big drink." Faith took the fountain drink from him and left the window down. Gas vapors poured in from around her. She took a long sip then guzzled more, having not realized how parched she really was.

Within minutes, he was back in the car and looked over at his daughter. He managed a smile and placed a hand on her knee. "Ready?" he asked, taking a more upbeat approach.

Faith smiled a more relaxed grin and nodded. As they drove, her eyes became heavy. Louis kept a close watch on her as she continued to sip the drink he had prepared for her. He took the long way around town. When he knew Faith was completely knocked out, he left the Tampa Bay city limits and headed north.

Chapter 31

Richard knew he was close to a breakthrough and shut his office door. He hunched over the letters on his desk.

Just as it had done to Chelsea, the last letter in the pile caught his eye and he read it over and over trying to figure out what it was that was bothering him about it. The greeting was different. *Darling. I'm not scared anymore. Our love will see us through this mess. By this time next month ...*

Richard was certain that this letter did not fit with the others. This unfinished letter had not been meant for Louis, he deduced. Sissy had been writing to Gabe and Richard could envision Louis startling Sissy halfway through the letter. He could imagine the rage that Louis would have shown her upon finding out that Sissy was planning on leaving him for Gabe.

With Gabe's daughter.

Louis' pride would never have allowed it. Looking back, Louis played the role of the hero by raising Faith on his own, even if it was at arm's length with the help of nannies and boarding school.

Next, Louis picked up the letter written by Gabe to his parents. Aspects of the penmanship screamed truth as Richard compared the letter to Gabe's parents with Louis' own signature on the police report from the robbery investigation. Louis had forged a letter to Gabe's parents.

Sissy had written her letter to Gabe. Louis, in turn, wrote a goodbye letter to Gabe's parents from Gabe. He recalled Chelsea's question and the Louis' own words from the night his first wife disappeared.

How did Louis' wife die?

Richard, they're dead to me.

Richard picked up the phone and dialed Louis' house phone. Chelsea picked up.

"Chelsea. Is Louis home yet?"

"No. And I haven't been able to reach him for twenty-four hours. Something's wrong. I know it. I called Faith and I can't reach her, either."

“I think you better make an excuse and find a hotel for the night. Let me know where you end up. In the meantime, I’m tracking Faith and Louis to bring them home.”

Chapter 32

Waxy waterfalls poured over slanted shelves and dripped onto pine floorboards in the ramshackle fish camp. Crickets and bullfrogs welcomed dusk while a nearby owl wondered about whose arrival the woman anticipated. Mojo bags were spread about inside and out and the overgrown trails were littered with morning glory petals for additional protection. The time was near.

The green-eyed sorceress busied herself with her precious trinkets as she sat cross-legged on the rickety floor suspended over the murky shoreline. Her excited energy got the best of her as she lit the five pillar candles before her and laid a doll in the center of the altar. Placing her hand atop the stuffed token made of burlap, she closed her eyes and slipped into deep concentration. Then, slowly, she awakened.

"Are you ready to work for me? For us?" she summoned the cloth body. A smile spread across her face as she picked up a five-inch piece of twine. Her long blond tresses fell forward as she patiently circled a thin rope around the neck of the doll and prepared a loose knot. Laying the doll down again, she pulled two long, red pins from her shirt pocket and set them beside the figure.

"Now, for you," she cooed to a doll she pulled from her pleated skirt pocket, this one fabricated from soft, unbleached muslin. Meditating again, she focused her mind's energy upon this second doll. Satisfied, she turned her focus on a patch of black fabric from her other pocket which she lovingly swaddled around the doll snugly. She cradled the precious symbol as if lulling it to sleep.

"He won't hurt anybody this time," whispered the transcendent descendant of the Beaumont clan.

Chapter 33

Louis drove into the setting sun along highway ten through the Florida panhandle and into Alabama. Trapped between worlds, far from home and personal motivations, he saw his daughter in a different light for the first time. In the isolated cabin of the luxury sedan, with Faith slumped next to him, he looked at his sleeping daughter. She hunched forward with heavy breaths, her seatbelt holding her oblivious self in place. Her chopped hair bore a reminder of how far she had gone to hide herself from him.

"What have we done to you?" he sighed. "What do I do now?" Rage had pushed him to retrieve Faith from Tampa Bay. That fury had pushed him over the edge one other time in his life, but he could prevent that from happening again. On a wild mission to find her, deep down he knew his intentions couldn't be trusted and he hadn't cared. She hadn't deserved the soda laced with a strong sedative, let alone whatever else he was capable of. A shudder ran through him and, in a rare moment of lucidity, a tear escaped his eye. Holding tightly to secrets while charging toward devious goals over the decades had finally exhausted his assaults. He considered the ways he and Faith could start over.

He collected his thoughts. When she woke, he would convince her. She would understand. She would finally appreciate all he had done for her. Where could they go? The only logical answer, in Louis' mind, was back to the start. Back to where his life with her had begun. There was an undeniable pull to return there after all this time of trying to forget it. A new force pushed him in a new direction. Inexplicable, but undeniable, he would follow the urge to return to the Bayou.

After another stop for gas and countless miles on the road, Louis and Faith had arrived back in Louisiana. Faith began to stir and Louis braced himself for her reaction. Dusk brightened the lights upon the highway now as they rounded the northern edge of New Orleans. The scenery was different from Tampa and a confused Faith would soon realize her father had not honored his promise to take her to Tampa General. He was protecting her, he assured himself. Protecting her from dealing with death just as he did years ago. Long ago, he had given her a better life and he would do it again. Faith's eyes fluttered open and she squinted to make sense of her surroundings. She arched her back slightly and moaned a little. Turning, she fixed her gaze on Louis.

"Dad? Where are we? I have such a headache," she mumbled, rubbing her temples.

"You're awake. Hi, dear. How did you sleep? You must have needed some kind of rest," he said in a more exuberant tone than was normal for the circumstance.

"Yeah. I guess so. Where are we? How's Patrick?"

"Patrick? That's his name? So, I have to talk to you. To show you something."

"Show me what? Dad, what is going on? Where are we? You never stopped at the hospital, did you?" her voice became stronger and was laced with irritation as she recalled the events leading up to the moment.

"There was no need, Faith. Why would I put you through that? You've been through enough and I'm going to change that. We're going to start over. Maybe move. Wherever you want to go. We'll start over. Just you and me. How does that sound?" Louis' voice was oddly jovial.

"Dad, are we back in Louisiana?" she asked with frantic eyes staring out over swamplands surrounding the familiar highway spanning the murky countryside. "Why? Let's just go home, okay? Where's Chelsea?"

Still disoriented and desperately trying to sharpen her mind, her hands were numb and her legs tingled with weakness. The car exited the highway and sped through crossroads flanked by tall pines. Approaching headlights became less frequent. She reached for the door handle, he pressed the auto lock. The hard click was a jolt to her heart.

"Chelsea? Oh, home I guess. It doesn't matter. You and she never got along that well anyway, right? I'll protect you. I know you stole the jewelry. I won't let her find out or press charges against you. Don't worry. Just you and me from now on, right? If anyone can cover your tracks, it's me." His manic laugh elicited her panic.

"Where are we going? Please tell me where you're taking us." She fidgeted with the beads around her wrist for focus and Patrick's lifeless body being carted from the hotel room filled her mind. The sun had sunk behind the pines by now and the scene beyond the car window was completely unfamiliar. Turn after turn, the road turned to dirt. Louis looked at Faith with trepidation as he prepared his words. The unfamiliar scenery was nothing compared to the look of uncertainty on the face of this madman.

"Faith," he began slowly, "I know I've made mistakes. I know I've not been the best father to you. I'm gonna change that. I promise you. I know of a place we can talk. It's actually …" he trailed off.

"What, dad? Actually what?" Anger replaced her fear. "I am so tired of all these games. Everyone having an agenda. No one telling me the truth. No one caring about anything except their own precious ego and image." Faith exhaled disgust before adding, "There's only one person I know who cares about others more than himself. I didn't think anyone like that existed anymore. And now he's gone. He's gone and I didn't even get to say good-bye. Thanks to you, that is." She was screaming realizations and accusations by now.

Louis gripped the steering wheel tighter and accelerated down the dark dirt road. The halogen lights illuminated the swampy surroundings in a surreal blue haze. Finally, Louis spoke up. This time, his voice adopted ire.

"You are so ungrateful. You do know that, don't you?" He looked at Faith with a venomous glare. "I gave you the finest schools and bank account of spending money to do as you pleased with. A beautiful home. Food on the table. A closet full of clothes. You ungrateful brat! What do you do?" he growled. "You take on an alias, use that alias for fake ID's and credit." She looked at him with shock as he raged on. She gripped the door handle as the Cadillac swerved along the dirt road. "Yes, of course I know about all that. Your so-called connections are my connections, sweetheart. You're nothing without me." The words stung and Faith blinked back tears. "Then, you run off with the first guy who pays any attention to you and not only ignore my calls, but flat out lie to me."

It was his turn to yell now and his words bruised tender places. Faith swallowed frustrations and watched the narrowing road ahead, afraid looking at her father would elicit more fury. She yearned to react, the lump deep inside forming a pit of frustration and despair that reminded her of the times she would cause her own pain to distract herself from never having a parent's love. Love. She turned her thoughts to Patrick and his caresses and supportive words while Louis started back on his rant. She had found love and it was a reminder of her worthiness as Louis droned on.

"Being a single father is not an easy job, you know. Sorry I wasn't up to the task in your entitled mind. It doesn't help that you act just like your mother. I don't need it. You've both caused me enough trouble." Louis paused then blurted out a crazed, demented question.

"Maybe you'd like to meet your mother? How 'bout it?"

By this time, Louis had stopped the car at a dead end in the darkness. A thick wall of cypress was visible by the light of a full moon and Faith scrambled to free herself from the seatbelt then the car. He was anticipating her moves and locked her door with the key fob as he walked to the trunk. She heard the trunk creak open then slam shut. Soon, Louis appeared at the passenger side door and she tried to jump into the driver's seat. It was too late. In no time, Louis had thwarted her attempts by quickly opening the passenger door and applying a firm grip on her wrist. With his other hand on her other wrist, he pulled her outside as she tried to use her feet to hold her inside the car. Unable to complete with his strength, she resorted to other methods. Faith kicked at his shins as he pulled her toward the woods.

"You sure are feisty. Just like she was after I disposed of him."

"Who are you talking about, dad? Why are you doing this?" she screamed, all the while fighting against his efforts.

"Who?" He laughed at her question. "You mother. And, your father of course. I brought her here after I got rid of him. Why? They deserved it. You deserve it, too." His casual banter continued as he pulled her wrists behind her back and pushed her along the path with a tight hold.

In moments of despair, it's odd what one observes. For Faith, she noticed that the dirt path was dotted with white magnolia petals that reflected the glow of the moon. She considered her options as she derived strength from the sight of the peaceful petals randomly appearing along the way. They were reminders of the jars of petals and beads lining the shelves of the crude shop off Bourbon Street. Faith breathed in scents of curious floral perfumes on breezes that kicked up around her. The crickets sang to her and the bullfrogs croaked their disapproval of the disruption of their peace. Faith felt the harmony of a world that gravitated toward peace. She floated above the scene, finding perspective, finding her strength against a man she knew would fall when she showed him what she was made of. She would not let this be the end. She had confidence in a knowing universe that rewarded good.

"You know, it's not too late to start over," she started as she began to conserve energy and devise a plan.

Her words registered with him and he answered softly.

"Start over? Yeah. I'm gonna start over all right. But, first …"

Faith gasped as she realized they were at the water's edge. He released his hold, knowing the swamp was her only escape.

In his outstretched hand was a flashlight that he clicked on to bathe the top of the swamp in light. A light mist rose from the dark, warm water. Sets of yellow eyes appeared one after another. Alligators. Lots of them. Louis shined the light directly on them one by one.

"That might be your mother," he laughed. "Or maybe that one?" he added as he shined the light on another set of eyes. A few of the curious creatures swam toward them. She stepped back and began to shake uncontrollably. Louis laughed harder and Faith noticed the shape of an abandoned bayou cabin on the far shore, its tin room illuminated by the full moon. Alligator eyes deterred any plans to swim for safety and she whirled around to face him.

For the first time, she noticed concrete evidence of her despair. Louis towered above her naturally, however with her desperate position closer to the shoreline, she appeared smaller than ever in his shadow. She could see loops of rope hanging loosely from his forearm partially covered by rolled up sleeves. He let the flashlight drop to the ground, using on the moon's light instead and Faith considered how unwilling the peaceful moon would be as an accomplice to his intentions. A roll of duct tape positioned on his wrist and the discarded flashlight showed the mud on the soles of expensive shoes and a pile of rocks placed strangely at the edge of the path.

"Well, let's not drag this out," Louis said matter-of-factly as he methodically wound the rope around her wrists.

"So this is all you got left?" she asked flatly.

He shifted his gaze at the sound of her regained voice.

"You've resorted to controlling me with a silly rope. I would think someone as powerful as you would have at least one more respectable trick in his bag."

He froze, his stare passed through her as her words resonated. The night sounds applauded her.

"You've taken everything away, but you still can't control me. A sedative and a rope? That's what you've been downgraded to?" As she continued her lecture, his eyes went wide. "You're pathetic."

Last words uttered, she reached with her fingers to grasp the rope he had suddenly weakened his grip on. Gathering at the slack, she tugged a last effort to escape Louis' hold on her.

With the slippery soles of his shoes along with her pull on the rope, he lost his balance and slipped, first to his knees then the rest of the way down until his head landed upon the pile of rocks. The rope slid with him and her hands were free. As Faith leaped past him, she could have sworn she witnessed the rope slither like a snake toward Louis' ankles. There was certainly no time to investigate and she ran with a flash of green light at her back.

She stole one last glance behind her as she ran to confirm she was not being followed. Louis LeBlanc remained in a heap at the end of the dirt path, but someone else caught her eye. Someone was clearly standing on the porch of the old cabin. Her green eyes glowed like the eyes of the gators and the wisps of light hair floated in breezes.

Faith's heart outraced her run from the pines and the pounding in her ears drowned out the swampy sounds of the Bayou. Her legs strengthened with every step and guiding moonlight intensified along the path. Its glow caused strange magnolia petals to glow and Faith followed the discarded petals out of the swamp. The black Cadillac waited but her heart sank as she realized Louis had the keys. She could not go back.

The road ahead was her only option and she ran until she thought her heart would burst. Her quick steps added sufficient distance from a past she had left at the edge of the swamp. The sound of sirens were barely audible, but her desperate senses picked up on them long before the flashing lights came into view. A fleet of squad cars approached to rescue Faith after she had already rescued herself.

Chapter 34

It was not long until papers across the country excitedly revealed the coroner's opinion. Voodoo Death. A case of sudden death brought on by a Voodoo curse combined with extreme fear or shock. News outlets salivated over photos depicting the candlelit altar in the neglected cabin and the peculiar tokens lining the path. Only in the deep south could such a diagnosis be official word. Only one city would bask in this notoriety. New Orleans defended her loved ones with ways most would deem sinister. She shrugged in the face of judgement.

Within hours of receiving the box of Sissy's letters from Chelsea, Richard had summoned the official help of his New Orleans police station and tracked Faith and Louis to the bayou, the same swampland where Louis had murdered Sissy and Gabe. By the time Richard had triumphantly placed the clues together, Chelsea was on the road for her mother's house in Charleston. She had grown tired of Louis' selfish ways but had no inkling of his true capabilities. When Faith had a chance to talk to Chelsea, she explained the events of that fateful Friday night with half-truths and remorse. Chelsea was ready to move on. Richard, ready for retirement and in response to Chelsea's request, was more than willing to close the missing jewelry case once and for all. After all, she had provided the imperative pieces to the puzzle and he was happy to concede to her wishes. The house on Prytania Street was sold and in a gracious gesture, Chelsea split the proceeds with Faith, each looking toward the future with modest hopes and occasional dreams.

The woman on the cabin porch remained an enigma. The rookie detectives assigned to track her down were quick to declare a cold case on the matter after tasked with visiting one too many occult shops laced with long needles. The Voodoo regulars and local priestesses claimed no knowledge of the woman with the kind green eyes. Faith had her thoughts on the subject after seeing pictures of her green-eyed mother with long blonde hair.

Faith rented a second-floor apartment in the French Quarter where she crawled into the folds of her city, seeking anonymity. When she did dare to dream, she imagined Patrick returning to her. When she woke, his absence produced heartbreak on repeat. Not wanting to tip the police off on Patrick and his escapades, she had waited for privacy before making attempts to reach him by phone. Back in New Orleans, and after Richard and his squad had pulled her the rest of the way to safety, the hospital operator had promised to put her through to someone who could answer her question. Unable to make good on the promise, they blamed it on patient confidentiality.

Patrick was not alone in his disappearance into thin air. No one answered the phone at Francine's shop and eventually the line stopped working. The country club had hired a new manager who could not recall any former employees with the name Patrick Morris. The tavern remained padlocked and she checked on it every day for weeks. None of the other barkeepers in town claimed to know Hawk. Eventually, to prevent madness, Faith stopped asking.

In the days following her dramatic return from Tampa, depression seeped in through the walls of the Pyrtania Street house where Faith was stuck with the ghost of Louis. Having to stay in the vacant mansion may have been the worst part of the entire ordeal, so, Faith spent her afternoons walking through the streets of her city. New Orleans' was a gracious hostess as she welcomed the girl back with clarinets and trumpets as chicory coffee was offered up on shaded park benches and strolls through narrow alleys allowed her mind to come to terms with a new reality that, she discovered, was liberating. She could be whoever she wanted to be now and by August she had moved into a studio apartment three blocks west of the cathedral. The handmade For Rent sign had caught Faith's eye, along with the little hoodoo shop on the first floor. The landlord recorded her new tenant's name as Faith Beaumont and also, surely knowing more than she let on, hired her to work in the shop she owned downstairs where piles of ribbons, herbs, candles and beads lined shelves and Faith felt right at home. Day after day, Faith dispensed the apothecary case by case to those in need who walked through the parlor doors. She soon found she had an innate knack for the profession.

Richard had departed for a retiree's life in Florida but first he struck a deal with Faith, whose wellbeing he felt some responsibility to. If she would see a trusted therapist and actively work on overcoming the past, he would abandon pursuance of the stranger Faith had handed the jewels to. After work one evening, as Faith sat alone with her thoughts, Louis' booming voice returned. He pointed out a pathetic perception of her plight and before his memory could succeed in making her believe, she called the first professional on the list from Richard. From the first session in September until the most recent talks in June, Faith blossomed while memories faded.

Still, her past naturally caught up to her from time to time. Now, she walked slowly from her apartment to the therapy session, this time following a route down Pirate Alley. Faith had grown accustomed to the stale disappointment that quietly waited ahead. What once brought eager butterflies had now turned cold on her. She needed that connection, however. She wanted to ensure his memory had not completely faded. As she passed the wooden doors, she noted the oversized padlock and chain still in place. Faith pressed her ear against the splintered wood and all was quiet inside. With eyes closed she could still see him and warmth grew inside of her at the thought of his smile. She was satisfied that his memory was still alive. She knocked with the base of her fist on the ragged door. Her knocks were desperate attempts to reach he who she had so much to tell, so much to share, so she banged louder, begging for an answer. There was none. Once more she resigned to face what she did not want to believe.

Two more blocks and Faith arrived at the therapist's modern office housed within walls dating back to the seventeen hundreds. Faith had downgraded her sessions to once a month since beginning her therapy nine months prior.

"Hello, Faith. Nice to see you, as always." The therapist was trendy and fresh. Her ebony skin taut against high cheekbones and the inverted bob framed her beauty nicely. Faith was always impressed by her intelligent mannerisms and kind approach.

"Nice to see you, too, Regina," she greeted.

Regina Sanders led them to her open office door and Faith took take a seat on the plush leather sectional. Regina took a seat at the far end, facing her client. It was one of Faith's favorite aspects of the sessions that were more like having coffee with a friend. A friend who doled out useful conversation notes now and then and listened while Faith took a little break from ever-increasing daily responsibilities since she had embarked on this new chapter of life.

"Have you given any thought to what we spoke about last time? A way to find closure and peace by honoring your mother and father's memory?"

Faith still thought of Louis when anyone mentioned the word, father. After a second she recalled that this discussion revolved around Sissy and Gabe.

"Well, you know I took my mother's maiden name, Beaumont, when we began our sessions last year. Becoming Faith Beaumont was therapeutic."

Regina nodded politely as she listened.

"And my little business has been paying the bills." Faith's dried herb and gardening business was a top seller at the city's farmer's markets. Regina, like most, remained unaware that Faith's biggest clients had become the Voodoo and white magic parlors throughout New Orleans. "And, getting to know my grandparents and uncle has been nice. So, at first, I thought that was all. But, I agree I probably do need more closure."

Faith inhaled sharply before continuing.

"I'd like to have a memorial erected in one of the city parks. A tree, a magnolia, planted with a plaque along with a service to dedicate it. Maybe even a community garden in honor of my parents."

Regina clapped as she rolled back against the armrest in delight. "I love it! Oh, Faith. It's perfect." Her eyes moistened as she went on. "And Patrick? You should consider his memory as well."

Faith picked at a piece of topsoil embedded in her fingernail. She shook her head. When silence remained between them, Regina continued.

"Should we include him in the memorial plans?" Regina's voice softened as she tackled one of the heavier matters between them.

"Once I know for sure." Faith looked up and Regina noted the fear in her eyes.

"Knowing he has passed is hard, but knowing might also give you complete closure and freedom to move forward."

"I'm not afraid of his death. I'm afraid to know he never really loved me. It was only a week. What if it all meant more to me than him."

"Very insightful," Regina pointed out. "It has been a year."

"I know. I told myself, told you, I would give the search a year."

"And then move on," Regina finished.

Faith shoulders sagged in defeat. She ticked off reasons for not finding her. "I did change my name. I was given a new cell number when

I got a new phone. I have a new home and the old house on Prytania has sold to new owners since I moved." Her eyes widened with hope. Regina took on a look of pity, but Faith was undeterred. "I think I'll give that a few more months."

After the therapy session had concluded, Faith made her way back home to retrieve her car. Her grandparents were expecting her. The thought of her new little family was still odd, but it had softened her. She left the bustle of the French Quarter to head a few neighborhoods west into Audubon, a gracious neighborhood built around the largest of the city parks and two universities. Of all the grand mansions and quaint shotgun houses restored in vibrant colors, her grandparents' modest, colonial home was her favorite. Maybe because of waited for her there.

She pulled into the concrete driveway and admired the piles of jasmine blooms cascading around the dark green, wooden garage door. The blooming aroma intoxicated and lifted her spirits higher than any shot of liquor had in her previous life. She smiled as she walked to the front door and gave a little knock. When no one answered, Faith walked around the front of the house to the side garden gate. Peering over the pickets and though a trellis was one of the most beautiful sights she had ever laid eyes on. She remained at the gate, careful not to disturb.

Sitting comfortably on a free-standing swing under the shade of a mighty oak was her dear grandmother who had shown nothing but love and support to Faith since she entered her life a year ago. Feet barely touching the ground, Faith could see a side view of the woman with crossed ankles, pointing to a mockingbird arriving home to a nest. Faith's grandfather sat on the opposite side of the gently swinging bench and as he turned to his wife, his love was clear. He leaned in to kiss her cheek. Faith swore she could see the eighty-five year old blush from afar. Faith eased the gate open slightly, not wanting the old hinges to creak, and softly latched it closed behind her. Soft grass padded her approach and the mocking birds took flight from the tree, teaching their young to fly under June's afternoon sun. Excited coo's mixed with birdsong. Tiny bare feet kicked from the old woman's lap. The great-grandmother turned to see Faith coming near.

"There's mommy," she announced.

Faith beamed with outstretched arms, unable to wait another second to cradle her baby in her arms. At three months, the baby retained her rosy, chubby cheeks that made her look like a cherub. Faith laughed as the tiny hands reached for her mother's shoulder-length blonde hair and gave a tug with tight fists.

"Patricia. Always going for mommy's hair, aren't you?" She smothered the tiny knuckles with kisses and pulled her baby in close as she placed her lips to the round cheeks and breathed her in. Remembering her grandparents, she looked up. "Thank you for watching her this afternoon."

"Are you kidding? We ought to thank you! I mean to tell Violet to be sure to tell you she's not available more often," the grandmother said of her daughter-n-law. "It is just too hard to compete with Brookes and that wife of his, but we intend to get our fair share of time in with this sweet baby girl, isn't that right, Gordon?" By now, the great-grandmother had eased up from the seat and laid a wrinkled hand upon Patricia's tiny head.

Gordon Thibeaux remained seated, comfortably looking on with contentment. "That's right, Betty. And if that apartment becomes too much, dear, you know you and that little angel are welcome to move in here. Like I said, we have plenty of room."

Faith smiled at the same offer made every time she visited. "Thank you, grandpa. I appreciate that. But, we would just keep everyone up all night, wouldn't we, baby girl?" she added in a tiny voice directed toward the tiny child. Patricia cooed again and kicked long legs inherited by her father as if to agree.

"Oh, we don't sleep well anyway," Betty Thibeaux waved off. "A sweet baby to rock in the middle of the night might actually help me to sleep more. You'll at least stay for supper?"

"I'm afraid we can't. We have some work to do. We'll be back on Sunday, though, if you're still up for our visit?"

"Of course! Sunday spaghetti dinner. I already have the sauce and bread dough made." They began to walk Faith and her baby back to the gate. "What work must you get back to? Do you need any help?" she asked her granddaughter.

"Just some deliveries to get ready for to a few … flower shops … in the area tomorrow. I need to bundle some dried sage and lavender. I'll put a few aside for you and bring it on Sunday."

"Oh, how wonderful. That lavender just fills the room with the most beautiful scent." Faith smiled knowingly at the accolades. The version she grew did have a particular potency she had never experienced and neither had the shopkeepers who kept her in business.

Faith had been waiting until Sunday to share her plans for the memorial, however, decided to open up about it then. "I also need to put together a plan I have in the works. A memorial. For my mother and father."

Not wanting to make an awkward misunderstanding, the grandparents urged her to continue. "A memorial for Sissy and …"

"Gabe. Of course!" she confirmed. Patricia squealed and kicked again at her mother's voice. Faith focused on her child's green eyes, eyes that were unusual for a baby of three months. There was a connection between them that Faith presumed her own mother's green eyes would understand. Upon hearing her grandmother's gasp, Faith quickly went on to keep anyone from developing expectations too grand in nature. "I have no idea if it will work out and if it did, it would be pretty simple – like a tree planting or something. I'm thinking a magnolia tree would be perfect."

"Oh, dear. How wonderful. Please come inside for just a quick second. I need to show you something." Faith exchanged a quizzical glance with her grandfather, and they followed her back though the patio door and into the rear sunroom. Faith took a blanket from the rattan couch and spread it out for Patricia to stretch out on the carpeted floor. As the baby reached and kicked and looked about haphazardly, Faith and her grandfather immersed themselves in the infant's actions until Mrs. Thibeaux returned. She sat down on the couch beside where Faith sat on the floor, leaning against the piece of furniture.

She had returned with a photo album which she quickly opened on her lap for Faith to see. "This is one of my favorite pictures of Gabe. He just looks so happy."

Faith turned to see the photo better. Gabe Thiboux was dashing in a tuxedo. The sepia photo proved that he shared the same sandy blonde hair and smile as his daughter who presently gazed upon the photo twenty-five years later. With him, under a blossoming magnolia tree, was a woman with long hair in a lighter shade of blonde and a smile just as bright. She wore an ankle-length, canary yellow chiffon dress and a wrist corsage made of lilies.

"They had gone to prom together. You probably didn't know that?" Betty extended her arm to pat Faith's shoulder.

"No," Faith whispered.

"Just as friends, they said," Gordon sneered in amusement. "I remember that now."

"Funny what the mind forgets, isn't it?" Betty said wistfully. "Funny how the world works."

"A magnolia tree. Probably the backdrop for a very special evening for the two of them. What a coincidence," Faith asserted.

Betty shrugged as she showered baby Patricia with smiles.

"I guess you could look at it that way."

Chapter 35

Patricia cried from her car seat on the short trip back across town and her wails broke Faith's heart. Like any good mother, Faith shushed and sang and consoled with kind words to no avail. When she did arrive home, Faith grabbed the first open spot she could find on the block. There had been no fancy shower to laden her and her baby with gifts, and the unexpected pregnancy had gone by so quickly, a backpack served as a diaper bag. It did the trick, since it allowed the single mother's hands to remain free. She slung the backpack to her back, hoisted the baby carrier car seat out of the back seat and heaved her little bundle down the block to her apartment. The painted blue door to her apartment was to the left of Tilly's Tonics and Charms, dark for the evening, and Faith set her crying child, still buckled into the car seat carrier, down to unlock it. The door led to a set of narrow, steep stairs which led to interior door to the little apartment. By the time she reached the top, she was winded, and her arms threatened to give out under the strain of the baby in her carrier. Faith huffed and puffed like the wolf and the lock gave way under the pressure of the key. The lavender bundles hung throughout the kitchen to dry welcomed them home with syrupy perfume. Faith breathed it in. Her daughter did too, and soon enough wails were reduced to staccato breaths and hiccups. Relieved to be home, the tired mother gently placed the baby in her carrier down on the pine floor to unbuckle the innocent bundle. Patricia's tiny cheeks were as red as strawberries due to her tantrum over car seat restraint and Faith kissed the stale tears from her baby's face. Stubby arms punched the air while chubby legs kicked in excitement.

"Okay, okay. I'm working as fast as I can, little one," Faith soothed as she blew air to move long strands of hair from her eyes. Patricia's green eyes met her mother's and Faith knew she had all she really needed in life at that moment. She eased the warm body from the seat and cradled her as she moved to the nearby secondhand couch. They settled into the corner of the sofa together, the baby finally relaxing, knowing her tiny hungry belly was about to satisfied. Tiny fists made demands and Faith could not help finding a touch of amusement in the dramatic actions. As the baby suckled, peace was fully restored. Faith leaned her head back against the soft, freshly laundered, cotton cushion cover and embraced harmony that flowed as her body nourished her baby. Faith, too, was hungry, but her own needs would have to wait. She felt her stomach growl its own frustration and she thought through her options. A baloney sandwich with a side of chips and pickles was the best she could do. Once Patricia was satisfied, and still awake, Faith held her upright to pat her back. Fully content now, Patricia was willing to allow her mother to satisfy her own hunger needs.

"All better now, baby?" Patricia looked about the room with wide eyes, taking in her familiar surroundings. Faith relished the quiet moment, despite her empty stomach still raging. Her baby's soft movements were too enticing to part with. "How did I get so lucky to be chosen as your mommy?" she whispered.

A blanket on the floor served as the baby's exercise mat. Faith eased the child on to the blanket and sat near as Patricia stretched and extended her head. Faith thought back to the picture her grandmother showed her of her father. A pang of sadness occurred with the thought of not having a picture to share with Patricia one day. How would she convey his smile to their daughter? On cue, Patricia flashed a crooked grin that brought tears to Faith's eyes.

A glass of tap water complimented the sandwich plate Faith prepared while Patricia entertained herself with the corner of the blanket. Faith sat next to her on the blue area rug and devoured the meager meal, knowing she had limited time before the baby made her next request. With one bite left, Patricia tired of her current situation and Faith took the plate to the sink before returning to her motherly duties. It was early, by the baby was rubbing her tired eyes, no doubt from the fresh air provided courtesy of her great-grandparents. It would mean being up most of the night, but Faith would pay that price to have time to wrap her lavender bundles in paper and ribbon that evening.

"Shall we check on our garden before sleep, Patricia?"

From the balcony, Faith caught sight of a red sky.

"Red sky at night, sailor's delight," she mused aloud.

Staying close to the wall as she held her baby in her arms, she took a seat at the bistro table and scanned her pots to take stock of her plants. The next batch of lavender was doing well, and the white sage was ready to be cut. The evening was quiet, air was still. A baby's yawn took her back inside to rock the child to sleep.

Monday morning in the French Quarter allowed the neighborhood to lick its weekend wounds. Hoses sprayed the sidewalks clean and some storefronts remained closed for a day of recovery. Something was shifting in Faith. She was recovering, too. That morning, she filled her cup of coffee half full and felt a renewed determination filled with good hope. While Patricia slept soundly after being up most of the night, Faith focused on finding out Francine's last name for her usual internet search session. If Regina knew the habitual way Faith searched for Patrick most days from a laptop or smartphone screen, she would most certainly disapprove, so Faith always made sure to leave these stalking tendencies out of the therapy sessions. The connection she had with Patrick was more than anyone would understand. She needed to find him and know that the love they shared for one glorious week had been real. It was impossible to doubt anytime she looked into her baby's eyes. The shock of finding out she was pregnant, preparing a home to bring a baby back to, and the bouts of morning sickness that had plagued her throughout the pregnancy had prevented her from doing much more than survive. Once Patricia was born, focusing on keeping the tiny, demanding infant healthy and content was all she could do. Now, she and her daughter had settled into a rhythm and having never known Francine's last name, she decided to find out. The Cut was still closed, but the owner's information was still listed online. In ten minutes, she had it. Whitley.

Praying that Patricia would sleep for a little bit longer, she dialed the number as she sat at the metal and Formica kitchen table and chair set she had found at a flea market. The retro boomerang pattern worn from many meals shared before her on the gray tabletop. Faith traced the parts of the pattern that remained as she waited for a Tampa General Hospital receptionist to answer. This time, she would remain vague with her questioning in order to get whatever information might be divulged from the unsuspecting employee. She had asked for Patrick in her other attempts. This time she would focus on Francine. In her most pleasant and professional voice, she made her inquiries when the receptionist answered the call.

"Hello, I'm calling to speak with a patient, but I'm not sure what room she's in or if she has been discharged."

It was a new approach. She hoped it would get her though to someone who could answer questions about Patrick. The receptionist transferred the line to an employee in the admissions office. This was normally where she hit a dead end.

"Uh, yes. I'm calling for Francine Whitley or Patrick Morris. I'm not sure of the room number."

She waited as she heard the employee type the names into the data base.

"Yes. I have no record of a Patrick Norris. I do see a Francine Whitley, but she has been discharged. I'm sorry I can't provide more information to help you."

"Morris. With an M!" she exclaimed. Had all of her attempts failed because of this misunderstanding? Her heart raced as the typing started once more.

"Okay. Yes. Patrick Morris. I have a discharge date here of June thirtieth of, oh, last year. Francine Whitley was discharged on the same day."

"June thirtieth?" she repeated in shock. The air left her lungs. Her heart raced. That was a little less than two weeks from that fateful day she left him. And now she knows Francine had been admitted, too. The pieces to the puzzle began to fill in her mind.

Knowing the answer already, she tried anyway. "Do you have contact information for either of them? I wanted to mail a get-well card."

She waited with closed eyes. "No, ma'am. I'm unable to provide that personal information."

She thanked the employee before hanging up, stunned to the core. There had been a hospital stay for both and a discharge date for both. A constant search of obituaries had turned up empty. Her call today had not yielded anything to suggest that Patrick had died from his ordeal on the last day they were together. In fact, she had more proof than ever that Patrick was not only alive, but quite possibly very well.

Tiny cries summoned Faith to the bedroom she shared with her baby. Lifting her from the pillow-protected spot on the bed her weary mother had resorted to at five that morning, she moved on to diaper duty on the thick area rug at the bottom of the bed before retreating to the couch for the morning feeding as her coffee turned cold. Faith was exhausted. The past three months were taking its toll. Her eyes were red and puffy and barely able to stay open. The baby's eyes were so full of innocence. Faith was astounded by the lack of any ill-will in the child's eyes. Patricia was not able to survive on her own, of course, so her tiny outbursts served only to meet her needs of survival. Such a sweet, innocent creature had only love and a will to survive in her little heart and mind. After all she had been through, Faith found that to be encouraging. She needed her baby as much as her baby needed her.

As she sat alone in the quiet apartment, feeding Patricia from the couch, she glanced around and felt a warm affinity for the modest décor. Creamy walls with fresh paint, varnished wood trim, oiled pined floors with throw rugs provided the backdrop of the one-bedroom apartment with a tiny efficiency kitchen. A white, slip-covered sofa found through a Craig's List ad and from a fine home in the Garden District. The woman had claimed it had been in their exquisitely furnished home for less than a month when she decided it did not fit well with her newly planned décor. Free to anyone who was willing to move it, Faith had secured a comfortable centerpiece that had initially cost a thousand. The sofa barely fit up the stairs and Brookes and Violet had the hardest time getting it inside. Once in, Faith thanked them profusely. She appreciated the little couch more than anyone could imagine. There was no television before the couch, like most would have. Television was too expensive, and Faith had no interest in any shows that were on anyway. The news was too depressing to watch, especially being the focus of the local channels for a week. Instead, a thrift store trip had led to an oil painting of the sun setting over the sea. Having loved the painting already, when she noted the pencil notation, *Sun Setting Over the Gulf of Mexico*, she was sold and handed over the twenty-five dollars it took to take the piece of art home. From the couch, the painting was a view she would take over a television any day. A wood coffee table left over from the seventies, a few used lamps, a wrought iron bed, and a plain dresser she painted mint green made her apartment complete. The first night under a comforter set purchased at Wal-Mart proved to be one of the most luxurious nights she had ever experienced. She made up her cozy home by herself and she intended to keep the positive energy swirling for her baby girl.

The basket of wrapped lavender sat by the door as a reminder of deliveries needing to be made before work and once Patricia was ready for her blanket time on the floor, Faith brought the baby back to the bedroom where she pulled her own messy hair into a bun and pulled on clothes from the day before. Life with a newborn rarely permitted self-indulgence, but it did indulge one's spirit. Since June of the previous year, Faith learned how easy it was to transform your outward appearance. Eventually, true colors shine through. With Regina's help, Faith had bonded with her new family and as she worked to be the best mother to Patricia she could be. Faith was grateful for the chance.

The phone rang and seeing it was the contact she had recently made at the mayor's office, she answered the call.

"Simon?"

"It is. Have a second, Faith?"

Faith glanced down at Patricia who was content to stretch about.

"I have to leave shortly for work, but yeah, I have a few minutes."

"Great. So, after hearing your idea for a memorial in one of the city parks, I took the liberty to pitch an idea for you. I hope you don't mind."

Faith did not have time to answer before Simon continued, obviously proud of himself. Faith listened closely as he rattled off recent events during a weekly staff meeting.

"And then she mentioned there's a poor old oak that has seen better days. Termites have gutted it to the core and it must come down. No one is happy about this and protesters, who apparently know nothing about the effects of termites nor what can happen if a tree falls on someone," he sighed his frustration away before continuing, "are already planning a protest to save the tree. The mayor needs a PR boost for multiple reasons – including past dealings with a certain maniac senator." He came up for air and added that last bit hoping it would strike the comic chord he intended. It did and Faith surprised herself by chuckling at the dark humor. Maybe her mind was coming around. "So, I seized the opportunity and revealed your plan for the memorial." He stopped there and Faith could barely take the suspense. She heard him tell a co-worker he would be with them shortly. She could hardly breath while waiting for him to go on.

"Sorry," he finally began. "I'm trying to keep this quiet. Okay. I'm in the elevator now. Yeah, so I pitched your idea. The room loved it – especially the mayor. It turns out she has a quite a soft spot for you, as we all do," he added sheepishly. She blushed. The support that was finding its way to her in these times of need was humbling and it warmed her heart. She touched the tiger eye beads still worn around her wrist in a display of gratitude and focus. "The tree is coming down next week, but a magnolia tree with two concrete angels are going in along with a memorial service that you are asked to help plan." She could hear his excited smile through the phone.

"When?" She squeaked out the word.

"Nobody wants to give the protesters a chance to organize. The sooner the better. They were saying it'd be nice to have everything wrapped up by mid-September and they said the more publicity, the better."

"Where?"

"Jackson Square. Back by the cannon display."

Faith sunk to the floor with weak knees. It was a place she had avoided at all costs since re-settling in New Orleans. The memory of meeting Patrick on that bench had been too hard to go back to. The tavern, the marina, the Maurader's slip, for unknown reasons, were comforting to her when she ventured out to check for signs of him or his friends. That bench overlooking the park and the cathedral was too much. Now, she would have to face the fact that she would be revisiting that bench, alone. Her eyes welled and she reached for Patricia's tiny fingers.

When she didn't respond, Simon feared he had overstepped boundaries. "You there, Faith? I'm sorry if I spoke up about your plans too soon. The timing was too perfect."

"Thank you, Simon," she managed to say through tears. "What do I need to do next?"

His voice showed relief as she heard horns sound and the clatter of the St. Charles Avenue streetcar clatter by his presumed perch on the steps of city hall.

"You're helping me, too, I should say. If you trust me, I can organize your plans with the city. It would be a feather in my cap and a healing endeavor for you. If you don't mind, we can meet up asap so I can write up the official plans to submit it?" he suggested tentatively.

"Of course. I'd appreciate your help."

Chapter 36

Miss Tilly hunched over a cash register where a hundred jars of dried herbs were about to swallow her up. She punched the cash drawer open to pull three twenty-dollar bills from the slot. The priestess allowed her dark locks to brush the tops of her middle-aged hands. Her gentle ways were an indication of pleasant demeanor. She dealt in the lighter side of the voodoo religion, focusing on peaceful intentions.

"Faith, dear. Let me see that baby." Her quiet voice soothed. Patricia, comfortably swaddled in a pink blanket, allowed the transfer without a fuss. Faith balanced the basket of herbs on one arm while she leaned toward Tilly who cradled the tiny human in her arms. Lovingly, she looked down at the child. "My, my. What a dear," she tutted.

Faith sunk into an oversized upholstered seat and rested her head against the soft wing on the back of the pastel blue chair. Tilly noticed Faith's reaction to her comfort and continued stand, swaying to the rhythm of an unsung song. As the child's eyes closed, so did the mother's. A bassinet sat nearby for Faith's visits, on and off the clock. The shop owner eventually laid the sleeping baby down and went about her business. Faith succumbed to deep sleep. Dried sage, delivered to Tilly from Faith's own balcony, sat in a pearly oyster shell where burning incense dripped ash. The concoction swirled from the deep windowsill, sedating the already-tired mother. Her breaths grew heavy as she began to dream. Tilly quietly moved the basket to the butcherblock counter and lifted twelve of the fifty parchment wrapped packages. Six bundles of dried sage and six bundles of dried lavender, each tied with a black bow and ready to sell for double of similar offerings around town.

Tilly went about her business for the next hour, enjoying the companionship of her tenant and friend along with baby Patricia, even as they slumbered. She always thought her shop would fit better in Salem versus New Orleans, but the voodoo culture was widespread in New Orleans and her niche brand of unorthodox magic was well-received. Tilly believed in the positive and healing side of magic so day after day and year after year she continued to refill jars with beads and hang herb sachets and crystals from hooks, just as she did now while her guests rested. She believed it was bad karma to spend time in negative environments, so she refrained from stocking her shop with tokens that only brought harm. The dolls she did carry had been stuffed with flower petals and designed to strengthen bonds rather than break them. Of course, Tilly knew there was a place for darker intentions and sometimes good reasons to venture to the dark side of their beliefs. She peered over her glasses to the prime example slumped in the corner of her shop. There were places she could refer those seeking a stronger power on a need-to-know basis.

Velvet ribbons in an array of moody hues swayed upon an updraft from an unseen source. The candlelight throughout the shop flickered. Tilly wondered who entered from the other side. When the baby giggled in her sleep, she knew. Love knew no boundaries – even after death. Coincidentally, or not, the shopkeeper began stocking a row of true love candles. The seven-day candles were poured in a tall glass container and dressed with the appropriated herbs to attract love's truest and most genuine form. This particular batch had been made with Faith's delivery the prior month. It was a potent batch, one that those with highly tuned sensibilities would pay top dollar for. As Tilly refilled her stock on the shelf, she experienced a touch of sadness. True Love was the candle sought by most who walked through her doors.

A whistling tea kettle sounded from the back room and Tilly was startled by the sound. She had forgotten about the kettle on the hot plate. Removing the angry pot, it hissed as she poured two cups of scalding water over her own batch of tea leaves. The mint from her garden swirled in the cup made on a potter's wheel and Tilly could clearly read the heart shaped by the leaves. She added a sliver of lemon to intensify the refreshment. By the time she took a seat on the matching chair, her friend was beginning to stir. She placed the mug on the small table between them.

"Oh," Faith gasped. "Patricia."

Tilly patted her hand before lifting a dark finger to her red lips. "She is asleep."

Faith sunk back in relief. Tilly passed her a warm mug. They sipped in silence until the drink was reduced by half, all the while breathing in restorative steam.

"I'm not sure how that happened, but it felt good."

Tilly shrugged. "Sissy's Sage is resting beside you. It could be the culprit."

Faith turned to see her mother's namesake product upon the light blue sill. The photo of Sissy and Gabe came to mind as did her recent dream.

"Your sleep was peaceful," Tilly whispered knowingly. "You had a visitor in your dreams."

"You knew?" Faith asked the question but was hardly surprised. Tilly had a way of knowing most things. The woman's thoughtful nod as she sipped her tea was her only answer. Faith sighed. "I didn't want to wake from it. My mother and father looked on as Patrick held his daughter, and me, close. It was just too real. I want it to be real."

The sleeping child uttered a delighted cry and Faith and Tilly halted their quiet discussion in hopes the baby would continue her needed rest. They looked on as a baby fist reached from the bassinet then outstretched fingers reached for invisible affection. The candles flickered upon the breeze once more and Tilly leaned forward, interested to see what others could not. She tilted her head and a lock of black curls slipped from a wide headband adorned with embroidered flowers. She was trancelike and unaware of Faith's scrutiny until the younger woman spoke.

"What is it?" Faith breathed.

Tilly resituated her red-rimmed glasses and watched over the baby who continued to coo and gasp excitedly. Thick little legs kicked in approval. Tilly stood and walked over the white bassinet where the baby's jade eyes glowed with happiness. Faith stood to join them.

"You wanted your dream to come true," Tilly told her. "You, of all people, should know to be careful what you wish for." Tilly's expression turned sweet as she picked up the baby and handed her back to Faith. "Why not sit a spell and feed Patricia. I can deliver your orders for you."

Chapter 37

Hope. It encouraged every step since that fateful day in June when a curious visitor entered her life on dubious conditions, enticing her to follow. Along the way, she realized people are rarely who they seem. Yes, many did place two hats upon one head. She remembered his words and, more often, his actions. Patience and kindness in place of harshness and fear. Together, they confronted their demons and chased down a new reality. Separately, she was better for it. She hoped he was, too.

Home. No longer a mansion on a coveted block in the Garden District. Nor, a place of turmoil and deceit. Faith's apartment was meager. It had to be sparse to make room for the love.

Love. A mother's love is a supernatural power. Faith now knew her mother, and the mothers before her, had given her the strength to thrive in an often-harsh world. Faith would do the same for her own daughter, who would no doubt face her own havocs in time and would rise from the grave to do so. That notion proved not as outlandish as she had once considered.

The spin of life's merry-go-round had slowed just enough for Faith to stop and smell the flowers and she did so every chance she got. Including this July morning as she pushed Patricia in her stroller toward Jackson Square. Her steps a march to a beating heart and her chiffon yellow dress a flattering thrift store find. She drew looks from men and women sipping chicory coffee in moody cafes. They had to wonder about this sunny soldier on her way to lay her past to rest. A gardenia vine extended aromatic tendrils of intensity to halt her charge. She plucked a showy bloom to let her baby discover one of life's more beautiful moments before inhaling the sweetness herself. She placed the stem through the buttonhole on her dress to encourage the perfume to distract her from the battlefield ahead. The spinning may have stopped, but the dizzying effects of years past remained. She arrived in Jackson Square with a light head and nervous palms, unsure of her ability to handle the heaviness of the memorial in a place so full of the past. She was afraid she might collapse from the rush of memories that piled atop what must be done next as she stood in the shadow of the familiar white cathedral, preparing the enter the park's tall iron gates.

Focus. Faith recalled the trick she used in the past to ward off anxiety's threat. Surprisingly, it was the first time since Louis left her life that panic went on the attack. As she eased the stroller up and over two small, stone steps, she glanced down at Patricia, dressed in a cool cotton romper yellow to match. Her baby's eyes met hers and Faith's emotions no longer had a hold on her. This was her focus. Her baby was all that mattered now. She pulled away from her child's stare, brave enough now to look up at the familiar cannon display in the rear of the park. Tourists stood capturing pictures of the park below from the cannon area. She could see the silhouette of someone on the bench. Someone on their bench. She squinted to gain a better look. No longer in mourning, only wanting to relish the future. She considered walking to the bench to relive the memory before moving on for good.

Closure. It was a word used often by her therapist and that bench was the last stronghold from her old life. Sitting there without him would bring the closure Regina told her she needed. However, she was not prepared to close that door, yet. Still, seeing the shape of a familiar frame on that familiar bench urged her to walk there and sit in Patrick's memory. The stranger began to rise from the bench and Faith saw her chance to reclaim their meeting place from that Saturday morning a few months ago. Her heart ached. His memory was not enough. How little time it had taken her, with Patrick's help, to find a new perspective on life and on herself. New memories took the place of old and she smiled at the thought of that morning. His perplexed expression at her changed appearance then that crooked smile that was easily on hand to lift her spirits. The ride out of town. As she had held on to him that morning on the back of the motorcycle, she had no idea of the places he would take her. She longed to be at his side again, even if in spirit. Before she could act on desires, someone was gently grasping her hand.

"Are you ready? I can't wait to show you," Simon beamed as he waited for Faith to retrain her eyes on him.

"Simon," she greeted warmly and squeezed his hand in return. "Thank you for being here. Thank you for everything."

Simon waved her off and gestured his intent to push the stroller the rest of the way. Faith gave in, walking beside him and taking in the more immediate surroundings. The paved sidewalk weaved through the center of the grassy park.

"Wait until you see it," he gushed.

She opened her mouth to question him and what she witnessed left her jaw agape.

Gray clouds moved in to cover the sun and hundreds of flowers shined in place of the sun. Heaps of yellow, red, orange, purple and white encircled the angelic stone statue that would one day find itself sheltered by broad magnolia branches. The flowers bequeathed in respect for the memory of Faith's parents as the memorial service had been widely publicized throughout the city. She caught glimpses of strangers smiling at her as she passed, some raising plastic cups of morning cocktails and wearing parade beads. She found that sight a little inappropriate until the lighter side of her new self found it amusing. Why shouldn't the event feature a festive air? It was similar to the reasons she chose yellow over black. It was hard to hold a sad expression in the Big Crescent. Behind the stone angel, amid the bunches of blooms piled upon the ground, stood a modest yearling with waxy leaves. The little tree stood at attention from its newly planted position and ready to grow roots. A steady stream of early risers had passed through the park to deposit the blossoms and she turned as another bouquet was gently discarded next to her feet. She smiled at a young couple who paid their respects without words. Faith admired the angel's gentle face framed by waves of carved tresses. Her heavenly wings ready to take flight. She thought about how she, in contrast, no longer wished fly away. She was at home in her city. Faith teared up at the show of love from a community her mother and father had never had the chance to know. She crouched to move a few stray bunches of blooms from the granite plaque and read the inscription.

In memory ... Savior "Sissy" Beaumont LeBlanc and Gabrielle Joseph Thibeaux

Faith read the names repeatedly. The weight of the moment sunk in. Her parents had shown their love for her in ways she could not rationalize. She felt their love every time she visited her grandparents and aunt and uncle. She felt it when she held her baby. She knew another dimension of love exists – even if she could not explain it. Tilly would understand, she thought. At the same time, Faith recalled the woman with the green eyes and long hair and as she did, she touched the beaded bracelet. In a desperate time of need she had allowed herself to heed calls from those unseen bonds. Unable to explain any it, but able to feel it. A shiver went through her.

Suddenly, her world alit in color. Faith stood slowly and took in the blazing colors around her. She was grateful to be alive and grateful for a chance to live her own life, on her own terms. She breathed in a good dose of oxygen just because she could, and she basked in the beauty of it all. The crowd grew around her as she stood before the stone marker. Simon remained quietly beside her, softly bouncing the stroller as Patricia fell asleep with her bottle. The mayor and other politicians and clerks filed in around him. Moving her gaze from the statue momentarily, she noticed Regina taking her place at the edge of the unorganized congregation and as she turned all the way around, she gasped at the sight of a hundred or so people standing with her in support. Her heart swelled. The Thiboux's arrived and those around her parted to allow the elderly couple, along with Faith's aunt and uncle, walk to the front of the crowd. They embraced Faith in a long group hug, and she felt her heart expand to even larger proportions. She welcomed their presence on this day like she never had before. A day of new beginnings and finding peace. Love. It was often shown without words.

All attention turned toward a woman who delivered sunflower seeds to the stone angel's out-stretched, cupped palms. A white robe draped her petite body and her salt and pepper hair was cropped in a sensible style. Her wire glasses made her appear scholarly and her short stature made her non-threatening. Simon had arranged the details of the day and had mentioned he was particularly fond of this sweet person who had reached out to him upon hearing of the plans. She had asked to deliver blessings for peace and appreciation at the service and he found he was unable to do much more than agree to her request. She had introduced herself as Miss Margie. Her spiritual beliefs knew no religious boundaries.

"How are you doing, sweetie?" she asked while gently squeezing Faith's hand. Faith smiled at the gesture and leaned into an embrace with this serene woman. Her calm presence melted away any tense energy.

With a knowing wink, Margie stepped before the newly-formed family in the heart of the supportive crowd that has assembled. The mass of people hushed in her presence and she began.

"When we die, we should want the living to be glad to have known us. To celebrate us. Those that are taken from this earth will leave connections and bonds behind. The universe works in ways we may never know; however, we are foolish to ignore the gestures. Channel your energies to do good. Sissy Beaumont and Gabe Thiboux, we hope you may rest in peace and feel the love being sent to you on this day. May this site be one where family and friends can always greet you."

Faith reminded herself to stay strong as she felt for the tiger's eye beads burn against her wrist. At the same time, her grandparents each wrapped an arm around her from where their flanked positions. Painful memories slipped away as good intentions took their place.

"I ask that you now join me in a moment of silence as we reflect and look forward to a promising future. A future that is ready to be granted by a loving and nurturing universe."

Faith bowed her head and as she did, she caught sight of a familiar face that, in the heat of the moment, she could not place. She whipped her head back up to gain a better look. With all heads now casting downward glances, she was unable to confirm what her eyes had told her. Francine? Was the vision a hallucination? Was she seeing only what she wanted to see? She inhaled a shaky breath to regain her senses.

Miss Margie sprinkled red rose petals on and around the statue and little tree before standing as tall as she could to deliver her final words.

"Please carry this love with you and spread it to others in the memory of Sissy and Gabe. May you find your own kind of peace and happiness from this day forward."

As the ceremony ended, the rain began. A sudden downpour that caused everyone to leave as quickly as they had assembled.

"Oh, dear," Betty Thiboux started. Simon, always ready to serve, popped open a large umbrella he had on hand to shelter the old couple, along with Faith and Patricia in the process. Others soon rushed forward to do the same for Miss Margie and any others who were unable to quickly escape the weather. The passive fall of rain held no thunder.

When the mayor's assistant handed Faith an umbrella, Simon moved his to cover the grandparents and himself. Faith moved to stand with the stroller, her sleeping baby unconcerned with the shower.

"The mayor reserved a few tables at Café DuMont for us," Simon shouted over the pelting rain. "Are you coming?"

She remained, unable to tear herself away just yet.

"There's something we have to do first. You all go," she encouraged.

“Can we at least take Patricia along?” Brookes’ wife, calm as always and a picture of beauty with olive skin and thick, shoulder-length brunette hair, offered. Betty nodded her eager agreement.

“No, we’ll be fine,” Faith answered. “We’ll meet up with you there shortly.” As the rain came down harder, they ran off toward the exit and for the dry café. The oversized, black golf umbrella shielded mother and child from the strengthening pour.

Miss Margie moved closer to Faith in passing with the mayor and her entourage. “A cleansing rain,” she said with a knowing nod. “You are indeed loved, my dear.”

With those parting words, Faith was alone. Before leaving the site, Faith transferred a kiss with her fingertips to the engraved names of her parents. She watched a dainty vine of morning glories extend toward her hand. She refused to believe the motion was a result of the breeze. The world was certainly magical. As the cleansing rain continued, she knew her mother and father were finally at peace and would always be looking out for their only daughter. It was up to her to watch for their signs of love.

Regina had been right. Closure was an important part of healing and Faith was determined to heal completely that day. Before joining the others, she knew there was one more stop she had to make. Unable to walk easily through puddles with her white sandals, she continued the trek barefoot. Her breathing grew heavy from the onslaught of nerves and keeping the umbrella over the stroller as she forged on. Then, the last step arrived. She looked down upon the park and at the St. Louis Cathedral now boldly a beacon of strength. How many storms that structure had weathered? The face of the massive church was a white sheet of light against the darkened sky. She looked at the memorial and it seemed so small now from this vantage point. Faith sighed and turned her attention to the old iron bench. The last piece of her past needing to be addressed.

It was that moment when their eyes met again. That same crooked smile that melted her heart last June, and under wildly different circumstances, was widening across his face. He was waiting for her just as she hoped he would be, although she was too afraid to admit it. He was wet with rain and, despite the Chesire grin, wore a look of defeat as he spread his elbows across the backrest and gave in to the rain and anything else that was about to be lobbed his way.

“I tried to find you. I’m too late,” he admitted.

"You're not late. You're here," she cried. Weak with emotion and shock, she moved to the bench where they had met once before and sat in close to him, using the black umbrella to shield all three of them from the downpour. "I thought you had …," Faith whispered between sobs that crept into her voice. He huddled in closer, wanting to pull her to him, but resisted as he had deduced she was now with another man. She had a family now and he suffered as he came to terms with the realization in his mind. Faith reached for his hands, holding them in hers.

"You found someone else. I know." Still, instinctively, he smiled at the baby who was slowly waking in a state of amazement over raindrops bouncing out a melody all around her. She reached toward him. He allowed her to grip his finger as he smiled wider. Faith's sobs were drowned out by the storm. Patrick continued to talk, never taking his hand, or eyes, off the baby. "She was a match. I got to New Orleans as soon as we could travel after the surgery. I've been trying non-stop to find you. Your old number wouldn't work. There was no trace of you anywhere in the city." Faith nodded her understanding through cries. "You saved my life, Faith. You saved me."

"You saved me, Patrick. I need you. Patricia has saved me. She needs you."

Wanting to hold on to the hope, he held onto his questions. "Patricia? You have a strong grip, little one."

Beginning to understand his misconceptions, she chose her words carefully. "She is strong. Strong like her daddy."

He huffed a response. "How did you meet him?"

Her grin turned sly and she increased her voice over the dancing droplets. "When he broke into my house and stole my heart."

And just like that, his slanted smile returned to her. She nodded and eased Patricia from her seat after setting the umbrella down. The rain ceased as Patrick held his daughter for the first time. Mockingbirds rushed from the trees and the clouds parted as life went on around them. The father cradled this renewed purpose in life and kissed the only one he had ever loved. She returned his love and sealed a fate in harmony with a universe quite persistent at pulling the strings. The storm had passed.

About the Author

A member of the Florida Writers Association and the Space Coast Writers' Guild, Dana weaves decades of east coast, deep south, and international travel into playful storytelling tinged with bigger ideas and the often-inexplicable ways of the universe. Countless backroads, waterways, small towns, big cities, odd occurrences, and curious characters have wandered into her fictional and first-hand accounts published by outlets such as: Florida (An Anthology), Trail Towns, The Pittsburgh Post-Gazette, and various travel and tourism publications.

She currently resides in Cocoa Beach, Florida. Readers can connect with her through Instagram, Facebook, and Goodreads.

About The Tallest Timbers

5 Stars ... Dana Thomas Weber creates a timely portrait of "the American dream." Heroine Lacey Williams blindly accepts that ideal with all of the trappings, the right car, the right clothes, a posh address, yet is sadly unfulfilled. Dana takes us on a wonderful journey with Lacey, as she seeks authenticity in her life and creates a new American utopia for herself...this time, dreaming with her eyes wide open.

Is the simple life so simple?

Lacey Williams is a driven and disciplined Annapolis real estate agent who has created success from scratch. It is, however, a life she has become disenchanted with. Yearning for a simpler way of life, she follows her heart and less-practical intuitions for the first time in order to seek out her version of a fulfilling life.

There is no turning back once she sells her home, walks away from her career and moves to a rustic cabin in upstate New York. Eerie nights in the mountains, modest living quarters, harsh winters, and repeated sightings of an apparition in the woods become the least of her concerns when a river guide with a past crosses her path.

Things are not always what they seem, though, and her strength and independent spirit fosters a new drive. Lacey Williams is focused more than ever on discovering her true self while carving out the life she was meant to live.

The Tallest Timbers is available online and select booksellers.

www.ingramcontent.com/pod-product-compliance
Lightning Source LLC
Chambersburg PA
CBHW030618310726
48979CB00003B/769

* 9 7 8 0 9 9 6 5 4 9 8 7 5 *